To,

Lynn,

love,

Chassa

x

Warm Orange Glow

Chrissa Mills

authorHOUSE®

AuthorHouse™ UK Ltd.
500 Avebury Boulevard
Central Milton Keynes, MK9 2BE
www.authorhouse.co.uk
Phone: 08001974150

First published by AuthorHouse 3/17/2009

ISBN: 978-1-4389-2964-4 (sc)

Printed in the United States of America
Bloomington, Indiana

This book is printed on acid-free paper.

Dedication

Graham, my adorable mentor
All my wonderful inspirational family
Especially Embo whose support is endless
And my brother, Roger - an avid Chelsea fan

1969

Neil Armstrong set foot on the moon
Concorde's maiden flight
Human egg made fertile in test tube
John Lennon and Yoko Ono promote peace with bed-in
Paul McCartney marries Linda Eastman
Judy Garland died
Prince Charles investiture at Caernarvon Castle
Chelsea football team doing well

Sky Blue/Grass Green

I wasn't your average teenager. Camilla once said I was a geek and all because I commented on how blue the sky was and how verdantly green the grass.

Even in those days I always thought in colours so being with friends, as Camilla suggested, and going out didn't appeal to me; it was no colour and, anyway, Newmarket wasn't cool; not then. But I adored my after-school life helping my father out-of-doors and in his position as head-gardener he was never happier than when nurturing roses and fruit trees and growing the finest and most delicious vegetables. I knew more about mulching and pruning than was probably beneficial to me at that age.

My father was the antithesis of a smart man and the warmest orange imaginable. With his wild hair and shabby clothes I felt so at ease in his company; don't tell me why because I wasn't like that myself; I was inclined to be neat. He had two assistants, apart from me that is, and we all busied ourselves on this rather smart stud-farm east of Newmarket; it was a labour of love. I should add that my interest in the outdoors started with a tricky relationship with my mother; I did everything to avoid her.

1969 changed all that. My father died two days before my eighteenth birthday in February; a brain haemorrhage meant he went from being a big and strong gardener to 'gone'. Snap your fingers; it was as quick as that! I was bereft. It seemed as though my most special friend had been snatched away from me and within days he was replaced by his superiors and my help was no longer welcome.

We lived in a charming thatched cottage in a village called Ashley but the house went with my father's job. My mother and I walked round in a daze for a while both knowing we had to look for somewhere else to live. That was when I turned to reading and studying and my mother could find no complaint with that. She worked in Barclays Bank in Newmarket, nothing special, just an accounts clerk, but thought she was extremely clever. She wasn't, not really, but my relationship with her was fundamentally based on exam results so when in the early summer of 1969 I gained three A's in my A-levels I suppose you could say our relationship hit an all-time high. Perhaps gaining such results was a positive colour; say indigo, but it was nothing like sheer happiness; it didn't give me a warm orange glow. Indeed it would be many years before I experienced a warm orange glow.

Hot Red

I was now self-assured and very positive about my future; I would earn as much money as I could then go to university after which I would travel and experience life; all away from my mother. Camilla was proud of me. Meanwhile I went from part-time shop assistant at Ashfords in the High Street of Newmarket to full-time worker in a very busy office in Bridge Street near the round church in the middle of Cambridge. I travelled in every day on the bus from Newmarket where my mother and I now lived in a small flat in Granby Street. The flat wasn't so bad, only five minutes from the middle of town.

I thought of my job as a means of saving as much money as I possibly could. The business was called H-G Properties Limited and all to do with property developing both home and abroad and I did whatever was asked of me. I suppose I was a dogs-body but I didn't care. The man who owned the business was called Ben Herriott-Greene, which was odd because Ben certainly wasn't green. In my eyes he was hot red even though he was considerably older than me at thirty-two. Unfortunately his reputation preceded him, out and out womaniser, love 'em and leave 'em sort, so I was well and truly warned, but feelings are feelings and my youthful confidence allowed me to ignore anything I didn't want to hear. Besides, I was desperate for affection.

From the start he showed an intense interest in me. As he passed by he would touch my hair and comment on its warm colour and soft texture and he would quite openly stare at my legs; I only had myself to blame; I had a tendency to wear *very* short skirts. I was warned that Ben showed an interest in every pretty face and to watch out. Needless to say I didn't watch out and became infatuated. Ben was quite short and not particularly good-looking with his snub nose and thin lips; he was even starting to lose his light brown hair but he had the most enchanting blue eyes and he wooed me with a skill and charm that I'd never come close to before because where I came from you called a spade a spade in every sense of the word. Anyway, I was enormously flattered.

On reflection he played a crafty game; I should have been a baby in his eyes but hindsight is sobering. Anyway, on our first date he didn't even kiss me. We ate in a small bistro off Trinity Street, very trendy, and

I wore a white dress I'd found in a boutique near the office; it had a mark on the shoulder so I got it at a reduced price but it was quality; short, crepe de chine and figure hugging. I chalked out the mark and felt like a million dollars. We ate pate, coq a vin and crème brulee all washed down with Chablis and Beaune and I was very drunk but somehow able to focus. He gazed at me across the table adoringly and when I went to the ladies loo I looked in the mirror and believed that my donkey brown hair was luscious and my brown eyes mesmeric and that my skinny frame exactly right for a modern girl.

He drove me home to Newmarket. I was grateful; the last bus had left ages before. On reflection I think he might have been expecting where I lived to be rather more impressive than the seen-better-days Granby Street that I directed him to. At the time I hadn't given that fact a thought.

His face was stern as he leapt out of his Mercedes sports car and came round to my side and opened the passenger door. He held out a hand which I took and we both stood on the pavement looking at the run-down block of flats. I pointed to the top left hand window and said,

'We live in that one there but please don't set any store by what you see on the outside.' I smiled and sighed, 'Because it's *much* worse on the inside.'

He stared at me for a few seconds before smiling broadly. I'd scored a point; he liked my sense of humour.

'How worse?' he asked.

'Care to come up and see? I make an extraordinarily

good mug of cocoa.'

'Cocoa!' he hooted. 'Whoever drinks cocoa in this day and age?'

'We do all the time.'

'I'll pass, thank you.' He looked down at his car keys and then again at me. His wonderful eyes were fathomless as he nodded a farewell. 'See you tomorrow, Diana.'

I was devastated but struggled not to show it. 'Of course. Thank you for dinner.'

He smiled warmly. 'My pleasure.' Then he climbed back into his car and was gone.

It was a week before he asked me out again. We went to the cinema to see James Bond: On Her Majesty's Secret Service. George Lazenby had taken over Sean Connery's role as James Bond and Diana Rigg played his female counterpart. I loved the film; up until then I'd hardly been to the cinema and I remember crying at the end when Diana Rigg's character was shot dead wearing her beautiful wedding gown. I was embarrassed but Ben wasn't. He even suggested we went back to his place for a nightcap and of course I agreed. He promised to take me home afterwards. He lived in a beautiful penthouse apartment overlooking the backs of Kings College. I looked around at the vast expanse before me (compared to the pokey flat where I lived) filled with ultra-modern furnishings and it occurred to me then than Ben was rich. Within minutes of arriving in his flat I was given a large glass of white wine and as we looked out of the sweeping window to the panoramic view before us he kissed me. I'd never been kissed before and it was delicious and so rousing. Feelings I'd never experienced flared within me and I was putty in his hands but sadly that was all he did; that evening.

On our fifth date I met his sister. Her name was Angelica and I knew she thought I was ridiculously young for her brother and not in the least bit worthy. But Ben was obviously close to her because although there wasn't any outward sign of affection his demeanour with her was very respectful. Ben's demeanour with people in the office was curt and off-hand. He was always kind to me though.

We ate with Angelica in Ben's flat; it was a casserole she had made and very tasty; I praised her for it but she didn't acknowledge me at all. Then she went home and I was relieved. Ben visibly relaxed when she'd gone and it wasn't long before we were kissing but it went much further this time, all the way, starting with something I was never to forget; a technique that was extremely erotic. As we lay on the carpet kissing and stroking he rolled away from me and shifted so that he was behind my head. Very slowly he pulled back my hands so that I was lying with totally outstretched arms. He stroked the under-flesh of my arms from my wrists all the way to the swell of my breasts sending shivers through my entire body. He moved back again to my side but still with his hands pinning back my arms; then very gently he raised himself on top of me. It awakened all manner of cravings within my body and even when he moved his hands to cup my breasts I still kept my arms stretched behind me. It was then that he started to strip away my clothing.

Ben didn't just take away my underwear; he held it to his face and drew in his breath and to this day I

7

know he derived some deep joy from the ritual. When I was completely naked he quickly removed his own clothing and for the first time in my entire life I saw the body of an aroused man. By this time I was yearning for more so when he plunged himself inside me I was not expecting the pain and yelled out like a baby! But it was short lived and followed by the most exquisite hurt and his eyes stayed on my face continually as he enjoyed my virginal response to his lusty behaviour.

I thought I came close to a warm orange glow that night but with hindsight not at all. However, afterwards we spent many a wondrous hour in his flat and I felt impervious to the outcome of our affair and lavished my love on him to the extent that he became my whole life. And he thoroughly reciprocated those feelings in the beginning.

Warning Red

The fly in the ointment was Angelica. Her name conjures up someone quite ethereal; beautiful even, not short, plump, bossy and the female version of Ben. She was nearly thirty-four and their weird closeness had evolved because of the acrimonious break-up of their parents at an early age. Apparently the father took Ben and the mother Angelica but when this didn't work they swapped. It still didn't work so both children were packed off to boarding school. Consequently Ben and Angelica corresponded constantly and whenever they did meet started to depend on each other, or rather Angelica depended on Ben. Ben went to great lengths to explain all this to me pointing out that Angelica would always be his responsibility. But she disliked me and went out of her way to make me aware of this. I remember she asked about the bloodstain on the cream carpet; virginal bloodstain. We'd tried to get it out but a sludgy mark remained. Ben was irritated but I was hardly to blame; then again perhaps he thought I was. Angelica took a disquieting pleasure in asking what the stain was; yes, she asked me and I knew she knew. It crossed my mind that she'd never had sex in her life and considered it dirty. Some people did in those days.

I tried everything to make her see that I was friendly but in her eyes I was the opposition and as I was to later find out Angelica never changed her opinion whatever the circumstances.

Things jogged along like this during the summer. When Angelica was on the scene I stayed quietly in the background, just giving the odd encouraging smile to Ben although we still giggled like crazy at something totally ridiculous which would leave his sister cold. My relationship with him only began to wane when I mentioned not going to university. I wasn't even sure if it was what I wanted but I'd seen a different way of life and was sick of studying. Studying was all about keeping my mother happy.

Ben said vehemently, 'Of course you must go!'

That was my first warning. Not because he wanted me to go to university, as any sensible bloke would, but because of the terror in his eyes if I should stay. It shocked me and my childish confidence started to crumble away.

Then I didn't see him so often and gradually not at

all and I was heartsick and moped around like a zombie. Nobody could persuade me that he was no good and I chased after him in a way no decent girl should. He cold-shouldered me relentlessly and I couldn't for the life of me understand his behaviour or what colour his feelings were. Icy-white perhaps.

I was so wrapped up in misery that I didn't see what was happening to my body. Even when I started being sick reality didn't set in. Somebody at work said, 'You're not pregnant, are you?' So I went to the doctor as there was no such thing as a home-test in those days and I remember the disdain on his face when he told me I was pregnant. A termination was recommended. They always were to single girls in 1969.

I baulked at the idea; didn't like it at all. Strange really, because I was terrified of what my mother would say and do; most likely throw me out. And Ben? I think in my heart I clung on to the slimmest chance that he might be pleased. He once mentioned that he feared he'd never have a son; that the chance would pass him by; he even implied that a man like him deserved a son. It did cross my mind that my unborn child might not deserve Ben Herriott-Greene but I pushed such thoughts aside. I was good at burying my head.

Finally, when I did manage to confront him with my news he shrank from me like a scalded cat and I didn't see him for a week. I felt wretched and humiliated.

Then he reappeared looking slightly weary and sad and he even managed to smile at me. He surprised me further because he arranged for us to meet in his flat to discuss the situation. It was then that my whole being went into fantasy mode. I had been right to hang on because he did want a son. I had brought him round; we were both still hot red, after all.

Even so, I didn't take the lift to his penthouse flat and my legs were leaden as I walked up the stairs. I think I wanted to keep my worst fears away for as long as possible. When I rang the bell and he answered the door I knew it was useless because the coldness in his eyes spoke volumes and I remember looking out over the backs of Cambridge and feeling a terrible sense of loss. It was over; my wild, mad love affair was over and now I ought to be sensible and terminate what was left - our child.

He faced me, his now cold blue eyes staring into mine and he spoke in a partronising manner. 'You know,' he said, 'you're terribly young, darling, and should not be shackled with a kid.' He made a noise in the back of his throat, a sort of chuckle, a bit like my mother might make. 'And you also know I'm not the settling down kind.' He held out one hand and with the other pulled on the cuff of his shirt. I remember distinctly that his expensive cuff-links sparkled in the autumnal afternoon sunlight. Then he flicked both hands dismissively and lied through his teeth. 'Besides, I don't want children, never even contemplated the idea. My world is about business, the next deal...' He looked at me. 'I thought you knew that.'

'Ben, I never planned this,' I said.

'Maybe not, but I honestly thought you had more sense.' He sucked in his breath and added, 'And I think you should have an abortion.'

It was my turn to stare now. What a horrible word abortion is. Perhaps it was his use of this particular word that made the scales finally fall from my eyes and allowed me to see him for what he was - a cruel, ruthless man. I decided then and there that I wasn't going to let him off the hook so easily. Instead I played him at his own game having watched his antics and tactics so adoringly for months.

I said, 'I'm not getting rid of our son.'

He blinked and took a deep breath. The word son definitely struck a chord. He stroked his chin and said, 'What do you intend to do then?'

I placed my hands on my stomach. 'Have him. Love him.'

'Jesus,' he sighed as though in pain. 'You're crazy - and what's this son stuff? How can you possibly know it's a boy?'

I smiled smugly as his tough stance slid a little. 'I just do.'

He turned and walked to the window. Peering outside he deliberated over his next words before saying, 'I still think it's a very bad idea because I can't offer you any help with this, and I don't want it hanging over my head for ever more.'

I was stung but remember staying perfectly calm because he had always admired my calmness. I said, 'You know, for once you should stop thinking business and start thinking reality. Our son is part of your future whether you like it or not.' As I drew a trembling breath I remember thinking how grown-up I sounded and he was actually listening. 'If you leave me now what will you do in all those lonely years to come when you're past it and pretty faces don't find you quite so attractive anymore? Maybe you'll reflect upon your son but he *won't* be around and most probably won't want to be.'

He got angry. 'You keep talking about my son! How do I even know it's mine?'

I choked, 'How dare you say that?' Never had I expected him to doubt my honesty. I backed off immediately, stumbling towards the door. He chased after me, grabbing my arm.

'Diana! Wait!' He looked away from me towards the table where a large brown envelope sat. I'd noticed it straight away but thought nothing of it. Ben let go of my arm and walked towards the envelope scooping it up with his left hand. He handed it to me.

'What is it?'

'Open it and see.'

I did and inside was so much money that I gulped.

'There's two thousand pounds there. I suggest you get an abortion and then take yourself off on holiday, but it's up to you. Like I said, I can't be accountable.'

Oh, boy, what I could do with all that money. It was a lot in those days. I held it in my hands briefly before raising my eyes to his and seeing a kind of relief there. He thought he'd got away with it!

It was then that I did the fateful thing and tossed the envelope across the room. I couldn't have created a better scene if I'd tried as fifty-pound notes fluttered everywhere like feathers after a pillow fight. The colour silvery-white dazzled my eyes and I realised it was my own anger. He thought he could pay me off! What an atrocious man he was.

'*I don't want your money, you ape.*' I pushed him away, 'And I don't want you either!' I stormed out of his flat and even though I heard him call my name in a frantic way I had no intention of ever going back.

A darker shade of blue

I went to stay with my God-sister-cum-best-friend Camilla in London. Briefly, I'd gone home to my mother but only to pick up a few things. She had shown some concern, seen my distress but I was anxious to get away and my behaviour wasn't enough to unsettle her.

Camilla, on the other hand, was wonderful. She plied me with comfort food and lashings of alcohol. Yes, in those days, I drank while pregnant.

Perhaps I should explain about Camilla. She came to live with us when I was nine. Her parents died in a car crash and as my mother was Camilla's Godmother she took her in. She soon regretted her altruism because at fifteen Camilla was a handful. Although extremely beautiful with her curly red hair and green eyes, and she was clever, she was also wayward. She later told me it was because she knew she was different sexually and didn't know how to handle it. Anyway, she loused up at school and hiked off to London where she lived rough for a while before coming home quite repentant. My mother allowed her back in; much to my father's and my surprise; and that was when Camilla and I became close. Even though I was only twelve she confided in me and I felt very grown up. Eventually she found work in a hairdressing salon in Cambridge and did extremely well. It soon became evident she was a whiz with peoples hair and before long was winning all sorts of competitions, one of which took her to London again. Here she used her brain and found work in one of the best salons in town. She progressed and began accompanying the owner on all sorts of trips doing famous folks hair.

We stayed in constant touch and even though she regularly chided me on being boring I still had enormous respect for her. She was my mentor so six years later when I was pregnant she was the obvious person for me to turn to and she offered me time to reflect.

She was shocked, I can tell you, but in all honesty I think she was impressed that innocent little Diana had tasted the forbidden fruit. Anyway, we both came to the conclusion that I should have the wretched termination but Camilla did give me the option of moving in and us both parenting my child. I'd always suspected that she rather fancied me but never felt threatened, and didn't even then but that wasn't what I wanted and *I'm* certainly not a lesbian.

I made her choke. 'I'm thinking of swallowing my pride and asking Ben for that money.'

'Diana, don't you dare! If you need money, I'll give it to you but don't go crawling back to that swine.'

It was then that the phone rang. Camilla answered it and pulled a face. 'Deborah, how are you?'

I covered my face with a cushion because I didn't want to talk to my mother, but an insistent Camilla handed me the phone.

'Diana,' said my mother in her matter-of-fact way, 'so there you are. Now, this chap's been bothering me, constantly ringing. Even called round last night. Ben Herriott-Greene - isn't he the man you work for?' My mother was always vague, never listened to me properly.

I sat up straight. 'Yes, well, he was. So what did he say?' I panicked because I didn't want my mother knowing anything about my condition.

'That he was most anxious to see you.'

'Did you tell him where I was?'

'I didn't know! You left in such a hurry.'

I felt a strange sense of relief. She obviously knew nothing and Ben might just be having second thoughts. 'Yes. Sorry about that. So why are you ringing?'

'Because I promised I'd find you! He wants you to get in touch as soon as possible.' She took a deep breath. 'You're not in any sort of trouble are you?'

'Of course not.' I lied.

'Well, the way he spoke anyone would think you'd run off with the petty-cash or something.'

My heart plummeted. 'I expect it's something to do with work. There's no need to worry, and while we're on the phone, I thought I'd stay here with Camilla for a week or so. Is that okay with you?'

She hesitated. 'I suppose so. But what about all this money you were supposed to be earning for university?'

'Mum, give me a break.'

'Typical! Just like your father; all talk no staying power. Anyway, do give this chap a call. I promised, and I do like to keep my promises.' She hesitated. 'Actually it's just as well because Aunt Fi is coming to stay next week. But what about your job with this Herriott-Greene chap?'

I sighed in exasperation. 'I've packed it in but don't worry, I'll sort everything out and do give my love to Aunt Fi. Bye for now.' I replaced the receiver and Camilla gave me a sympathetic look. I wiped imaginary sweat from my forehead. 'Lucky escape, Aunt Fi's due for her visit next week.'

'Blimey, they come round quickly.'

'I swear she'd like to live with us if she could.' I

shuddered; in that pokey flat; me, mother and Aunt Fi!

'So tell me, what did Deborah want?'

I brightened. 'It's Ben. He's been asking after me.'

'Perhaps you're the only person who's ever thrown his money back in his face so he thinks he'd better marry you!'

I stared at her. 'I doubt that.'

She shrugged. 'Ring him and see.'

I thought about it. But no, I wouldn't be doing that. The swine could wait.

Purple

It was about a week before Ben turned up at Camilla's flat. During that time Camilla had given me a complete overhaul. My hair had been highlighted and cut to shoulder length with a long fringe and she'd shown me how to use eye-liner and shadow to the best effect making my brown eyes seem almond shaped and rather sexy. I liked it.

The look on Ben's face when he saw me was similar to how it had been when we first got together. Anxious, keen even. He didn't waste any time; said he'd found a beautiful house in Brooklands Avenue in Cambridge, a house fit to bring up *his* son; not *our* son.

'So what about your flat?' I queried out of interest. 'Are you going to sell it?'

'Why should I?'

'I just thought…'

'Diana, I own the whole block; in fact I own a whole lot more as well.'

Rather humbly I nodded and if I am completely honest I was impressed. He owned all that property and there was my mother and I living in a tiny flat in Newmarket. Actually I was perplexed. 'What are your intentions, Ben?' He hadn't mentioned marriage.

'Intentions?'

I knew him so well. It was the baby he wanted, not me. But at eighteen years old a new me was emerging. Was it because I was pregnant and over-protective or was I selfishly looking out for my own.

'Look, Angelica can look after the baby and you can go to university, do whatever you want to do. It won't be a problem.'

I was right. Angelica looking after my baby! No way!

'I'll look after my own baby, thank you.'

'Diana!' Ben moved closer to me and reached out for my hand which I withdrew. 'I'm so sorry I behaved as I did. It was the shock. But I've had time to reflect and I know now that I want to have this child. Just tell me what I have to do to make things right between us?'

'Marry me for starters.'

He swallowed hard. 'Yes, yes, I agree to that - if it's what you want.'

I was stunned. He'd just agreed to marry me! No more pokey flat.

'And Angelica?'

'There's a separate basement apartment in the house. It's three storeys, for God's sake! It won't be a problem.'

Wouldn't it? Angelica permanently in my life. 'But she doesn't like me.'

'She will do as she's told.'

Of course; but what about me? 'Will I have to do as I'm told as well?'

He hesitated and smiled. 'You haven't so far.'

I smiled too as I reflected; if I married Ben Herriott-Greene it would be a very strange union. Ben, me, our baby – and Angelica. She hated me, would she hate our son as well?

I had no choice. The alternative seemed much worse.

1970

Gay Liberation Front begins
Lester Piggott wins Derby on Nijinsky
First Jumbo lands at Heathrow
Edward Heath becomes new Tory Prime Minister
Major oil field found in North Sea
Tony Jacklin wins US Open
Chelsea win FA Cup 2-1 against Leeds

Pale Blue

Pale blue: does it conjure up a beautiful sky on a mid-summer's day? Or is it a man's crisp and freshly ironed shirt with a contrasting coloured tie? Or a colour waiting to change into something far more magnificent? When I reflect upon the time up until the birth of our baby I think of a colour where I was living in hope. I had a lot of time on my hands because Ben didn't allow me to work in his office anymore, or anywhere else for that matter, but things would change when our son was born. They had to.

We all duly moved into Brooklands Avenue. I loved the house, early Victorian with high ceilings and deep casement windows, especially the garden which seemed to go on forever, sort of narrow yet far reaching. Angelica took over the basement space and turned it into a shrine for her carefully sought after antiquities. It was her main hobby going to antique auctions and sitting with her thermos flask and ham sandwiches waiting for her specified lots to come up. I have to give her credit, the things she bought were quite beautiful and 1970 was certainly a time for picking up such treasures cheaply. Everything then was supposed to be ultra-modern with weird and wonderful shaped furniture and with furnishings in bizarre colours like bright orange mixed with purple and chocolate brown. And because Angelica loved her antiques so much I wanted to be different so encouraged Ben in his love of modern furnishings even though secretly I coveted Angelica's purchases.

Oh, yes, and Angelica did nothing to endear herself

to me. Shortly after I married Ben (in Shire Hall's Registry Office in Cambridge with only him, me, my mother and Camilla present – Angelica couldn't make it!) she told me in no uncertain terms that her brother secretly despised me and had only married me because he thought I was going to give birth to a son. But she thought I was expecting a girl and that Ben would hate me for duping him. These words chilled my bones, and briefly the colour nightmare black clouded my mind without the tiniest hint of a light and I was afraid. I spoke to Ben.

'But you assured me it is a boy?' he said matter-of-factly.

'But what if it's not?'

He smiled then shrugged. 'I won't trust another word you say.'

I walked towards the door and he called after me. 'Diana, if it's a girl - we'll just have to try again.'

I pushed Angelica's words aside and convinced myself that all would be well once our son was born. You can convince yourself of anything if you try hard enough. I was young, vulnerable and pregnant.

The silly thing is Angelica did not work either, she quite comfortably lived off her brother and still her position was held in high esteem whereas mine seemed not to be; I'm sure Ben saw me as the cook and cleaner.

My mother thought that Ben was wonderful. Well, she would, and she loved our home in Brooklands Avenue. In fact, she sucked up to Ben in a way that I never would and still he didn't offer to re-house her. He could have easily afforded to. I often wondered about that. With all that property he could have put my mother into a new home without it making the minutest dent in his profits. But he didn't. My mother thought none-the-less of him, but I did. I learned never to expect anything and it was as well that I did.

Nightmare Black

'Push! Come on now, just one more really big push!'

I was exhausted. Ben was nowhere to be seen and I was being shouted at by a middle-aged spinster mid-wife who was treating me like a machine. I'm quite sure she'd never come close to sex let alone giving birth!

But I pushed with all of my might even though the pain was excrutiating and I remember feeling as though my insides were being forcefully shoved out of my body - and then the mid-wife shouted,

'Good girl! Stop! Stop now - it's a girl! Yes, a girl! You have a daughter!'

If I said my heart sank it would be the biggest understatement of my life. I think in that instant exhaustion manifested itself into sheer panic and I actually wanted to die. How could life treat me so cruelly, this was so disastrously unfair.

She was placed in my arms and I looked down at my daughter. I stared at her hardly able to believe my eyes because this crinkly faced little mite bore a striking resemblance to the person I hated most in my life.

'Angelica!' I said pitifully.

'What a lovely name.' The mid-wife cast an eye over my newborn baby and I knew she was thinking that the name didn't suit the face.

'No! That's not her name. It's just - she looks like someone…'

'Poor baby.' The words were out before the mid-wife had time to think.

I searched the face of my offspring; I must have been looking for something of myself. She screwed up her face and squealed, or at least made a noise like a squeal, no it was more like a rabbit in a trap. She hates me, I thought. My baby hates me. The midwife whipped her out of my arms.

'The doctor will be along soon to sew you up,' she said.

I just wanted to die.

He arrived at the Rosie Maternity Hospital in Cambridge without so much as a single flower. If he'd bought me flowers I would have known I was forgiven. Hadn't I told him enough times that I loved flowers?

He peered into the cot and pulled a face. Then he walked round the bed and looked at me with something like disdain.

'Sorry,' I said.

'Why are you sorry?'

'Because I thought it was going to be a boy.'

'Hmm. I'll listen to Angelica in future.' Ben looked smug and I wished I'd never married him.

'Why?' I asked.

'You know why. Angelica *said* it would be a girl.'

I was exhausted and miserable and couldn't think of a single reason to be happy so I said, 'Your bloody sister cast a spell on me and that's why the baby looks exactly like her!'

He was shocked by my outburst. Normally I was

so calm. Ben walked down to the bottom of the bed once more and looked at our daughter. I watched and there was no doubting that he recognised his sister in the wrinkled features of our baby. Ben cast an eye in my direction and a sly smile crossed his mouth. 'I see what you mean.'

I repeated. 'I'm sorry. Truly I am. You can divorce me if you like.'

'Oh, I won't be doing that.'

'Why?' I brightened ever so slightly.

'Because I'll damned well hold you to your word. The next baby or the one after that will be a boy. We'll go on until it is. Okay? Do you think you can manage that?'

His tone was patronising and I stared at him aghast. I was miserable; trapped in a marriage that was only about bearing a son; there was no loving anymore. Having just given birth and writhing with the pain of the stitches than pinched like crazy his words filled me with absolute horror but how could I argue so I just nodded and agreed.

He left me then and our daughter started to squeal and all I felt was revulsion; no motherly instincts. I despised our baby because this was all her fault. One of the nurses plucked her out of the cot and started to hand her to me saying,

'She's hungry.'

I turned my head away and started to weep. 'I'm sorry, I can't feed her. I don't want to.'

The nurse shrugged but was sympathetic. 'Your decision. I'll give her a bottle. You rest, love.' She took her away.

I was so grateful. Thank goodness someone recognised my misery.

Amber Alert

It was visiting time. I woke to what seemed like a melee of people and in my dazed state of mind looked down to the end of my bed where my baby's cot rested. To my utter amazement Angelica was there and I'd never ever seen such a tender look on her face! I watched in fascination as she cooed over my daughter. Then she realised that I was awake and her face changed from soft to hard.

'Angelica.' I said.

'You're awake.'

I muttered, 'Didn't expect you,' as I tried to prop myself up with the pain of my stitches biting in.

She sniffed. 'Ben told me.'

'Told you?'

She eyed me in her haughty manner. 'That the child looks like me.'

I smiled in a resigned way. 'Indeed she does.'

Angelica looked into the cot once more and her face became a picture of tenderness as she ran a gentle hand over the baby's face. Then she surprised me even further as she reached into the cot greedily and picked the baby up cradling her and whispering endearments. I was staggered; Angelica actually liked something that I'd produced.

She looked at me and the switch in her expression took my breath away. 'You were telling the truth then.' She said.

'The truth?'

She looked once more at my child and smiled. 'She is Ben's.'

I caught my breath and stared at her. She put the

baby back into the cot and straightened herself but her eyes didn't leave the baby.

I slumped back into my pillow too exhausted to say anything.

She said, 'I must go. I shall look forward to your return.'

I swallowed hard and wanted to weep.

1973

Equality promised to Women Workers
Britain goes on a three-day week
President Nixon's Watergate hearings begin
Princess Anne weds Captain Mark Phillips
Picasso died
JRR Tolkien died
Noel Coward died
Chelsea – dropping in the first division

Spring Pink

It was early May and the spring blossom was on the trees. As a child I would have loved this time of year; helping my father nurturing the new year's growth and the prospect of summer. Natasha was almost three and about to have her first real birthday party. It was quite a highlight in our lives and although Ben was constantly away working and wouldn't be around Angelica and I had gone to great lengths to make this a special day for Natasha. Camilla was going to be there, as was my mother and Aunt Fi and several of Natasha's friends from nursery school.

Angelica and I now sort of rubbed along; if I remembered that she was the boss; whilst Ben and I seemed like ships that passed in the night and when he was around he usually found something to complain about. Our personal relationship was based on hurried sex, obviously to procreate because he didn't seem to place any importance on words of endearment. He never told me loved me, or that he even cared a little about me. He never paid me a compliment even though I looked after myself. Our home was kept pristine clean and his laundry beautifully cared for. I had taken myself off to cookery classes and if I say so myself the meals I produced were good, classy even. Very occasionally we'd throw a dinner-party and his friends and colleagues treated me with great respect and at these times so did Ben, but normally he ignored me except when procreation was on his mind. The irony was he never paid any attention to Natasha either and lurking in the back of my mind was my desire to leave Ben but as

Natasha grew it became an impossibility. She was very attached to Angelica; as was Angelica to her niece.

I was totally intrigued by their relationship because it was instant love that just grew and grew. Angelica knew exactly how to play my daughter along and did everything in her power to woe her away from me. For the first six months after Natasha was born I couldn't bond with her at all and was grateful for Angelica's help, relieved even to have my baby taken away and looked after. In truth I bitterly regretted marrying Ben and, shamefully, not having had a termination. Of course I only ever admitted this to my faithful friend Camilla who told me it would only be a matter of time before everything would come right between me and my daughter.

But Natasha only had to squeal (her favourite pastime, exercising her lungs to full capacity) and Aunt Jelly would come running. It was Angelica who chose the name Aunt Jelly and my daughter took to it with alacrity and love. Aunt Jelly never said no, Aunt Jelly would allow Natasha anything. Aunt Jelly bought all her clothes and Aunt Jelly organised bath-time and read bedtime stories. If I so much as suggested anything else Angelica would turn and ask Natasha what she would prefer and my daughter always chose what Aunt Jelly wanted. I gave in and realised that it was my punishment for making Ben marry me so I strived to make amends. Neither Ben nor Angelica noticed nor appreciated this but as my father had always insisted one had to make the best of a bad job.

Natasha's party went reasonably well, that is until one of her little friends, Sophie, decided that she wanted to play with my daughter's new pink doll's pram. Natasha wasted no time and pushed her away spitefully. Sophie decided to retaliate and quite a spat started with Natasha scratching Sophie's face.

'Now then!' reprimanded Angelica.

I watched, rooted to the spot. So did Camilla and my mother and Aunt Fi and everybody else. Angelica then proceeded to take Sophie's arm and tell her that she was an extremely naughty little girl. Our mouths fell open but not one of us did anything about it. Sophie wailed as though stung and Angelica made a big thing of cuddling Natasha. It was Camilla who went to Sophie and picked her up. She took her off to bathe her face.

My mother tutted and Aunt Fi nodded and I wasn't sure whether they disapproved of Camilla or Angelica. Well, I wasn't sure for about two seconds; because as they pacified darling Natasha who was in Angelica's arms I knew that they were under the same damned spell as I was. Perhaps it's called servility.

Camilla and I had a long heart to heart that evening. She moved into my bedroom and climbed into the enormous king-size bed I occasionally shared with Ben. Strangely enough Ben really admired Camilla and was always pleased to welcome her into our home. One of the few bonuses of my marriage was our annual skiing trip to Meribel in France and Camilla was always invited.

I have to say Camilla had done amazingly well. The early seventies did not boast breakfast-onwards television or the random designer personalities of much later years but she was personal hairdresser and adviser to many famous faces and had marketed several of her products which sold incredibly well. She was much sought after although she'd never found the love of her life and continued to live alone albeit in a smarter flat in Fulham. I valued her friendship enormously. She could have said many times, 'I told you so,' but she never did. What was extra special was the fact she listened to my moans and groans and although she never said as much I'm sure she thought my daughter was a spiteful minx who without stronger supervision could turn into an absolute horror.

'You're too soft, Diana, you should take control.'

Propped up against a myriad of pillows I sipped my red wine. 'It's all right for you but I'm no match for the might of Ben and his diabolical sister.'

'How can you say that? Angelica is a bully. Bullies always back of if confronted.'

'If only you knew. It's not like that. If I so much as voice my concerns Ben stares at me coldly and remarks on why I'm not pregnant. It's my Achilles heel and he knows it. He doesn't tire of commenting on how I managed to get pregnant so quickly before we were married and not afterwards.'

'So he's never guessed?'

I shrugged. 'Maybe, but somehow I don't think so. I've told him that infrequent and hurried sex is not conducive to child bearing.'

'So where do you hide your pills?'

I tapped the side of the bed. 'Under the mattress.'

'Have you ever considered having another baby? Perhaps if it was a boy…'

'Camilla! I couldn't possibly go through all that

again. It'd be bound to be another girl.'

Camilla sighed. 'I think your real problem is Angelica. You should have it out with her once and for all. Take charge of your daughter.'

Tears sprung into my eyes and I wondered how Camilla, my only friend, could not see how tricky all three members of this family were. 'I've tried so hard to befriend my daughter and Angelica will always outdo me. Can't you see the bond between the pair of them? They freeze me out and as young as Natasha is she enjoys the attention. Angelica takes great delight in turning my daughter against me and Ben doesn't give a damn. I've tried everything. If Natasha says she likes something I rush out and buy it but then Angelica will find something Natasha prefers. It's like a game with them and I'm at a loss to know what to do.'

Camilla considered this and said matter-of-factly. 'I know what I'd do; look after myself. Forget them all. Do something you like and to hell with them.'

'What do you mean?'

She tapped my arm with a beautifully painted forefinger. 'There must be something you'd like to do?'

'Ben would never agree to it.'

'There you go again! So defeatist! What is it? You have rights in this household as well, you know.'

'But it would cost a lot of money.'

'Of which he's got bucketloads. Think of Angelica's antiques for starters. How can he deny you anything?'

'It's the garden. I'd like to revamp it. Do you know, I could make our garden look stunning.'

Camilla looked at me her eyes widening. 'Fab! Do it then!

'He'll say no. He'll say the time is not right or something equally negative.'

'Don't give him the choice. Just do it!'

I looked at my friend. 'What - present him with quotes and stuff?'

'Yes! For goodness sake, you know more about gardening than anyone I know.' She rolled her eyes mockingly.

But already I was feeling better. 'Fancy another bottle?'

She grinned. 'Yeah, may as well get smashed. I'll get it, shall I?'

And with that she was off the bed and padding downstairs to the kitchen to bring back another bottle of Ben's finest burgundy.

Bronze with red

In the end I decided not to consult Ben at all about the garden. During the summer of 73 he was away a lot in California. Sometimes I didn't see him for weeks on end. In fact, he was fine with me about money; I had a cheque book and a personal allowance but I never abused it, on the contrary I lived quite frugally, I don't know why. Food was the big item in our house and I never scrimped on that.

I contacted two landscape gardeners and liked the first one immediately. I just went through the process of seeing the second so that I could produce two quotes if Ben were to later ask. But Ivor Stanford arrived with his big smile and amiable disposition and he listened to all of my ideas and gave me just a little advice and I knew he wouldn't try to change my plans. He told me how he'd been a gardener all his life and his father before him, and now his fifteen year-old son Charlie was helping him during the summer holidays.

Then I worked a bit of magic. I took my daughter Natasha by the hand and led her all the way down to the bottom of the garden telling her of my ideas. I knew that there must be something of me in her but was beginning to despair until I mentioned that the picnic area at the bottom of the garden which would be surrounded by tall exotic leaved plants and flowers was going to be called the teddy-bear's picnic area. As simple as that! She was caught and her imagination began to move on as rapidly as mine. We then went over the whole of the garden and I painted in her mind an enchanting picture of Toby turnips and Mrs Poppy Pumpkin in the vegetable patch. The small lily pond set high within stone steps would have ducky doolittles and Freddie fishes and then – my piece-de-resistance – the play area with its sand-pit and swing dangling from the sturdy old oak tree would also have a small slide descending from a tree house, well, it was more of a raised house on a platform within a swathe of prunus.

Natasha's mouth was open in awe; that is between question after question. And could her friend Jakie play with her in the garden? 'Of course', I said. Jakie was Natasha's invisible friend, a friend that Aunt Jelly disapproved of and rubbished at every opportunity, but somehow Natasha knew I would never do that.

As we walked back into the house Natasha rushed towards Angelica who had been peering out of the kitchen window with inquisitive eyes. It was ironic how she used my house as if it was her own yet I was never allowed into her pad unless invited.

Natasha's words tripped over themselves as she explained to her beloved Aunt Jelly about our new garden. I noticed how my sister-in-law's face remained rigid before she glared at me.

'Ben never said anything about a new garden.'

I remembered Camilla's words of encouragement. 'Maybe because he doesn't yet know.' I smiled in my most disarming way.

'Isn't that a bit presumptious of you?'

'Why?'

'Gardens like that cost money as you well know.'

I looked at the confused face of my daughter. I winked. I'd never done that before but instinct told me to. Her face, so like Angelica's, creased into a lop-sided smile.

'Who cares; it's only money, and Daddy earns loads of that.' I reached down and picked up my daughter. I added, 'And we are going to have so much fun in our new garden.' I also added. 'And when we get us a brother like Jakie he'll love it too.'

Natasha's face flooded with glee. 'A brusser?'

'Yes.' I replied. 'Not too long now.'

Speechless, Angelica looked at me with absolute loathing in her eyes.

I have to admit, it was Camilla who had put the idea into my head. Tonight I would throw away my pills and to hell with it. I'd been a good wife and my penance had been paid. Surely a boy was owed to me now.

Ben arrived home and Angelica couldn't wait to speak to him. She was hopping mad since the garden incident and had shunned me completely whilst being all over Natasha making sure attention was taken away from me. It wasn't hard, Natasha so adored Aunt Jelly.

Ben paced himself and climbed into bed next to me. Quite casually he said, 'So, what's all this about the garden?'

'The garden? Who told you about that?' Innocent little me; I was learning.

He cleared his throat. 'Angelica; she's a bit upset.'

'Why?'

He shrugged, 'Just that you seem to be doing things without telling anyone else about it.'

I laughed out loud. He was bemused. 'You're hardly ever here and I certainly told Natasha and she is delighted but Angelica didn't like that. She takes over our daughter and what am I supposed to do?' I looked at my husband and tried to remember how I used to feel about him, how I adored him. Surely it wasn't so hard to feign love. 'I'm just going to redesign our garden, it's not a problem, is it?' I smiled, then giggled, remembering how we used to laugh together. 'You know, lots of childrens things. Ready for when we get our boys.'

His demeanour changed. 'Boys?'

'Isn't that what you want?'

He stroked his chin; his manner vulnerable. I'd never seen him so and I was to think about that later in my life. Then his manner switched like a chameleon. 'You've changed.'

'Have I?'

'I'll say. The original ice-maiden you've been.'

'That's unfair. You're hardly here and you take no notice of me.'

Ben sighed. 'And now you want something.'

I decided to remain positive. 'The garden is going to look sensational and I have a strong feeling we are going to have a son.'

'I've heard all this before.' But he could not hide his excitement. 'Are you pregnant?'

'I aim to be.'

He slumped, disappointed, and said nothing.

I drew him closer. 'But I promise I will be soon.'

'How much is it going to cost?'

'The garden? Just a few hundred. I can take it out of my allowance if you like.'

'No need for that.' He pushed his hand between my legs and I fought to suppress my antipathy. To survive I needed to give this everything so I caressed his face as I would have done in the early days. He said, 'Put on your high-heels.' It was a command, not a saucy request.

He made me feel sick, but I did as I was told.

Ben left for California two weeks later, which was as well because Ivor was about to start work and I didn't want my husband making endless criticisms. Ben's accountant Sean Jackson was travelling with him this time and arrived at our house to pick Ben up. I was introduced and very surprised by this extremely good-looking divorcee; I'd heard Ben talk about Sean quite a bit, caught snippets of telephone conversations and I knew he had a seventeen-year-old daughter so assumed he would be a lot older and never expected to be bowled over by this tall very masculine man with searching brown eyes and dark curly hair. Perhaps I was more intrigued by the way he looked at me. How old could he be? Middle thirties maybe; it had been years since anyone had looked at me like that. After they'd left for the airport I went upstairs and peered at myself in the mirror. I took the bulldog clip out of my hair and noticed how my highlighted hair, thanks to Camilla, tumbled around my shoulders and had been further streaked by the sun. It looked good, and undoubtedly the light tan over my face and body made me look healthy. I reflected; I was twenty-two years old and most probably pregnant again now. Perhaps it would be a boy this time and Ben would change towards me. I'd managed to keep my figure even though at times I comfort-ate and certainly drank too much wine.

I went downstairs and out through the kitchen into the garden. It was a lovely July day and my heart lifted with the prospect of the work to be done on the garden. Ivor Stanford would be arriving the next day and said that with the paved terrace it would all take about four weeks. Of course after that the new plants and turf would need constant watering if the weather stayed dry but I was happy to do things like that, excited even at the prospect.

Red with Orange

In my mind real happiness is orange and in the early seventies I don't remember the colour even remotely emerging, until Ivor Stanford arrived to do our garden, that is. I'm ashamed to say there were other oranges in my head as well but I struggled to push such thoughts away.

Ivor arrived in a battered old white truck with all his equipment including a mini-digger and it was several minutes before I was introduced to his son Charlie. Both men wore orange overalls and that should have been a warning especially as Charlie was a very young man.

'Charlie, meet Mrs Herriott-Greene.'

'Diana, please call me Diana.'

Charlie looked at me briefly and then did a double take; his eyes now steady on my face and I noticed how enticing they were and that his blond hair was attractively tousled. 'Diana.' My name was said with surprised interest in his voice.

Let me describe Charlie: About 5'10", very skinny, beguiling hazel eyes, a generous mouth that curved into a stunning smile and lovely even teeth. His nose was his only irregular feature with a slight bump beneath the bridge but this only added to the charm of his whole face; and he had typical teenage skin but he was mature beyond his years and disarmingly polite. It was a whole week before the colour vibrant orange dazzled my mind but there were shards of it from the very beginning of our acquaintance. I had to remind myself that he was only fifteen.

I would take coffee to the workers. Ivor operated the mini-digger but his son was constantly busy. When I chatted to Charlie he was animated about my garden and knew all the Latin names of the plants I'd chosen and immediately we became kindred spirits. I'd never felt so comfortable with anyone since my father except this was very different. I found myself watching Charlie's face and noticing his hands, his long slim fingers and the way he rubbed the soil between them and then wiped his hands down his overalls. He had a naughty sense of humour and there was lots of laughing with the garden in such disarray. Even Natasha was interested when she managed to slip the leash tightly held by Angelica. Charlie was adorable with her, chatted away and when she told him to, 'Mind out! You're standing on Jakie's foot!' Charlie quickly stepped aside and apologised to her imaginary friend. He needed no prompting, just acted as though it was the most natural thing in the world to have invisible people in the garden. I started to fall dangerously in love with him then.

About a week later Angelica told me that Mrs Spencer wanted to see me. She said this with disdain. Why would Natasha's nursery teacher want to see me? Angelica always insisted on taking Natasha to nursery and picking her up. I had to fight for the privilege; it was seldom granted.

'Why?' I asked.

She turned on me. 'How should I know? Unless it's to tell you that Natasha hates all this fuss and palaver going on in the garden!' My sister-in-law's beady eyes glared at me and her thin lips pinched together as she continued, 'And I'm sure you actively encourage her with this ridiculous imaginary friend, in fact I know that you do. It's damaging, Diana, don't you know anything about children?'

I took a deep breath. Something I'd learned to do with Angelica. 'I'll take Natasha to nursery tomorrow, shall I?'

'I suppose you'll have to under the circumstances.'

I started to walk away. She called after me. 'You'll let me know.'

'Sorry?'

Angelica sighed indignantly. 'What Mrs Spencer is worried about.'

'Of course. I'll come straight back and speak to you before I do anything else.'

'No need for sarcasm.'

I looked at her and thought; I'd like to smash your face in but that was the imaginary me, a bit like my daughter's friend and that wouldn't do at all.

'We're seriously worried, Mrs Herriott-Greene. Your daughter can be very spiteful and it doesn't matter what is said to her she continues to be naughty. The other children are starting to dislike her and she is sidelined. I have to say it is very disruptive behaviour and if something is not done to sort it out there will no longer be a place for Natasha at this nursery.'

I was shocked and sat there for several seconds with my mouth open. Finally I said, 'When you say spiteful, what exactly do you mean?'

Mrs Spencer rolled her eyes. 'Pulling hair, pinching, and scratching are particular favourites of Natasha's. She is extremely obstreperous.'

'So what do you suggest?'

'Mrs Herriott-Greene, she's your daughter, you tell me?'

'Have you said anything about this to my sister-in-law?'

Again, Mrs Spencer rolled her eyes. 'To be quite honest with you, I think your sister-in-law might be part of the problem. She spoils Natasha in the extreme.'

I smiled, 'You've noticed.'

'She's your daughter, can't you do something about it?'

I was going to say no until I realised how pathetic it would sound. 'It's tricky and I'm sorry and will try to sort the situation out. It might take a while but I'll do my best.' I leaned back in my chair. 'You know, I thought you were going to tell me off about Natasha's imaginary friend.'

Mrs Spencer curiosity was aroused. 'Imaginary friend?'

'Jakie. Angelica thinks it's damaging, but, well, to be honest with you when I was Natasha's age I had an imaginary friend and I don't think he did me any harm.'

'You say Jakie?' Mrs Spencer sighed. 'Ah, that could explain quite a lot.' She too leaned back in her chair. 'It's just that one of the squabbles was because of Jakie, I remember the name well because we don't have a Jakie here.'

'Don't tell me someone sat on him?'

'Yes, exactly! That's exactly what happened!'

'I'm so sorry. Jakie has this way of getting trod on and sat on. Poor Natasha, to be honest I think he's the only friend she's got.'

'Hmmm. And *he's* in her head.'

I hesitated. 'Is it harmful?'

'To have an imaginary friend? I hardly think so but

I wouldn't really know to tell you the truth.'

'Will the other children laugh at her?'

Mrs Spencer looked wise. 'I don't think so and they might even be impressed. Perhaps they've got a friend or two of their own.' She looked serious. 'But that doesn't resolve your daughter's spitefulness. I'm sorry, but you do need to give Natasha some direction.'

'Oh, I will. I promise.'

'Good. Perhaps it would be better if you bought Natasha to nursery in future. Will that be a problem?'

'No; I'll tell Angelica that you've requested it.'

Mrs Spencer smiled. I like to think she understood my problem only too well.

As I walked back to Brooklands Avenue I weighed up in my mind what I was going to say. My sister-in-law was adept at twisting facts and making me look stupid and I knew she would not take Mrs Spencer's news lightly. She pounced on me when I walked in.

'Well?'

'It's just, Natasha hasn't settled so well.'

'Sorry?'

'She has some problems.'

'Such as?'

'Mrs Spencer says she's spiteful; to the other children.'

Angelica gave a derogatory laugh. I picked my words carefully. 'We should show her how to be kinder.'

'She called you in to say that?'

'Yes.'

'Ridiculous!'

'Actually, no, because Natasha needs guidance.'

'What?'

'Maybe she's confused.'

'You're confused, you mean. This is the most bizarre conversation I've ever had!'

'I'm not confused. What Mrs Spencer actually said was that the other children don't like Natasha and if she doesn't change she'll have to leave.'

Angelica was astounded and then her face contorted. 'So this confusion, it wouldn't have anything to do with this stupid Jakie friend you've encouraged her to have. I shall go and have a word with Mrs Spencer and give her a piece of my mind.'

'No! You mustn't. This is for me to sort out with your help.'

'And when did you ever sort anything out? All you ever do is wreck things – like our lovely garden for starters!'

I was reeling from her words. How quickly our relationship had degenerated since I'd taken some sort of control over my life. I retaliated. 'And if that's not spiteful I don't know what is.'

'The truth is always spiteful in *your* eyes!'

What did she mean? Where did she get such thoughts from? 'What's wrong with you? Don't you want Natasha to be liked by other children?'

'The reason she is not liked is because she has this stupid friend, it has nothing whatsoever to do with me!'

'Then why is it that Mrs Spencer thinks it has?'

For about two seconds Angelica was stumped for words. Then she said, 'There's nothing else for it, I shall take Natasha away from that ridiculous nursery and that will be the end of it – and hopefully Jakie as well!'

'No you won't!'

She glared at me. 'I beg your pardon?'

'I said; no you won't. You seem to forget that Natasha is my daughter, not yours.'

'We'll see about that. I'll ring Ben straight away and I know full well what he'll have to say.'

'I wouldn't do that! It's the middle of the night in California. And I'm warning you, if you upset things further between Ben and me you might find that I leave this miserable house and take my daughter with me!'

'No you won't!' She sneered at me. 'You're too scared. I know you, you wouldn't last a day without us to look after you.'

I hated her then because I feared she spoke the truth. I started to walk away. She called after me.

'I rule this household, not you.'

I didn't bother to reply, but one thing was for sure, I would take more control of my daughter from now on whether Angelica liked it or not.

Later that day Angelica did not come with me to pick up Natasha from nursery; I didn't see her at all until much later when she arrived home laden with new clothes for Natasha and several toys that I knew were intended to exasperate me further.

I thought I was pregnant and didn't know whether to be thrilled or filled with dread. I didn't mention this to Ben when I spoke to him on the telephone and it was obvious by the cursory conversation we had that Angelica had not spoken to him either. I was relieved. Who knows, being pregnant might change things. I lived in hope.

Deadly Purple/Shocking Orange

What happened next just added to my confusion and filled my head with shock waves of orange and deadly purples. It was a beautiful day and Natasha and I were in the garden. I had bought her a small spade and she loved digging in the now softly tilled soil and she talked to Jakie. I had spoken once more to Mrs Spencer and she assured me that an imaginary friend was harmless so long as it didn't become a weapon that the child used against others.

Charlie had been helping his father with the paving of the terrace but he wandered up to us and started to chat as he always did. These days I hardly dare look at him for fear of showing my feelings. What happened next was split-second; he just bent down to talk to Natasha and she turned on him; with her spade she smacked him in the face not once but twice lividly scraping his cheek and drawing blood. He shot to his feet and I yanked up my daughter by her arm and spanked her bottom hard. She yelped and scurried off screaming at the top of her voice for Aunt Jelly.

I looked at Charlie's ravaged face. Alarmed, Ivor came over and was shocked to see what my daughter had done.

I spluttered, 'I'm so sorry, I can't tell you how sorry I am. She's a very naughty girl.'

Charlie gave one of his heart-melting smiles. 'It's no matter. I suppose I stood on Jakie again.'

'Please, come into the house. I'll bathe your face. Come on, Charlie.'

Ivor patted his son's arm. 'Go on, go with the good

lady. You'll live, boy, it's only superficial.'

We walked into the kitchen and I went straight to the medicine cupboard in the top right-hand corner reaching for my box of tricks. I was about to start bathing Charlie's face with antiseptic when I heard Angelica's determined footsteps.

She pushed open the kitchen door; shoving Charlie aside, oblivious of him, and screamed at me. 'I think it's time you had a bit of your own medicine!' Furiously she raised her hand to hit me but Charlie reached out and grabbed her arm.

'No!' He said gripping her tightly. His commanding voice belied his years and his boldness catapulted him even higher in my estimation.

Like a vixen Angelica twisted free and faced Charlie about to hit him too but perhaps the shock at the sight of his face stopped her.

'Yes, see what Natasha has done.' I said.

My sister-in-law raged at me. 'And you know why!' She pointed at Charlie, 'He stood on her stupid friend!'

'I did and I'm very sorry.'

'It's you that should be sorry,' Angelica seethed at me. 'What a thoroughly useless person you are.'

I couldn't speak. I just stared at the woman who hated me so much. It was Charlie who took control.

'You know what? You're nasty. I feel mighty sorry for Mrs Herriott-Greene - and Natasha.'

Angelica blinked. I'd never seen her do that before. 'How dare you talk to me like that? Who the hell do you think you are?'

'Who do you think you are? Aunt Jelly? Is that what they call you? But it's Mrs Herriott-Greene I work for.'

Darling Charlie; he said it all in the most masterful way but it was lost on my sister-in-law. She practically spat at him. 'I'm glad Natasha whacked you in the face, it's no more than you deserve.'

He was appalled but made no reply. Very slightly he shook his head before looking at me. Angelica took a deep breath and left the kitchen. I watched her go and then couldn't stop the tears; they streamed down my face and I felt so stupid. 'Oh, Charlie, I'm so very, very sorry.'

He then did what he should never have done; or rather I should never have allowed him to do; he reached out and pulled me towards him so that I lay my head against his chest and I could hear his heart beating rapidly. He stroked my hair and I wanted to hug him with all of my being but how could I allow myself to do that. And yet with his right hand he raised my face to his ravaged one and pressed his mouth against mine and with sobs still catching in my throat I allowed him to do this. It wasn't a kiss; just a meeting of our lips and it was only when our tongues touched that I pulled away. He tried to stop me; tried to draw me back into his arms. He was one plucky young man and it crossed my mind that he was no virgin.

He spoke softly and meaningfully. 'I love you, Mrs Herriott-Greene.' His eyes held mine as he repeated, 'I love you, Diana.' These words thrilled me yet tore me to shreds.

Somehow I pulled myself together. 'Don't be silly.'

'I'm definitely not being silly.' His voice was breaking with emotion.

I fiddled about with the bathing swab. 'Come on,

you, I'd better do what I'm supposed to be doing.' I started to bathe the red raw scrapes on his adorable face. His eyes stayed on mine.

'You must know how I feel.' He whispered.

I stopped bathing and starting to apply antiseptic. 'I'm sure you'll be fine within a few days.' I turned away and he placed both hands on either side of my shoulders squeezing hard.

'I'll only be fine if you acknowledge my feelings.'

He twisted me round; so strong. Charlie pulled me once more into his arms and I couldn't resist it; I wound my own around his youthful frame. To be like this with him was both euphoric and dangerous; especially with Angelica so close by and like me he was aroused; I could feel it through our clothing and all it did was make me want more; never to let go.

Then there were footsteps and we separated like lightning. Ivor poked his head round the kitchen door. 'Thought I'd better check you're okay?' His face changed as he saw our embarrassment. 'Sorry…'

I gulped. 'No need to be sorry, Ivor. He's all fixed up.' I looked at Charlie's red face. 'Aren't you?'

He lowered his face and ran one finger beneath his nose. I looked at Ivor who just raised his brows. I have to say I was thoroughly ashamed.

Natasha left the nursery school, or rather Mrs Spencer requested that she leave. I had tried so hard to take control but at the risk of it soundly totally pathetic it wasn't possible for me at that time to battle against the wills of Angelica so you could say she won. I also got my period. I'm sure I was actually pregnant, but the turmoil in my life made my body say it had had enough.

And then my mother called. She was unwell and as Aunt Fi wasn't there could I visit; take some weekend shopping. This was no mean feat as I didn't drive. It would mean taking a bus from Cambridge to Newmarket, with all the shopping and Natasha, then getting a taxi from Newmarket's High Street to my mother's flat. I must learn to drive; it would be my next project and surely Ben would buy me a small car. I also knew that Ivor and Charlie would be leaving on the Friday and wanted so much to be there. Even though Charlie and I hadn't said a single word to acknowledge what had happened our eyes would meet and it was hard to look away. So I went to see my mother on the Thursday just about managing to wrestle my daughter from Angelica's clutches.

My mother was thrilled to see her granddaughter and she wasn't really ill, just feeling sorry for herself. However, I made a big fuss of her, offered to let her come and stay with us but she declined. I tried to get away in time to see Ivor and Charlie that afternoon but it was impossible. Then the next day Ivor told me that Charlie wouldn't be working because he'd had a last minute invitation to join a group of friends who were going to London. He could watch Chelsea at Stamford Bridge on the Saturday. The Blues was his football team; I knew that, he'd spoken of them many times. Ivor said Charlie had been very disappointed not to be able to say goodbye to me. Then he added, 'But perhaps it's as well.' He looked at me knowingly and I could feel the colour rising in my face.

All the same my heart sank. If only I'd known I

would have gone to see my mother on the Friday. I said softly, 'I won't see him again.'

Ivor said equally softly, 'Perhaps that too is just as well, don't you think?'

I found myself apologising. 'Nothing happened, Ivor. It was just, well, what with Natasha and everything. We only - hugged.'

Ivor nodded wisely. 'I know. But I feel I should tell you, Charlie's besotted with you and as you're married, a mother and, with respect, a good bit older I don't think that's a very healthy situation.'

I looked at Ivor and realised how it must seem to him. This was merely a teenager's fantasy and I should have known better. I'd allowed myself to get too carried away by it all.

'I'm so sorry; what must you think of me?'

'What are you sorry for?' He grinned. 'Charlie's got very good taste.'

I wanted to hug Ivor then. 'He's certainly mature for his years.'

Ivor nodded. 'He's been a bit of a lad one way or another.'

I felt wounded. 'Oh.'

Ivor touched my shoulder. 'If it's any consolation this was different. It's good we've finished here. No disrespect, Diana, but please don't try to see him again. Mature or not he is still only fifteen.'

My eyes filled with tears and I turned my head wiping them away with my sleeve. 'I wouldn't dream of it.' I looked at Ivor once more. 'I do have some integrity.'

'I know that and we've really enjoyed this job. You have a beautiful garden and great ideas.'

'Thank you.'

I felt thoroughly contrite and totally ashamed but whatever Ivor thought I knew in my heart that it had been real and I'd never forget Charlie for as long as I lived. It was just that the time factor was all wrong.

So I said my goodbye to Ivor knowing I'd also miss his craggy face and amiable attitude and I was saddened beyond belief. No more Monday mornings to look forward to even though my garden was now wonderful, and would continue to grow and flourish with every passing year, but what about me? What an absolute mess I managed to make of everything.

.

1974

Harold Wilson new labour Prime Minister
President Nixon resigns over Watergate scandal
Lord Lucan wanted for his nanny's murder
Great train robber Ronnie Biggs arrested in Brazil
Vanishing MP John Stonehouse turns up in Australia
British novelist Georgette Heyer died
Chelsea – is relegation on the cards?

Blues and Greens

In the middle of January we visited Meribel once more for our annual skiing trip. There were eight of us this time and Ben rented a fabulous chalet in the resort's Mottaret area. It was situated close to the piste and luxurious beyond belief. This time Ben had invited Sean Jackson and his daughter Mel, his new assistant Bethany, Angelica and Camilla and Natasha and me, of course.

Bethany ignored me from day one. Why did Ben respect women who thought it perfectly acceptable to be rude to other women? It wasn't as if Bethany was beautiful, she was far from it with her dumpy figure and ginger curly hair. She wore no make-up, like Angelica, and seemed to thrive on criticising women who did. Any sort of adornment was anathema to Bethany. And Ben appeared to approve and yet I know he admired feminine women. But he hung on to every word that Bethany uttered and skied with her every day (I have to admit she was a cracking skier, as was Ben) and I knew better than to criticise. I wondered if he was having sex with her. I'd had my suspicions about Ben on several occasions since we'd married but he'd never openly thrust any female in my face until Bethany. I mentioned all this to Camilla and she just looked at me and said,

'Ben respects women who are like men. Correction, he doesn't really like women at all. And do you really care?'

For some reason my thoughts flicked to Charlie. I'd never mentioned Charlie to Camilla because he was a precious part in my shameful memory. Besides, he was gone. 'Ben likes you.'

'I'm gay and very successful.' She shrugged. 'It's just a hunch, but I bet I'm right.'

I considered this and came to the conclusion she probably was but for some reason I did care. I cared very much. If I had a son, of which there was no sign yet, I didn't want him to be influenced by a misogynist. And why wasn't I pregnant? I couldn't understand it at all. And for some reason Ben was not giving me a hard time about it, perhaps because he was bonking Bethany.

Natasha was in ski school and as Angelica did not ski she took over the care of my daughter. I was filled with guilt because in all honesty I wanted to be able to go out with Camilla and sometimes Sean and Mel and ski all day long but the less I did for my daughter the more I lost her to her precious Aunt Jelly.

Then for some reason I found myself alone on the slopes with Sean. He was an average skier, like me, and great fun to be with. We loved the green and blue runs and on this particular day we'd gone over to Courchevel to ski. The skies were cloudless and blissfully blue and the mountains magnificent; everywhere shimmered in the sunlight. We stopped for lunch and drank a bottle of white wine and ordered another.

'I'm not sure I'll be safe to ski back.' I joked.

'You will. You're cautious. Not a risk-taker like that husband of yours.'

I watched Sean squinting against the afternoon sun. He was a joy to observe and I wondered why I didn't fancy him in the same way that I had Charlie. I mean,

Charlie didn't have the perfectly chiselled features of Sean, yet Sean did not excite me. However, he was easy to talk to and I had a strong feeling that he liked me.

I was bold. 'So do you think there's something going on between Ben and Bethany?'

He looked shocked and his eyes held mine. 'That's not a very fair question.'

My heart sank. 'Your reply just confirms my suspicions.'

He put his hand on my arm. 'Hold on there. I didn't say that.'

'But you didn't deny it either.'

'Because I don't know. Ben treats everything in life like business. We never have idle chit-chat.'

'Do you like her?'

'Bethany?' He chuckled. 'Not much. But I have to remember that she's part of the new team and if I want to get on I have to work well with everyone. Ben's one very shrewd guy, Diana, don't ever underestimate him.'

A shudder went through me. 'I don't. If you must know I'm terrified of him, and his blasted sister.'

Sean laughed out loud. 'I agree with you on that one! Isn't she a nightmare?'

We giggled together before I plucked up the courage to ask. 'So what do you think Ben thinks of me?'

'I can answer that easily. You're his wife and as long as you don't step out of line he'll always look after you.'

'What's stepping out of line?'

Sean drew closer. 'Having an affair with me.'

I swallowed hard. 'I take it you're joking.'

Sean leaned back in his chair and put his hands behind his head. 'Of course I am. But he's a lucky sonofabitch and that's for sure.'

I decided to take it no further but did say, 'Thank you.'

We were in Meribel for a whole fortnight. I was delighted to be away so long and enjoyed the endless days of sunshine and snow and the evenings of deliciously prepared food and bucket-loads of French wine. I must have put on a stone! Then it all went wrong.

Bethany had grown in stature as the fortnight wore on. She had everything going for her; she skied well (big on a skiing holiday); she was supposedly indispensable to my husband because she was adept at organising his every move (I wondered what that included), and she had him hanging on to her every word (most of which were snippety). So when two days before we left I walked past Bethany's bedroom in the middle of the afternoon and heard familiar noises and I carefully opened the door and peeked inside I cannot say I was surprised that Ben was screwing the ghastly Bethany. Standard position, nothing exciting, legs up in the air (Bethany) and Ben huffing and puffing for dear life. It may sound ridiculous but even in my humiliation I wondered why Ben was making such an awful noise. I quickly closed the door and I'm sure that neither of them realised I'd even entered.

But that night I turned to Sean and our relationship changed completely.

He was kind and I poured out my innermost feelings, my insecurities over Ben and my deep-seated guilt about my daughter. Between the sobs and sips of red wine I practically told Sean my life history and he listened, never interrupting; in fact he was loving in a way that is indescribable unless you've experienced it, which I had not until then. The only part of my life I missed out was Charlie; for some reason my feelings for Charlie were exclusive to me. Guilt again, I suppose.

So without a care for what Ben was doing that night I spent mine with Sean. I was the scarlet lady except we never made love but I do remember whispering to him, 'You could lose your job.'

He replied, 'Fuck. We'll survive.'

And I thought *we* meant more than it did.

Grey

Can you believe that after something so catastrophic life can return to normal? It did.

We all slipped back into our roles as though Meribel had never happened. When I returned to the normality of Brooklands Avenue in Cambridge Sean never so much as made contact with me and I was hurt; so very hurt. But within days I forced myself to stop thinking about him.

He came to me; I remember every detail; what he was wearing; how he looked; everything.

'I've something to tell you.' Ben cleared his throat as though he was in a board meeting or something. 'It's not very nice.'

Was he going to leave me? Were my wishes coming true at last? 'You'd better tell me.' I prepared myself; scared at the prospect.

He sat on the bed next to me. It wasn't often that we were in such close proximity. For some reason our sex life was always conducted in the dark after I'd gone to bed and he'd joined me much later.

He looked at me with a certain humour in his eyes. 'Do you want it straight, or should I couch it?'

My heart was beating very fast. 'Straight, please.'

Ben reached out desperately and I grabbed his hand. His voice broke, 'I'm going to die.'

I remember assembling his words in my head. They didn't make sense. I'd so prepared myself for something far more hurtful, but what could be more hurtful than this?

He spoke first. 'I have secondary cancers. Mainly, bowel cancer. It's bad.'

I stared at him, unable to take in his words. 'You?'

'Yes, me. I left it too late - should have gone to the doctors ages ago. I bloody left it too late.'

'Can't they; I mean, they can do loads these days.'

'Too late. It's got me.'

I remembered his huffing and puffing with Bethany. Perhaps he'd been doing that with me and because I blocked everything out I hadn't noticed. 'How long have you known?'

'Not long. At least, I've suspected something's wrong for a long time but the grim news has only just been presented to me.'

'Ben – why didn't you go to the doctors if you suspected something's wrong? If you'd told me, I'd have made you go.' I was panicking now.

He considered his next words. 'Too busy building my businesses. I thought it would go away.'

In the early seventies cancer was almost a banned word. It wasn't used, just referred to. My next question was blunt, but I was his wife. *'How* serious?'

'Six months – at the most.'

I gasped. 'Six months? Does Angelica know?'

He lowered his eyes and I knew that she did. How is it that when something as diabolical as this is presented one can still feel selfish. Why did he tell her first?

'I told her because she asked. She noticed I wasn't well.'

'And I didn't.' I felt even more selfish.

'Perhaps you were too busy with Sean.'

I stared at Ben. How could he say that at a time like this? 'Nothing happened between me and Sean and that's hardly fair; I caught you at it with Bethany.'

Ben looked surprised. 'When was that?'

'I walked…' I stopped myself. 'Does this really matter?'

Ben got up off the bed and it seemed to take all his energy. 'No. I guess not.' He faced me. 'I don't know how it's going to take me, but I'll carry on working for as long as I can. I've told Sean, and Bethany. They needed to know. I trust I can rely on your help as well.'

I practically flew off the bed and put my arms around him. 'Ben! I'm your wife. Of course you can rely on my help.'

He sort of patted my arms but it was obvious he was not in the mood to be hugged. I drew back; he half-smiled and then walked out of our bedroom. This was April. Nothing else was said about his cancer for another three months.

Browns and Blacks

I learned to drive. During this very sad period in our lives I found something I loved to do. I had twelve lessons over six weeks and passed my test first time. I didn't need to ask Ben to buy me a car; he threw his car keys at me and said, 'Here, it's yours. I've no use for it anymore.'

So I was the proud possessor of a Mercedes Sports. It was silver with black leather interior and I loved it. Angelica thought differently. She said, 'That's all you'll be getting. It'd pay you to look after it.'

'You don't change, do you?'

'People don't; and remember I have to put up with you.'

As always I was lost for words. When you hate someone you think you can't feel any more loathing but hate grows just the same as love. It may be wasted energy but, boy, does it grow.

Then there was Natasha. She was four now and about to start school in September. I wondered if Ben would still be alive. I tried not to think about it too much; besides he seemed alright. He didn't drive and he rested a lost but perhaps they'd got the diagnosis wrong. Miracles do happen. How was I to know that Ben forced himself to carry on; dragged up every last paltry reserve of energy. I didn't want him to die for selfish reasons. What a thoroughly selfish person I had become but I knew Angelica would get everything and me nothing. I had to start thinking about my future and what I was going to do. One thing was for sure, Natasha would not be seeing much of her precious Aunt Jelly.

But St Catherine's in Cambridge was a fee-paying

pre-prep school and how was I going to be able to afford such fees? This didn't worry me too much because she'd have to go to the local school. What did worry me was how Natasha would behave. She was not a pleasant little girl and I blamed Angelica for this. What am I saying; no I didn't. I knew it was my fault. I should have taken control and I didn't because I was afraid to. How could I possibly make amends?

Ben stopped work in late July. His health deteriorated considerably over the next few weeks and what was fascinating to watch was Angelica's behaviour. I thought she'd be fussing over him continually but it was as though she was disgusted. I wondered if he realised; I mean, he so adored his sister; she could do no wrong.

But he welcomed all of my administrations. At this time the MacMillan nurses visited once a day and he was on morphine to help with the pain and he bore it well. The incontinence pad changing was the most mortifying part of his life but I tried to make a joke of it. We sort of regained our mutual sense of humour during this time.

We decided to bring a bed down into the sitting room so that Ben could see out into the garden. I had neglected the garden somewhat but it still looked good for August. So there he lay, propped up with pillows looking at my garden and all the time I was remembering those special feelings I had nurtured for Charlie.

We had an alarm system set up against the bed so that if Ben did need me at any time he could press it and speak. It was connected to the kitchen and our bedroom upstairs.

Angelica and I had the most dreadful argument. I was in my bedroom and Natasha ran in. 'Mummy!' She put her hands on her hips and said petulantly, 'What are you doing?'

I was actually applying make-up. It might sound ridiculous but I wanted to look good for Ben. 'Just doing my make-up.'

'Aunt Jelly says you shouldn't do that. She say's it makes you look really horrid.'

I sighed. 'Natasha, Aunt Jelly doesn't like anything I do.'

'Yes and it's because you're very annoying.'

I looked at my face in the mirror and reflected; was this my daughter talking to me or some aged appendage of Angelica's? At least when Natasha's imaginary friend Jakie was around I could have some sort of conversation with my daughter but Angelica had managed to rid Natasha of him with bribes like, 'If you don't mention Jakie at all today I'll buy you anything you want in the toy shop.' Or, 'If you stop thinking about Jakie before your birthday you'll get a new dress, all the sweets you can eat and as many toys as you like!' It didn't take Natasha long to realise that all she had to say to Aunt Jelly was, 'If I don't mention Jakie can I have…?'

Annoying or not, I didn't need to reply because my sister-in-law appeared. 'Come on, Natasha, we're going out.'

'Where are you going?' I asked.

She looked at me as though I was a piece of dirt off her shoe. 'You must see that it's not healthy for Natasha to be here.'

I took a deep breath and looked at my daughter

who was fiddling with the alarm switch on the side of my bed. I was going to tell her to stop; I didn't want Ben hearing everything that was being said.

'Well? Are you going to argue as you usually do?' quipped Angelica.

'No, but I'd like you to remember that she is my daughter.' My voice sounded feeble but the declaration was as much for Natasha's benefit as my own.

'Diana, you don't have any possessions in this house.'

'What's that supposed to mean?'

'It means that you are going to get nothing. Ben's told me. You are going to get absolutely nothing and you won't be able to afford to look after Natasha so you won't get her either.'

Natasha stood there looking at her Aunt Jelly and then me. It was as though she was enjoying the conversation. Natasha enjoyed everything where she was the centre of attention.

I glared at Angelica. 'I may get nothing, but let me tell you - you'll get nothing as well because I will take Natasha away from you.' Natasha now sidled up to her precious Aunt Jelly and clung to her and I wanted to drag her off.

Angelica patted Natasha. 'How will you afford the school fees?'

'We'll move somewhere else.'

Angelica was really warming to the argument now. All these years and I still rose to it. My father would have said, 'Don't rise to the bait.' But I didn't have his good sense.

Angelica pulled Natasha forward so that she stood

in front of her. She stroked her whispy fair hair with the silly clip she insisted on putting bang in middle of her forehead. I hated that clip. It made her look like Shirley Temple without the pretty face.

'Natasha, tell mummy, who do you love the most?'

I was flabberghasted. I watched my daughter as she considered the question; but not for long. Natasha turned to Aunt Jelly and with a pout said, 'You.'

'See!' Angelica leered at me. 'Do you need any more proof?'

I looked at my daughter. Ideally I wanted to reach out and take her in my arms but I knew she'd reject me. I rose to the occasion. 'It doesn't matter. Natasha will still stay with me.' I winked at Natasha. 'That is, you and Jakie.'

I saw the glint in my daughter's eye. It was a shitty thing to do.

Angelica turned on her heel dragging Natasha behind her. She swung her head back at me. 'May you rot in hell.'

I thought: Yes, I most probably will.

He was sinking fast. I sat beside him filling in the Daily Mail's crossword and I detected that he was agitated. 'Can I get you anything?'

He sighed. As long as I live I will never forget the sound of his sighs. When somebody is in such paramount pain everything is significant and sadly memorable. 'I heard your quarrel. We need to sort things out.'

'Sorry?'

'Earlier. You quarrelled with Angelica.'

I remembered Natasha fiddling with the speaker

switches in the bedroom. 'I'm sorry. It wasn't intentional that you should hear.'

He smiled in his pained way. 'Look, if I promise to look after you, make sure you have *more* than enough to live on, will you give Natasha to Angelica?'

I sat there for several seconds considering his words. This was a dying man but I still despised the way he treated me; as though I wasn't important and my feelings didn't count.

'She's our daughter! You don't give away a daughter.'

He sighed again. 'Angelica has nothing. Natasha means everything to her.'

'But she's ruining her! In all of your self-centred bloody life, Ben, can't you see that?' I regretted the words as soon as I'd uttered them.

He laughed. In his pain he laughed. 'She's not ruining her! Natasha is a Herriott-fucking-Greene!'

'It might surprise you but she's also fifty percent me… And - one hundred percent herself! Somewhere she's going to be pretty damned good!'

'No she's not! One thing I soon learned about you is that you have a vivid imagination. Get real, your daughter is not going to turn into an angel.'

'I don't want an angel, I just want a well adjusted child.'

'She's not going to be that either.'

'Yes, she is.'

'Diana, let it go. I'm dying, for God's sake, let it go.'

I was stumped. 'What do you mean?

He took a long time to answer me. 'You might think I've taken no notice of Natasha but I have - since the day you said that my sister cast a spell on her.'

'On me! Not her.'

'Whatever.' Ben drew a heavy breath. 'Look, what I'm saying is, you have a beautiful face, Diana, you'll go far. Marry again and have more children. My sister will never marry and she'll never mother a child. She absolutely adores Natasha. It wouldn't matter what I give her - nothing could compare to my daughter.'

My ears pricked. In all the time we'd been married he'd never referred to Natasha as his daughter.

'So you admit she's yours.'

'She's more mine than she is yours and it is my dying wish that Angelica looks after her.'

'Never.'

'*Please?* Whatever you want you can have. I'm pretty rich. Name your price.'

I stood up and stared at my dying husband. 'There is no price. You're right, I do have a vivid imagination. I actually imagined that we could be happy together. I imagined that things would work out if I was a good wife and looked after you. I even imagined that your sister might stop hating me. But there is one thing that I imagine more than anything else and it's that Natasha will be a better person away from Angelica. There is no price you can pay that will take that thought away from me.'

'Noble words but you're hopelessly wrong. You should have learned that we Herriott-Greene's are a breed unto ourselves. You'll come horribly unstuck if you don't promise me this dying wish.'

'I started to walk towards the door. 'I think I'll go and make myself a cup of tea. Would you like one?'

'No. You'll regret this, Diana.'

I decided not to reply. He called after me. Where

did he get his energy? 'Tomorrow, *first thing*, ring my solicitor. Get him here… *Please.*'

'Whatever you say.'

I went into the kitchen and opened a bottle of red burgundy and drank the lot.

The solicitor came, stayed for about half an hour and then left. The subject of Natasha was never spoken off again but I knew that Ben was angry with me and I'd probably been written out of his Will completely; if I was ever in it!

As the days went past and September approached Ben's health was pitiful. He lost track of time and often asked about Angelica. I had to really persuade her to go in and see her brother.

She scoffed, 'I don't like ill-health. I can't help it.'

'But what if Natasha becomes ill?'

'That's different.'

I didn't want anymore arguments. I wanted Ben's last few days to be tranquil for both him and me.

The MacMillan nurses were dropping in twice a day and I kept a constant vigil. Ben wanted me there all the time and I should have been flattered but at this time I was looking forward to him dying because if I so much as moved he would beg me to stay, that is when he came out of his morphine induced stupor. I was now worn out and dreading my future.

I was alone with him when he died. I surprised myself; I wasn't frightened. He looked at me for several seconds and his eyes seemed to search my face and it was as though he wanted to say something. I moved closer to him being careful not to knock the bed because I knew what pain this could cause.

I whispered, 'It's all right, Ben, I'm here.'

He opened his mouth and I'm sure he tried to say sorry; perhaps not. I touched his mouth and said, 'I know, just go to sleep, everything will be fine. I promise.'

There was a weary smile on his face as he closed his eyes and he went to sleep forever. I cried; I really cried. Tears ran down my face prolifically and I sat there for about an hour feeling thoroughly sorry for myself before I went to tell Angelica.

Crisp White

Natasha started school and we went to Ben's cremation. Sean and Bethany, amongst a multitude of other people, turned up. I spoke briefly to Sean and before I had a chance to say anything he informed me that Ben had ordered both him and Bethany to stay away from his death bed. I must admit, I had wondered at the lack of visitors.

'You look tired.' He said.

'Yes.' I took a deep breath. 'In case you're interested, he died peacefully.'

Sean's eyes stayed on mine. 'You were a good wife.'

'Did he say that?'

'No, but he thought it.'

'I hope so.' I said and added flippantly, 'Perhaps he'll leave me a crust.'

Sean pulled a face. 'I wouldn't bank on it.'

'No.' I looked across at my sister-in-law who

somehow or other had managed to summon up bucket loads of tears. 'I think that would be very unwise.'

Sean touched my arm. 'When this is all over, you know, sometime in the future, will you have dinner with me?'

I remembered how he hadn't so much as lifted the phone to contact me after Meribel. 'Thank you, Sean, but I don't think so.'

He shrugged. 'Just a thought.'

I moved away before I had time to change my mind.

Natasha wasn't too sure about school; she was very quiet when she came home; perhaps the structure of it all tired her out or maybe she'd picked upon the gloomy atmosphere in the house. Angelica insisted on taking her everyday and I didn't argue. I was still exhausted after Ben's death; how pathetic does that sound? My mother fussed around me and Camilla was a great support but I couldn't get my head around what I was going to do. The reading of the Will was the next day and I dreaded it. In my heart of hearts I thought that Ben would have provided well for Natasha and maybe left me the house. If that was the case she could continue at St Catherine's and I could get a job. One thing was for sure, if Ben had left me the house Angelica would have to move out and I'd have more control over Natasha. It was all ifs and buts and tomorrow would give me the answers I dreaded.

There were a handful of us in the solicitor's office. I was nervous to see Bethany there; was I really going to be left with egg on my face? His assistant getting more than me? Anyway, there was me, Angelica, Sean, Bethany and another man, an architect, who had worked for Ben a very long time. But I didn't remember him.

The solicitor went through the formalities and explained that the Will was in no particular order; exactly as Ben had requested. He said that Ben had put a lot of thought into his Will. As a successful man who had died so relatively young he wanted it to make an impact. We all sat there looking at the solicitor not at all sure how we were supposed to interpret this.

And then to my surprise he launched in with all the details; Thomas Dean, the architect, was left ten thousand pounds! Then it was Sean's turn; he was left five-percent of H-G Properties; Ben's business in Cambridge. I figured that five percent must be a veritable chunk of wealth and I noticed Angelica looking across at Sean but not for the life of me could I tell what she was thinking. I don't suppose it mattered to her but Sean was very pleased. He nodded enthusiastically and I saw his mouth tremble in anticipation of his inheritance.

I have to admit I loved the next bit; Bethany was left Ben's cuff-links; the ones she'd so admired. Apparently they did have diamonds in so she wasn't so daft. But it was obvious she thought she was going to get a lot more.

Then it was Angelica's turn. Why not me next? For God's sake, why had they asked me to come? But the solicitor had said no particular order.

My heart absolutely sank. Angelica got the house! My house in Brooklands Avenue and, wait for it, a million pounds! She turned to me with a smug smile as if to say; told you so. A million! Never in my wildest dreams had I imagined that Ben was that cash rich! But my worst fears were now realised and I quite expected the solicitor to round things up, look at me and say, 'Who are you? Why are you here?'

Instead, he said, 'And now to Diana Herriott-Greene; my wife; the only person who has put no value on my wealth and who cared for me constantly in my dying days; I pass over to you the remaining eighty percent of my business.'

Angelica sucked in her breath making a hissing sound; she glared at me absolutely incensed. Bethany glowered too; had she thought that she was going to get a large chunk?

The solicitor continued. 'Diana also inherits the balance from the sale of properties and businesses recently sold in California.'

Angelica spluttered beneath her breath. 'Ridiculous!'

The solicitor looked directly at me. 'And I have a private letter for you, Mrs Herriott-Greene, from your husband which I will pass on to you later.'

I just sat there staring at him. I couldn't move a muscle such was my shock. Even so, I knew that Angelica was glaring at me, absolutely despising me, as I despised her. But I hadn't planned this. I hadn't planned anything. I'd just bumbled along as best I could. What on earth was I going to do with Ben's business? I hadn't a clue about business. It crossed my mind, even at this wildest of moments, that Ben had planned this with great precision.

It transpired that there was one other shareholder, apart from Sean Jackson that is ... my sister-in-law. The typewritten letter from Ben was short. In it he said that he hoped I would carry on with his business, that I needed something to keep my mind active as I was a bright young woman and Angelica could help me with regards to inheritance tax. Who knows, he wrote, you may even increase the portfolio of properties because negotiations were already underway for further prime-sites in Cambridge to be developed.

Ben also said that maybe if I took this opportunity it would mean that Angelica could look after Natasha while I worked. I smiled; he'd got it all planned.

I asked the solicitor, 'Was this dictated when you came to the house just before he died?'

'It was, yes. I think he was deeply concerned about your deteriorating relationship with his sister.'

'So he didn't change the Will at that point?'

'Oh, no. It was drawn up months before.'

'I was always going to inherit his business?'

'Yes.'

I thought; all those threats; why couldn't he be honest with me. I remembered his dying moments; perhaps he was trying to tell me the truth then.

The solicitor went on, 'It seems that Ben was impressed with your garden. He said that it showed how enterprising you can be.'

'My garden?'

'Yes, and according to him you did it all on a shoestring.'

A shoestring? I thought of Ivor and adorable Charlie; had I underpaid them?

Shakily, I asked, 'And the balance in California; how much is that?'

The solicitor smiled. 'It's a handsome sum indeed but very much tied up in a tax haven in the Cayman Islands.'

I was surprised. I expected a modest amount. 'So I can't get it out?'

'Tricky.'

'How much then?'

'Big bucks, this one. Over five million.'

'What! *Pounds?*'

'Yes, pounds.'

'Good heavens! You mean to say I have five million pounds in the Cayman Islands?'

'You do indeed but that's all I know so you do need to talk to your accountant.'

Shakily I said, 'I will.' I took a deep breath. 'So the business in Cambridge; how much, say, liquidity do I have?'

The solicitor opened out both hands. 'Again, you must talk to your accountant.'

'So what you're saying is I could be asset rich but cash poor?'

'I can't say because I don't know. But remember, you do have the opportunity to sell?'

I slumped back in my chair. Ben Herriott-Greene has had the last laugh. If I sold out I'd probably get a fraction of H-G Properties worth and if I carried on I wouldn't see much of my daughter.

The solicitor smiled. 'You can always emigrate to America.'

Yes, I smiled, I could, but Ben knew I wouldn't do

that, after all, money had never been my master.

I made arrangements to see Sean Jackson the very next day but when I arrived home Angelica was waiting for me.

I held up my hands defensively. How stupid am I? 'Before you say anything, I knew nothing about this.'

'I don't believe you. The business is *my* entitlement! Now I know why you nestled up to his deathbed you scheming bitch. You do realise it was *my* money that set him up.'

I knew this was a lie. Ben had told me years ago that she'd loaned him three thousand pounds when he was twenty-five and he'd used it as a down-payment for his first property. But he also told me he'd paid her back handsomely. I didn't know he'd also given her fifteen percent of his business.

She continued. 'I live by my dividends and if you think I'm going to trust you to run things you've got another think coming. I want to sell my shares immediately."

I took a deep breath. 'Angelica, I've been thrown in at the deep end here. I'm seeing Sean Jackson tomorrow. But aren't you forgetting something?' She looked at me blankly.

'Ben set this up so that you could share custody of Natasha. Don't you see, he cared so much about *you*.'

'Huh! I shall look after her anyway. In case you haven't realised you're homeless.'

I gasped at her nastiness. 'Do you know something, Angelica, you are one almighty cow.'

She walked out of the door. 'I'm going to pick up Natasha.'

I started to follow, I so wanted to take control

of my life but I stopped and watched her go. If only he'd left me the house and a million pounds. If only. I then poured myself a very large drink but vowed that Angelica would never have sole custody of my daughter whatever Ben had dictated.

Silver and Grey

I spent a little while with Natasha that evening but she was restless; anxious to get back to Aunt Jelly and all her treats (half of which I hadn't a clue about!) It was only then that I realised she hadn't been mentioned in her father's Will. All Ben had really cared about was organising us after his death. But what if I threw it all back into the melting pot, sold everything and scurried off to America, what then?

How did he know I wouldn't do that? The Will said I put no value on his wealth; was that true? I think it was more that I'd never seen myself as part of the family and was guilt-ridden. I considered the situation; I couldn't behave like a greedy coward now, could I.

Sean Jackson was ready for me when I arrived. H-G Properties office was still in Bridge Street and if anything down-sized; just a secretary, an accounts clerk, the architect and Sean and Bethany, except she wasn't there. Sean took me into his small office overlooking St John's Street. I looked out of the window watching students on their bicycles and others hurrying along with books tucked under their arms and remembered how it felt to work here all those years ago fancying Ben

Herriott-Greene like mad; except it wasn't so long ago. I looked at Sean's desk and noticed the photographs of Mel his daughter.

He held out a hand for me to sit down and started off the proceedings with a small apologetic speech. He had no idea I was going to inherit the bulk of H-G Properties shares and had surmised that they would go to Angelica and some to Bethany.

'Why?' I asked.

He looked at me guiltily and hurried his next words. 'Just that Angelica has always been involved and Bethany is very bright and canny and, well, knows the business inside out. To be honest, Diana, I thought it would be me, Bethany and Tom running the company and Angelica the sleeping major shareholder.'

'Tom?'

'Our architect.'

I weighed up his words. 'You'd have liked that?'

He chuckled. 'I dunno. Maybe; maybe not. Anyway, it's not going to happen is it?'

'Ben's pulling the strings even after his death.'

'Good ol' Ben.'

'I bet he's laughing in his grave.'

'Seriously though, what are your first thoughts?'

'To listen to what you have to tell me.'

'Right, let's get down to business. Currently we own three blocks of flats in Cambridge. Ben likes to build about thirty flats in a block and a penthouse, you know, keep it sweet. I say own, what I mean is we've maintained the freehold on all three blocks but sold half the flats on a long-term lease basis and rented out the remainder. We also own houses on Maids Causeway, opposite Midsummer Common which are rented out and then we've just bought another two sites; one in Chesterton and the other in Trumpington. On these we're planning to build high-spec houses. Other sites are of interest for the future. Had Ben been around I'm sure negotiations would be well underway.'

I hesitated, not quite knowing what to say. 'So all this is well funded?'

'Yes. We have a solid relationship with the bank although they are nervous with what's happened to Ben and anxious who is going to take over.' He leaned back in his chair confidently. 'But I get on well with them; they trust me.' Sean cleared his throat. 'Currently we have big borrowings with the new housing projects but there's absolutely no reason for the bank to get jittery.'

'And me? What about all this inheritance tax?'

Sean took a deep breath. 'Yes, bloody crippling, and the way Ben died didn't leave much room for manoeuvre. I'm afraid you have to pay it.'

'I can only pay it if I've got the money.'

'It's simple. I'm sure Ben intended that you sell some of your shares. I'd certainly be interested and so would Tom.'

I bet you would, I thought. 'Good. Angelica can't wait to off-load hers.'

Sean saw the resolute look in my eyes. 'Ben did speak to me about death duties but I thought he was referring to Angelica.' He laughed, 'And as we all know, she's got plenty of money.'

'But she'll have to pay death duties as well?'

'Of course.'

'And I don't think she'll be too eager to help me out

with mine.' I smiled. 'Ben left me a letter suggesting just that. What about me selling some of the properties?'

'You could if you could find a buyer; don't forget they have sitting tenants and you'd undoubtedly take a hit against their true value and, anyway, the vast majority of our properties are still secured against bank loans; at least for the next five years.'

'So could I get a bank loan?'

Sean looked surprised. He thought I was going to be a pushover, not a risk taker. I watched him swallow hard before he said, 'With respect, what bank is going to give you that sort of loan with your unproven record. I'm sure Ben assumed that in order to pay some of your tax you would sell shares to Tom and me, after all it's us who run the business.'

'No! Ben didn't assume that at all. I had a letter from him saying that he wanted *me* to take over. The solicitor told me; he liked the way I did our garden.'

Sean did a double take and looked at me cynically. 'He liked your garden?'

I realised how trite it sounded. 'You're not pushing me out, Sean.'

He softened. 'That was never my intention. You'd still be a majority shareholder but you don't know anything about this business and with respect you could upset the bank and they could call in the loans.'

'I wouldn't do that. I'd take a back seat.'

'You still have to pay your death duties.'

I took a deep breath. 'I'll find a way.' I added flippantly, 'And if it's too stressful I can always flee to the Cayman Islands!'

Sean chuckled. 'Aren't you the rich lady?'

'Not if I can't touch it. Is that right?'

'Let's just say if you tried to get it out of the States it could all be confiscated.'

'So how did he get the money in to buy property in the first place?'

'Therein lies a tale. Ben's methods were not entirely orthodox.'

'And why did he sell everything up?'

'Because he thought it would be too complicated to manage such a conglomerate of properties in California without him around and, believe me, he was bloody right.'

'Will we ever be able to get the money out?'

'For the time being I think you should concentrate on having some damned good holidays out there.'

'Alternatively I could bugger off with my daughter.' I was goading him. I wanted to see if he might encourage me to do just that.

Sean leaned across the desk. 'You're not going to do that, are you, Diana?'

I smiled. 'No, I'm not.'

He reached across and shook my hand. 'Ben must have known what he was doing. Welcome on board.'

His handshake was weak and I knew that he didn't believe I would ever be on board. I asked, 'And Bethany?'

'I think she might have left.'

'Really?' Was I surprised? No, but I was pretty damned pleased.

Our conversation was followed by a trip round Cambridge with Sean pointing out all the properties and land owned by the company. I queried, 'I need somewhere to live. Are any of these flats empty?'

He looked surprised. 'You've got the penthouse.'

'What penthouse?'

'Ben's. I'm sorry, I assumed you knew all about it.'

'The one off Grange Road, behind the backs?'

'Yes. As far as I know Ben's always had it.'

'Of course.' A lump came into my throat. Why had I not realised?

'The key's in the office. We could pick it up and go and have a look.'

I nodded. 'Yes, I'd like that. Thank you.'

Memories came flooding back as we stepped into the lift to take us up to the penthouse apartment where my love affair with Ben Herriott-Greene had started. I had to ask, 'So did he use this a lot?' I looked at Sean and fleetingly remembered our night together in Meribel. He had been very kind to me then.

He took a deep breath. 'I think so.'

'And I never knew. Funny that, there was so much of his life that I never knew about.'

Sean unlocked the front door of the flat and we stepped inside. I looked around and was overwhelmed with emotion. There was certainly an air of living in the flat. And then she appeared; Bethany. She came rushing out of the master bedroom looking flustered.

'Bethany!' Sean said.

'I was just packing a few things.' She looked guilty and I realised that this was their love nest. I wondered how many other women Ben had brought here during our brief marriage.

I heard myself say, 'Please, carry on.'

She walked back into the bedroom and I went into the sitting room and over to the window overlooking Kings College grounds. It was late morning and the sun was shining and although I wanted to cry for some stupid reason I smiled and thought, yes, I could live here for a while with Natasha. Get my bearings, sort a few things out.

I heard Sean talking to Bethany. 'Diana's thinking of moving in.'

Bethany reappeared with a suitcase. 'Fine. Don't let me stop you.'

'Not just yet.' I asked, 'Are you actually living here?'

'No. I just stay over sometimes; you know, when it's difficult to get home.'

I asked, 'Where is home?'

'Waterbeach.'

'Oh.'

She lugged the large suitcase to the front door and Sean stepped forward to open it for her. I called after her. 'It won't be for a few days.'

She shrugged. 'No matter. I'm done.'

Sean followed her outside and had a brief conversation with her. When he came back into the flat he put both hands on my shoulders. 'I didn't know. I wouldn't have brought you here had I known.'

'Please, don't worry about it.'

'She is leaving the company and won't be working out any notice.'

'Good.' I looked around and although the furnishings were not exactly to my taste, very Ben, very avant-garde, I knew it would be okay. Natasha and I would be all right. 'What sort of salary will I be able to draw from the company?'

Sean looked very surprised. 'You're the owner. Whatever you decide you need to live on.' He added with a smile, 'As long as you don't break us in the meantime.'

'I have to be able to afford Natasha's school fees.'

'But they're catered for in the school trust fund.'

I felt so stupid and stuttered, 'I didn't know anything about a trust fund. Nobody told me.'

'I'm sorry. I can't for the life of me think why not.'

'Oh, I can. Angelica would never reveal such information and it no doubt slipped Ben's mind, just like retaining this place.'

Sean reached out as though to pull me closer to him but I drew back. I didn't want any of that. I needed to gather my thoughts and prepare myself for a new future. At least I didn't have to worry about where to live or school fees. It was an enormous relief.

'So?' Angelica queried when I arrived home just before lunch.

'All sorted.'

'What's that supposed to mean?'

I ticked off the list with my fingers. 'Your shares will be bought by Sean and Tom. I've found somewhere else to live. And we will be moving in on Saturday.'

Her face darkened. 'We?'

'Natasha and me.'

'*I don't think so*. Ben wanted me to look after Natasha.'

'Angelica, we can share custody, but I'm afraid on a day to day basis she lives with me.'

'Now hold on a minute. No no no. Natasha lives with me. I won't hear of anything else.'

I could feel my blood rising. Calm down, I thought. This woman has no real control. 'Look, Natasha is my daughter and she is going to live with me whether you like it or not.'

'No! She is not! Shall we ask Natasha when she comes home from school? Is that what you'd like? To reduce her to tears and make her even more confused.'

I started to walk away. Angelica called after me. 'You're a fool, Diana; always have been. You won't win on this. Ben saw to that.'

I turned in rage. 'Sometimes I think you're evil! Have you any idea how much I hate you?'

'If it's anything close to my hatred for you it's mammoth.'

I took a deep breath and went to my bedroom.

Later it was a fight for whom should pick Natasha up from school. I gave in. While Angelica was out I would start to pack. I didn't need to take too much for myself and the bare minimum for Natasha. I could now afford to buy my daughter new clothes, clothes of my choice. We would start afresh. If Angelica would just listen she would see that we could come to a perfectly amicable arrangement whereby she could pick Natasha up from school, bring her back to Brooklands Avenue for tea and then I could pick Natasha up later and take her home with me. We could share her at weekends.

All I did know was that, at all costs, I must get my daughter away from the constant clutches of her dreadful aunt.

Fiery Crimson

When Saturday arrived it was horrendous. I had to practically drag a screaming and scratching Natasha through the house and when we finally made it to the hall Angelica tried to grab and pull my daughter away from me. I was amazed at my own show of strength because I picked Natasha up in my arms and with my backside shoved Angelica out of the way. She hit the wall with some force and was quite stunned. I strode outside and plonked Natasha on the backseat of the car and locked the door while I went back to fetch the suitcase which I'd left in the hall.

'This isn't the end of this.' Angelica seethed. 'Have you no consideration for Natasha's true feelings?'

For some reason her words struck home and I had no answer. Did Angelica really know more about my daughter's true feelings than me?

But I stuck to my guns and drove off with Angelica's fist waving in the air behind me. I had the key to the penthouse in my handbag and in my head lots of treats lined up for Natasha. She sat in the car yelping like a caged dog and calling for Aunt Jelly. I tried to calm her but it was impossible so I turned on the radio loud and did my utmost to ignore my daughter. If there was going to be any future for us I had to make a stand.

Then disaster! After I'd got Natasha out of the car and eventually into the lift with promises of all sorts and then unlocked the front door and pushed her inside the flat with the large suitcase I stood and stared. The flat had been stripped, absolutely stripped of everything! Every last morsel had been taken, not a solitary light bulb was left. Bethany! It must have been her. She'd filched the lot!

My daughter turned and looked at me and started to wail. 'I want Aunt Jelly! I want Aunt Jelly!' I wanted to gag her and tell her to shut up! At the same time I also wanted to shout and scream. At least Bethany had left the telephone and I rang Sean. 'She's taken everything, Sean! The lot! There's absolutely nothing left!'

Whilst I cajoled my daughter I waited for Sean. When he arrived he walked around scratching his head nonplussed. 'The thieving bitch!' he kept saying, 'The fucking thieving bitch.'

He looked at me and I could see his head reeling from the situation and also from my screaming daughter. 'She won't get away with this, I promise.'

I took a deep breath trying to calm myself. 'It's irrelevant at this moment, Sean. What am I going to do?'

'Come back with me. Mel's gone to Paris to see her mother. You can stay with me.'

'No!' I gasped. 'That won't do at all.' I couldn't give Angelica any reason to think I was behaving incorrectly. I walked over to the phone and rang Camilla. I can't tell you how relieved I was when she answered.

'Hey, calm down,' she said in her usual manner.

'Can we come and stay this weekend?' Then rushed on to explain as best as I could.

'Of course. I've a longish appointment later but no matter. You're very welcome, both of you.'

'I'll get the train.'

Sean looked so relieved. I asked, 'Is there any chance you could somehow get me a bed and some bed linen and, say, a television for Natasha?'

'Sure. I'll sort you out some furniture. You go and don't give it another thought.'

'Thank you, Sean. Thank you so much.' What a trojan he was.

Lugging my suitcase I got the train to Kings Cross and then a taxi to Fulham. Camilla was waiting for us with open arms. By this time Natasha had quite worn herself out and seemed pleased to see Aunt Camilla. We were made very welcome with Natasha being given chocolate biscuits, ice-cream and orange juice. Now wasn't the time to tell Camilla all that had happened and when she went off to her appointment I took Natasha to the nearby swings and slide and chatted as though we hadn't a care in the world. She seemed to warm to the situation and played happily enough. Other children were about and she even interacted with them in her bossy way. Eventually we went back to Camilla's flat after I'd stopped at the local shop to buy fish fingers and I later fried them and even made chips which I served with lots of tomato ketchup. Natasha ate it all hungrily, she'd never been a child to turn down her favourite food and I was relieved that she'd stopped asking for Aunt Jelly.

Much later I bathed her and put her to bed in the double bed that she'd be sharing with me. Only then did she ask, 'When are we going home?'

'Tomorrow.'

'To Aunt Jelly?'

'No. We don't live with Aunt Jelly anymore, but you'll love our new flat when you get used to it, I promise you will.'

Her face crumpled and she started to cry. Even

though she was my daughter and I loved her she looked liked a wizened monkey with her Angelica-like squidgy face. 'I don't want to live in a new flat, I want to live with Aunt Jelly.'

To say it broke my heart is not entirely the truth. I was tired and wanted to find the right words but hadn't a clue what they were. I thought of Ben saying that Natasha was a Herriott-Greene and always would be. It unnerved me.

'What can I do to make it right, Natasha?' I looked at the space beside her in the bed. 'Jakie's there. Will he make it right?' It was more desperation than wise.

She looked at the space beside her. 'Jakie's not here anymore. Jakie's very naughty and had to be put in the toilet.'

'The *toilet?*'

Closing her eyes as though I was quite stupid Natasha took a deep breath and sighed. 'Aunt Jelly said he was a horrid boy and deserved to be put in the toilet.'

'So what happened then?'

'We pulled the chain, silly.'

'So - he was flushed away for ever.'

She sighed again. 'Well, if he ever tries to get out Aunt Jelly said she'll chop him up into tiny pieces and bury him in the garden.'

I shuddered thinking that this was the stuff of nightmares. 'I'm so sorry, Natasha. That's not very nice.'

She took a deep breath and flopped back on to the pillows. 'Aunt Jelly said he wouldn't get out of the toilet because he can't swim.'

Perhaps it was the cold-hearted manner in which my daughter delivered these words that chilled me; or perhaps I was too tired to see the funny side.

Natasha gave a sort of grin. 'He's not real, silly. He's only a figlement of my 'magination.' She said all these words in an adult way; not like the four and a half-year-old that she was and then she sat upright looking at me with an unfathomable expression on her pinched face. 'It was *you* put him in my 'magination. You're very naughty.'

'I'm not naughty. I'm your mummy.'

'You're not my real mummy. Aunty Jelly is.'

I was astounded. 'Did she tell you that?'

Natasha sensed my anger. 'Umm - don't know.' She dithered. 'Umm - Aunt Jelly said when mummies are naughty they have to be made to go away and a good mummy stays.'

'And is that what you'd like?'

She thought about this. 'I think so.'

'What if I told you I love you very much and will never go away.'

She looked worried. 'You fight for me like this morning?'

'People shouldn't have to fight for what is naturally theirs, Natasha.'

'What does that mean?'

'It means you belong to me; you're my daughter. Nothing can ever change that, not Aunt Jelly, no-one.'

She frowned. 'But I love Aunt Jelly.'

'Of course you do, and that's good but I'm your mummy. Don't let anyone tell you any different.'

My daughter sighed again. 'H'okay.'

She was exhausted and I knew I could take this conversation no further, only hope for my daughter to come to terms with our new relationship in time.

'She's like a miniature version of Angelica.' I complained to Camilla later that evening. 'She acts like her and speaks like her.'

Camilla smiled. 'You mustn't beat yourself up about this. It may take a long long time to bring her round because Natasha's been indulged and petted and encouraged to blame you for everything she doesn't like. I suppose it's a bit like indoctrination.'

'Well I'll just have to indoctrinate her with the truth.'

She stroked my arm. 'You look so sad.'

'I am sad. I'm riddled with sadness and guilt because I let Angelica look after her in the first place.' I looked at Camilla. 'No! It's because I married Ben.'

Camilla smiled. 'But you have a chance now; a chance for a new future and Ben gave you that. This business thing sounds amazing. I'm so proud of you. You'll sock it to them all.'

'Or fall flat on my face.'

'Stop being negative. It's time to be positive.'

I thought of my meeting with Sean. 'I am trying.'

'And you're rich! Amazingly so.'

'On paper maybe, but I still have to pay a colossal amount of inheritance tax and how the hell am I going to do that?'

'I'm sorry, I'm really not rich enough to help.'

I reached out. 'I didn't mean that.'

'I know you didn't, but I wish I was.' She sighed. 'What are you going to do?'

'Get a loan. I'll fix it somehow. I just need some space to collect my thoughts. It's been crazy. Hopefully things will settle down. I hope so.'

Blues blue

When we arrived back at the flat I wanted to cry. Sean had furnished it completely. Well, not completely, but at least there were sofas and a table and chairs, and bedroom furniture. It wasn't quality furniture but what could be in such a short space of time. I would be eternally grateful to him.

I took Natasha to school the next day and explained to her teacher, Miss Darrell, that Natasha's address had temporarily changed until I found a house with a garden and that it would be me picking her up from school in the foreseeable future. Miss Darrell looked slightly confused but nodded. 'By the way,' I asked. 'How is Natasha getting on?'

'She's doing well; settling down. A very bright child but she needs lots of direction to keep her happy. We're getting there.'

I smiled broadly at such positive news. I went to the office feeling happier.

The day was pleasant enough spent looking at copious plans and drawings of the houses for the new sites. Then Tom, the architect, drove me to Chesterton and Trumpington and we thoroughly trudged the length and breadth of the sites as he explained where the houses would go. I liked Tom; he was about forty-seven, short, a bit tubby, not at all how you'd imagine an architect and I soon found out that he was married with three children; two girls and a boy. He enjoyed chatting and Tom had actually welcomed me into the office; I wasn't sure Sean had done that as yet.

I asked Sean. 'Any news of Bethany?'

'Yes. It seems she's vanished. No sign of her anywhere. But don't worry, she'll surface one way or another because she'll need to find another job eventually and we have her P45. I'll get her then.'

'She'll deny all knowledge of it!'

He looked at me as though that simple fact hadn't dawned on him. 'You're probably right. So what do you want me to do?'

'Nothing. We should have taken the key away from her there and then.' I smiled, 'But perhaps not. Perhaps she's owed more than she got.'

Sean snorted in an undignified manner. 'You must be joking. She had a whale of a time with Ben and loved every minute of it.'

'Now you tell me.'

He looked guilty. 'Sorry.'

I looked at my wristwatch. 'I really must dash. Don't want to be late picking up my daughter.'

'No, that would never do.'

I half-expected to see Angelica at the school but there was no sign of her. I grabbed a rather forlorn looking Natasha by the hand and whisked her off to the car. 'I thought we'd go to Joshua Taylors and buy you something exciting, how about that?'

She brightened a little. 'Like a new teddy-bear?'

'If you'd like.'

'Tessa's got a purple teddy with boots and gloves. I'd like one like that.'

Oh, dear, I thought. 'Well, yes, if we can find one.'

Natasha clapped her hands together. 'Goody. And can I have some choc'let?'

'If you're good.'

Natasha didn't answer but I saw the semblance of a smile on her face.

Needless to say we couldn't find the teddy and trawled round several other shops in the vain hope of seeing one but then, bingo, in a little out of the way newsagents cum post-office we found a furry lion cub that for some bizarre reason was purple and that seemed to do the trick. I realised then that it wasn't the teddy but the colour she liked. Good, I'd buy her a purple dress when I could find one. With a large bar of chocolate we went back to the flat and I later cooked sausages and mash with spaghetti hoops for supper. Natasha ate the lot, and then we did some drawing and reading before bath and bed. I was pleased with myself as I closed her bedroom door. There had been no real tantrums and without Angelica around life had become considerably less fraught.

When I dropped Natasha off the following morning she looked around. 'Where's Aunt Jelly,' she said with tears in her eyes. 'Why can't I see Aunt Jelly?'

'You can, Natasha. I promise you'll see Aunt Jelly this weekend. If you like you can spend a whole day with her. How does that sound?'

Natasha's bottom lip trembled. She took a deep breath. I'd seen her do this many times before and knew something awful was to come. 'You hate Aunt Jelly! She told me you hate her.'

I lied through my teeth. 'I don't hate Aunt Jelly.

Please, Natasha, don't be like this.' I tried to brighten the situation by saying, 'What shall we do after school? Tell you what, why don't we go to the pictures?'

She glared at me and the look on her face was so reminiscent of Angelica. 'Don't want to go to the pictures. I want Aunt Jelly.'

I took a deep breath and with my daughter's hand in mine walked towards her classroom. I unbuttoned her coat and gave her a kiss. 'Mummy will see you later.'

She whispered beneath her breath. 'You're not my mummy. Aunt Jelly's my mummy.'

I backed off and saw Miss Darrell looking at me. Then I did what I always seem to do in these situations, made a rapid retreat.

Worst was to come. When I arrived at Bridge Street Sean told me that the bank wanted to see me. He'd made an appointment for the two of us to meet the manager the next day at 10.00 a.m.! I panicked.

'Why does he want to see me?'

'Diana, you're the owner of this company. Ben's put you in sole charge. Why do you think he wants to see you?'

'What do I say?'

Sean sat back in his chair and looked at me. I hated that look! Smug git, I thought. 'It might be advisable for you to listen. I'll do the talking.'

I remember pinching my mouth together. 'Of course.'

I did what any woman would do! Took myself off to Jaeger and bought an incredible black suit. It looked wonderful, as though I'd been poured into it. The A-line skirt, snug around my hips, skimmed my calves and the jacket sleeves reached to just below my elbows; this I teamed with a lovely grey crepe-de-chine blouse which ballooned slightly beneath the sleeves and then tapered into fitted cuffs. It cost a fortune, the most I'd ever spent, but I had to have it. Then I needed shoes. No! Boots! I bought black suede boots, calf length with stubby heels but so sexy.

Where was Natasha? I searched! I was on time; not at all late, but there was no sign of Natasha. Mothers were milling around everywhere. I looked for Angelica but it was like searching through a sea of faces.

Then I saw her! Angelica! She was leading a delighted Natasha out of the playground. I wanted to shout out but something stopped me; instead I hurried towards them and then hesitated as neither knew I was there, such was their absorption in each other and I so aware of this. My heart felt squeezed and unable to beat but I continued and slipped my hand into Natasha's and held it firm. 'Come on now, darling. No messing.'

Natasha looked at me and opened her mouth protesting as loudly as she could. It was a nightmare. She had this way of sounding like a yowling animal in a death trap. I walked smartly on half-dragging my daughter away but Angelica pulled the other way. Everybody was looking at us now. I stopped and faced my sister-in-law. 'If you don't let go I promise you'll never see Natasha again! I have a flight booked for just the two of us to California. To be honest, I've had enough and we're off - if you don't let go I promise you, we're off.'

Her eyes widened in a way I'd never seen before. Maybe it was because in the past week she'd been faced with so much strength from me, I don't know.

'I only wanted to take her home for tea.'

Natasha was still wailing and mothers in the playground were starting to close in asking Aunt Jelly, yes, *Aunt Jelly*, if she was all right. How clever of Angelica to present herself in this personal way to the other children's mothers.

Holding on tightly to Natasha I said, 'I have no objection to that, Angelica, but you have to ask me first.'

In a desperate manner she said, 'You'd have said no.'

'No I wouldn't! I've told you, we have to compromise on this.'

Angelica drew her mouth back over her teeth but stopped short of speaking. Natasha stood between us and for the first time my daughter was afraid of me, don't tell me how I knew this, I just did.

The other mothers were glaring at me now with hostility written all over their faces. I spoke to my daughter. 'Come on, Natasha, come with mummy, there's a good girl.'

She stamped her foot. 'Don't want to.'

Angelica bobbed down and put both hands on my daughter's shoulders. 'Go with mummy now, Natasha, and I'll see you soon.'

'Pwomise?' She said and even I gulped.

'I promise.'

With my head held high I walked back to my car a sobbing Natasha beside me.

We went straight back to the flat and whatever I tried to do I couldn't console my daughter. I almost took her back to Brooklands Avenue but how defeatist was that? I had to ride this out. So I made shepherds pie for supper but Natasha took barely two mouthfuls. Her eyes were red and swollen and her short breaths the result of constant sobbing. In the end I bathed her and put her to bed with her new purple lion cub. She did cuddle that. I left her and went back into the sitting room. I thought of California and I have to say it was like a safe light at the end of a dark and dismal tunnel.

She ate sugar puffs for breakfast and I drove her to school chatting all the way. She clutched *purply*, as the lion cub was now called, in her hands and hardly spoke. I walked my daughter into school and turned quite a few heads in my new smart suit. I hung Natasha's coat on her peg and was about to leave when Miss Darrell appeared from nowhere.

'Mrs Herriott-Greene, could I have a word?' she asked. Her tone was clipped and put the fear of God into me.

'Of course.'

'If we could go through here; I'd rather Natasha didn't hear.' She said.

I said goodbye to Natasha and followed Miss Darrell into the music room which was cold and empty.

'Mrs Herriott-Greene,' she said. 'I am extremely worried about Natasha. She is absolutely traumatised by your recent move, and I have to say I am not surprised. The little girl has just lost her daddy and now it seems she has lost her home and garden and, of course, her beloved Aunt Jelly.'

I wondered how long it would be before she was mentioned. 'I know,' was all I could say at that point.

'Do you really think it wise moving her away from everything she loves? She's barely four and a half years old and although she's very mature in a lot of ways her home life should be her foundation.'

'But there's so much you don't know, Miss Darrell.'

'And probably don't want or need to know. Natasha is my priority and she is quite distraught.'

'But with time ...'

She cut me off. 'I don't think so. She obviously needs to go home to Brooklands Avenue and Aunt Jelly. *Whyever* did you leave?'

How impudent but I smiled. 'I didn't leave out of choice; I was told to leave.'

A cynical expression crossed Miss Darrell's face. I realised then how I must appear in my fine suit and somewhat flighty manner. I was not yet twenty-four; how did that compare to the more solid and dependable persona of my sister-in-law.

I stumbled over my next words. 'It's been extremely hard for me too, Miss Darrell. But Natasha is my daughter and I care about her very much.'

'In that case you should seriously consider what you are doing to her.'

'Has Angelica been in to see you?' I asked.

'Angelica?'

'Aunt Jelly. *Miss* Herriott-Greene.'

'No, not since this all happened, but I understand there was a tussle in the playground yesterday. Again, this is not the sort of behaviour I expect from parents.

Do you understand, Mrs Herriott-Greene?'

Loud and clear. 'It won't happen again.' I started to walk away.

'Please take my advice. Please return your daughter to where she is most happy. If you want a well-rounded child you have to make sacrifices.'

Well-rounded child! How I kept myself from telling this jumped-up teacher what I thought of her I do not know. Maybe guilt. Maybe Miss Darrell had a point. Maybe I was in the process of making a huge mistake and Ben had been right all along. There were so many maybes. California beckoned.

I arrived at the office in Bridge Street quite flustered. I had been allocated Ben's old office which was very nice indeed but with no windows. Apparently he liked this because there were no distractions but I found windows therapeutic; to gaze outside and watch people going about their everyday lives. I looked at my wristwatch; it was nine thirty. I went in search of Sean.

'He said he'd meet you at the bank.' The secretary said.

'Oh, I see. Thank you.'

How very supportive of Sean I thought as I walked back to my office. I was hardly there a minute when the secretary buzzed through to say that Miss Herriott-Greene would like to see me. Should she send her in? 'Erh, yes, of course,' I said and took a deep breath. *Please,* this was all I needed.

Angelica walked into my office and my first thoughts were she looked as though she hadn't slept. In fact, I'd never seen her looking quite so haggard.

'Angelica,' I said.

'Diana.'

'What can I do for you?' She looked me up and down. 'I've a meeting with the bank shortly. I need to make an impression.' Hopefully she would take the hint and not hang about.

'I see.' She slumped down into the chair opposite my desk. 'But I didn't come here to argue, quite the opposite. I came to make peace.' She looked at me earnestly and tears welled into her eyes. 'I can't bear it, Diana, I miss her so much. I'll do anything, *anything* to have her back.'

I took a deep breath and said softly, 'That's not possible, Angelica, but we can compromise. There is no reason whatsoever why you can't see her often; as often as you like, but Natasha lives with me.'

'You are *so* stubborn.'

'And so are you.'

'But the difference is Natasha loves *me*; I'm the one she wants to be with and if you can't see that you must be blind!'

I swallowed hard as I allowed her words to sink in. 'I've made some big mistakes but I'm not going to give in to you about my daughter.'

'In that case come back, both of you. I'm begging you, come back to Brooklands Avenue and I won't be nasty to you ever again.'

I actually laughed and then rubbed the side of my nose. I always did this when something preposterous was said to me. 'I'm afraid I don't want to live with you anymore.'

'There's no alternative! You have to so that Natasha

can have a happy life. If you continue to let that child live apart from me we'll both pine to death - or I certainly will.'

I stared at my sister-in-law. 'That's blackmail.'

'It's the truth! I'm telling you I miss her *that* much.'

'It wouldn't work.'

'It *would*,' she insisted. 'I'd make it work. If you have a heart at all please come back, *please.'*

I actually started to feel sorry for her. How can you feel sorry for someone you hate so much? I remembered Miss Darrell's words and Ben's before he died. I sat down heavily into the seat opposite the aunt of my child and put my head in my hands. She did something then that sent a shiver through me. Angelica reached out and squeezed both of my forearms.

She implored, 'You might remarry, have more children, but Natasha is all I'll ever have. My insides ache with the loss of her. I've made a promise to God or whoever's up there that I'll be good and look after her with all of my being if you'll just let me *share* her with you by coming back to live with me.' She slumped into her seat. 'And I've money; *lots;* I've saved all my life. I know you need it to pay your inheritance tax.' She added with a flick of her hand. 'You can pay it back; whenever.'

My eyes were on stalks now as I stared at her. 'You'll lend me all that money?'

'For Natasha I'd do anything.' She stood up pushing her seat back clumsily. 'I must go now.' She took a deep breath and the tears were back in her eyes as she insisted, 'Just promise me one thing? You won't take her to California?'

'I'm not promising you anything, except - we will

come and see you after school, so, please, no more shenanigans outside the school gates.'

She nodded and stumbled out of my office. I felt so sorry for her. It was the strangest feeling I'd ever experienced.

I arrived at the bank before Sean with Angelica's words still ringing in my ears. Had Ben talked to her about my inheritance tax? Is that why he mentioned in his letter that she could help me out? But that couldn't possibly be right because she was so shocked when I inherited the business. Maybe he knew his sister so well; maybe he surmised that it would be her bargaining stick.

Sean arrived with minutes to spare before our meeting with the bank manager. He looked me up and down and nodded his approval. 'You look nice,' he said.

'So do you.' He wore a navy blue suit, crisp white shirt and red tie. He was a handsome man and I wondered again why I didn't fancy him more.

The bank manager, Roland Chambers, stood behind his desk looking every bit the banking patriarch. He was older than I'd anticipated with a mop of greying hair and bushy eyebrows over twinkling bright blue eyes and I didn't so much feel intimidated as relieved that he wasn't the big bad wolf I'd expected him to be.

Sean and I sat down and were served coffee which was gratefully received by me. 'So,' he said looking directly at me, 'you have taken on the mantle of H-G Properties. A tall order, Mrs Herriott-Greene, how do you think you can live up to its esteemed reputation?'

This was easy for me. 'I don't." I said. 'All I can do is listen and learn.'

Sean briefly glanced at me and then nodded at the bank manager. 'I think the business is still in safe hands, Mr Chambers. We don't intend to change anything in the foreseeable future. In the meantime Diana will be well schooled in our modus operandi.'

'Fine words, but *Mr* Herriott-Greene did have the Midas touch. It counts for a lot in these uneasy days.' Mr Chambers flexed his hands; 'He kept his finger on the pulse; I liked that. That's why we maintained good financial business. If you don't mind my saying, this isn't about modus operandi, it's more about us relying on H-G being able to keep up its payments.' He directed his gaze at me once more. 'For instance, have you decided what you are going to do about death duties?' He narrowed his eyes. 'Aren't they dreadfully onerous for you?'

Sean interrupted. 'We've talked about this.' He looked at me, 'Haven't we, Diana?' I didn't like his patronising tone.

'Yes.' I looked at Mr Chambers and it was so easy for me to say, 'My sister-in-law is helping me on that one. It seems she has deep pockets.' The words slipped off my tongue like velvet and I smiled.

He chuckled knowingly. 'Oh, yes, indeed she does.' He obviously knew Angelica well and was relieved. So was I.

Sean's eyes stayed on my face as if to say you should have told me that but I didn't know myself until a few seconds before. Yes, I suppose it meant that I was going to trade in my daughter for payment of my inheritance tax. Everyone has a price, Ben had once said to me, even me.

'So what do you think you might bring to the business?' Ronald Chambers asked. 'Apart from being a pretty face, that is.'

Again Sean jumped in and his words took my breath away. 'You're going to make the gardens pretty too, aren't you, Diana?' He looked at me and grinned. He was irritating the hell out of me.

Mr Chambers was surprised and Sean went on. 'It seems Ben was very impressed with the way Diana did their garden in Brooklands Avenue.'

The bank manager was now hooked, I noticed, and asked, 'What did you do?'

'I landscaped it, or rather paid someone else to do it. But it was a labour of love as far as I was concerned.'

'And Ben was impressed?'

A lump came into my throat. 'Yes, it seems so. He spent his last days gazing out of the window. I like to think it gave him some peace of mind.'

'So where does your knowledge of gardening come from?'

'My father; he was head gardener on an estate in Ashley near Newmarket for several years before he died.'

'Was he really? How very interesting. I'm a keen gardener.' He smiled broadly, 'As I approach retirement I spend more and more time nurturing my plants. So tell me, what do you know about roses?'

I grinned. Why was it that everyone loved roses? 'I know that I absolutely adore roses.'

Mr Chambers leaned across the desk. 'You see, I've had the most amazing display for several years, but this year - pooh - the poor things look as though they've been eaten alive; all black spots and mildew. I've tried everything and nothing's worked and now they look as though they need digging up and putting on the compost heap!'

'Are they in a rose bed or within your border?'

'In my border, but it hasn't been a problem before.'

I too leaned across the desk. We were so close to each other that he drew back ever so slightly but I knew he did this for comfort not because he found me unattractive. 'Next spring cut them back and then when they start to flower spray them with a third part household bleach and two parts water. It will knock them back for several weeks but I'm sure you'll find they bloom amazingly well for the whole of the summer.'

'Bleach? Sounds a bit drastic; are you sure?'

'Let's just say my father swore by it.'

'In that case thank you. I'll try it. Thank you very much.'

'A pleasure.'

I faced Sean whose mouth had dropped open. I smiled and he closed his mouth.

Mr Chambers composed himself. 'Is there anything else, Mrs Herriott-Greene, that you'd like to discuss with me?'

I scratched my neck; I was nervous. 'Actually there is. You see, I remember a conversation I had with Ben when he was constantly flying backwards and forwards to California. He told me that it had all started with a holiday when he'd noticed that the place was ripe for development. Anyway, last weekend I was in London, Fulham, and I noticed this derelict site near my sister's flat. It was big; say, an acre and I rang up about it; just to see if it was for sale. It was but nobody's interested.

I'm sure it would take a block of flats like the ones here and I thought wouldn't it be a good idea to carry on my late husband's work in London? There must be loads of similar sites around.'

Mr Chamber's looked at me quite astonished. 'Yes, my dear, how very venturesome. I'm impressed.'

'I think we might get this site at a reasonable price and it could be my project.' I looked at Sean. 'With your help, of course.' I looked at Mr Chambers, 'And yours.'

Sean went up in my estimation because he gave me a very warm smile, sat back in his chair and folded his arms. I knew then that I'd won him over.

'So, you'll be in touch, I think.' Mr Chambers said.

I smiled with great relief. 'We will. Thank you for talking to me and good luck with your roses next year.'

He stood up and shook my hand, and Sean's. 'Good luck yourself, my dear. You come across as a plucky young thing. I can see why your late husband put his trust in you.'

I could only incline my head as his approbation. Ben's trust, I'm sure, was more based on his sister's happiness.

'Fancy lunch?' Sean asked as we left the bank.

'Bit early.'

He looked at his watch. 'A drink then. I could murder a beer.'

It was eleven-thirty. 'Yes. A Gin and tonic wouldn't go amiss. Let's go and have a drink.'

We sat in the Berni Inn next to Eden Lilley's department store and it was like Meribel all over again. Sean let down his prickly façade of the last few days and chatted to me as an equal; at least I like to think he did. We talked about the business, his daughter Mel who was now nearly eighteen and very beautiful, and my daughter Natasha. I didn't tell Sean too much about the recent conflicts except to mention that I might be moving back into Brooklands Avenue.

He looked surprised then said, 'You've still got the flat. Do what Ben did; have the best of both worlds.'

I stared at him in amazement as though he'd just lifted a weight off my shoulders. 'Goodness, how right you are. Why didn't I think of that?'

He tapped my hand with his forefinger. 'You see, you do need me.'

'Oh, I need you all right and what a brilliant thing to say. I mean, I have to move back into Brooklands Avenue for Natasha's sake but if I keep the flat I have a bolt hole; somewhere to call my own. They need never know.'

I studied Sean then and asked, 'I've always wondered why Mel lives with you and not her mother?'

'Liz left me and buggered off to Paris and it was hardly the place to take a fourteen-year-old with well-established friends at school. Anyway, Mel didn't want to up-sticks and move to France, plus I don't think she was welcome. Liz was too involved with her ex-lover.'

'Ex?'

'Oh, yes. It didn't last long, but Liz likes Paris and Mel gets to see her quite often. Trouble is it messed up her exams. She scraped through her 0-levels and her A-level grades have been abysmal. She will not be going to university.'

'What will she do?'

'Not a lot if it was up to Mel.' He smiled in a fatherly way. 'She's talking about doing a secretarial course, or something similar, meanwhile she flits about doing a bit of this and a bit of that.'

'Who'd have daughters?'

'Too interested in boys, my Mel; too attractive by half.'

'How do you feel about that?'

'I've had to let go. She's almost nineteen and entitled to live her life the same as I do.' He finished his beer. 'I just wish I'd been able to buy a few of your shares to really set me up in the future but now I see there's no chance of that.'

'Don't forget Angelica's fifteen percent.'

'But will she ever really sell?'

I scoffed. 'Can't wait to get rid of them!'

Sean pulled a disbelieving face and as we sat in the bar I looked at the food now being served in the restaurant. 'I don't know about you, but I'm hungry.'

'Good. Let's do lunch.'

We did and both ate steak and chips.

I picked Natasha up from school and before she had time to grumble or whine about precious Aunt Jelly I said, 'We're going to see Aunt Jelly.'

Her face lit up as though she was the luckiest girl in the playground and I have to say an enormous lump came into my throat. Natasha clapped her hands together gleefully. 'Are we going home?'

It was no good denying it. No good kidding myself any longer. 'Yes, Natasha, home.'

'Goody!' She plucked her purple lion cub out of her school bag and kissed him. 'We're going home, Purply, we're going home! Just wait 'til you meet Aunt Jelly.

You'll love Aunt Jelly. Everyone loves Aunt Jelly.'

Natasha made herself very comfortable in the back of the car with Purply placed very firmly in the middle of her lap looking ahead. 'This is the way,' my daughter said keeping up a conversation with her furry friend. 'It's the mostest lovely house in the whole wide world and we'll have so much funnykins in the garden. You'll *love* my garden.'

I braced myself; in all of this at least I'd done something right.

As we walked into the house I was overwhelmed with misgivings. It was as though I had stepped right back into the lion's den. Then my mother and Aunt Fi appeared from nowhere and a shudder went through me.

'There you are,' my mother said. 'We've been waiting for you. Where have you been?' She made a clucking noise in the back of her throat. 'Goodness, aren't you decked out. All this money gone to your head, Diana? Whatever next.'

'Whatever next.' Aunt Fi repeated as she stood behind my mother like a nodding donkey. She always agreed with my mother and had this habit of repeating her last few words. Consequently Camilla called her Aunt Fi Fi. She was skinny and appeared frail whereas my mother was plump and hearty looking; the combination quite comical; or it was to me.

I lied through my teeth. 'How lovely to see you both.' I noticed that Natasha had taken off and flung herself into Angelica's warm and welcoming arms.

My mother was insistent. 'So why are you dressed up like that?'

I took a deep breath as if it was any of her business. 'I had a meeting with the bank manager, mother.'

'Oooh la la!' She said sarcastically.

Aunt Fi said more softly. 'Oooh la la.'

'Not oooh la la at all. More sink or swim.'

'And will you?'

'Will I what?'

'Sink?'

I smiled; why was she never supportive? Why did she enjoy making me squirm at her comments? I consoled myself with the fact she had done this to my father as well. 'I'm hoping to swim. Time will tell.'

My mother looked at her watch. 'Come on, Fi. If we don't get off now we'll miss the bus.'

I took a deep breath. 'I'll take you home.'

My mother sighed in great relief. 'It would be very nice dear, if it's not *too* much trouble.'

I beamed at her. 'No trouble whatsoever.'

On the way home she asked outright. 'So are you rich now, dear?'

I laughed. 'Only on paper.'

'Angelica said you're loaded and that you somehow or other managed to cream everything off Ben.'

Here we go again I thought. What was it Angelica had said about not being nasty anymore? 'I'm not even going to honour that comment with a reply, mother.'

She coughed. 'Well, just remember me. I've spent my whole life struggling and living in squalor!'

I glared at her. 'Hardly squalor! What are you talking about?'

'I'm talking about your father. As you well know

lie was useless when it came to money and us having a respectable existence. All he cared about was his stupid trees and shrubs.'

'Stupid trees and shrubs.' Repeated Aunt Fi who was sitting in the back of the car. I took a deep breath and was so pleased to see Newmarket's lights approaching. 'As soon as I get sorted you will be my first priority. I'll make sure you're comfortable and have a lovely house to live in, I promise.'

She became quite excited and craned her neck to look at Aunt Fi in the back seat. 'Did you hear that, Fi?'

My mother tapped my arm. 'Promises are all very well but I do hope I can count on that?'

'You can, mother. You most definitely can.'

She looked ahead. 'Hmm, well, perhaps you're not so bad after all.'

How can you reply to that? I decided not to try.

I was glad that Natasha was watching television when I returned to Brooklands Avenue. The first thing I said to Angelica was, 'You said this morning that you would not be nasty to me anymore?'

She was immediately defensive. 'Yes. So?'

'You told my mother that I had creamed everything off Ben. You know that's a nasty lie.'

I saw her gulp. Good. She was unsure of her next words. 'That's how I see it. I only speak the truth.'

'No! Let's get this straight here and now or I leave forever.' There was panic in her eyes and I was glad. 'You don't speak the truth; or at least only your truth. I didn't cream anything off Ben. Before he died he begged me to let you have Natasha; told me to name my price but I refused. And then when he did die as far as I knew he'd left me nothing. That is the real truth and if you can't accept it I'm not staying here and neither is my daughter.'

She was lost for words. Tongue-tied.

I continued. 'I saw your misery this morning and I'd have to be blind not to see Natasha's. I've been left all these shares by Ben and a letter *directing* me to run the company and let you look after our daughter. I'm tired of fighting a losing battle; I just want her to be happy. So I've gone full circle and today, in that bank manager's office, I decided to give in to Ben, you and my daughter. Okay? Do you understand?'

She sneered ever so slightly. 'Nothing to do with me paying your death duties then?'

'Yes!' I exclaimed. '*Yes!* But do you blame me? Sometimes I think my head is going to explode with everything that has been put on my shoulders!' I drew closer to her. 'Sometimes California with all its millions beckons like crazy!'

'Oh, I wondered when you'd mention that again. Is it going to be the stick you beat me with when you don't get your own way?'

I stopped in my tracks and looked at my sister-in-law; at her pinched face and sallow complexion. It crossed my mind; why did my daughter love her so much but, of course, when someone loves you with all of their being it's easy to love back.

'No. It's not. I'm sorry. I'll never say that again. I'm also very grateful for your offer of a loan and I accept it. I'll pay you back as soon as I can with interest. I'll also live here with Natasha. That's the deal, isn't it?'

She softened and took a deep breath. 'In that case I won't be nasty anymore.'

'Angelica,' I said, 'could we at least try to be on the same side in the future. I love my daughter and genuinely want what's best for her. If that's *you* then so be it, but I am her mother and please don't tell her any different. If you promise me that - I'll always call you Aunt Jelly in the future.'

Her eyebrows shot up in surprise and I saw the delight in her eyes. I'd really hit the jackpot on that one.

She spluttered slightly, 'Yes, I - I think I might like that.'

It gave her status, and for whatever reason security with my daughter. She was *Aunt Jelly*; and as close to being Natasha's mother as damn it. 'Well, Aunt Jelly, one other thing.' Her eyes held alarm once more so I said quickly, 'Nothing to worry about; on the contrary. Your shares, you'll be pleased to know that Sean is very interested in buying them.'

She frowned. 'Sean?'

'The accountant; he's very keen.'

She folded her arms. 'I'm not sure; I'm not going to sell them to just anyone.'

'But you have to offer them to the share-holders first and if you remember Ben left Sean Jackson five percent.'

She sniffed and looked pensive. 'In that case I might hold on to them.'

I was surprised and yet not surprised. It was one piece of power still left with her and she was going to hang on to it. I decided to be positive. 'You may be very pleased with that decision in the future, Aunt Jelly, because I intend to make Ben proud of me.'

She was going to say something sarcastic but obviously thought better of it. We were saved by Natasha who appeared between us as if from nowhere. She looked up at her beloved aunt and said.' You said I could have some choc'let.'

Angelica threw a look at me, bobbed down and said to my daughter, 'As you've been such a very good girl of course you can have some chocolate.' She took her hand and led her through to what used to be my kitchen. I watched them go, shrugged and followed.

1975

Margaret Thatcher new Tory Leader
Charlie Chaplin died
Oil begins to flow in from North Sea
Chinese archaeologists uncover terracotta army
Dutch Elm disease kills 6.5 million trees
Chelsea relegated to second division

Warm Red

It was late September and there we were showing all sorts of Cambridge dignitaries, decked out in their finery, around our new development in Cambridge. Thankfully it was a bright sunny day and the weather had been dry so everyone's shoes remained relatively clean. This was followed by a champagne reception at The Cambridge Lodge hotel in Huntingdon Road.

I was enjoying myself. Aunt Jelly was there and Natasha had been given time off from school to accompany her. Both clung to each other like limpets but I'd come to accept this completely now. Ronald Chambers, our bank manager, looked at me beneath his daunting eyebrows and if not exactly praising me he was at least letting me know he was wise to put his trust in me. The honour that H-G Properties had received from no less than the Duke of Edinburgh in recent weeks was much deserved, he said.

I fell over my words pathetically. 'Honestly, this was all going ahead before I arrived on the scene.' I tapped his shoulder, 'But just you wait 'til Fulham starts to happen.' I bit my lip remembering the hassle and detail I'd had to endure to secure the site. Thank God for darling Sean. He'd been an absolute wonder.

'I know, my dear. And by all accounts it's looking good.'

I took a deep breath remembering that the champagne had gone to my head. 'I think so. I hope so. I've been so lucky to be involved in all of this; privileged actually. And thank you for your support, Ronald, I can't tell you how much it means to me.' I realised immediately that I'd used his Christian name. It was because Sean always referred to him as *Row'land,* and I'd forgotten that one should be polite to bank managers and always use the mister prefix.

He moved closer. 'My dear, if my support means as much to you as your presence lighting up my life does to me then we're quits.'

I was delighted and wanted to laugh out loud and for some obscure reason thought of Ben. How we would have chuckled about this in the very early days of our relationship. 'Do you know, I think that's the kindest thing anyone has ever said to me?'

'In that case, I'm honoured.' He nudged me. 'Now, my dear, you must leave me and mix. It wouldn't seem right for you to be spending too much time with me.'

I was bold and plonked a small kiss on his cheek. 'Thank you. Your guidance is invaluable.'

He just squeezed my arm. I would remember that feeling forever. How precious it was.

'You seemed to be very cosy with our Row'land,' said Sean.

'He was just being the avuncular bank manager.' I looked around at everyone drinking and eating and seemingly enjoying themselves. 'It's going well, isn't it?'

'Better than we could have expected in our wildest dreams, don't you think?'

I was contemplative for a few seconds. 'Do you know who I'm really thinking about?'

He said, 'Let me hazard a guess. Ben?'

I was pleased he understood. 'Yes. I can't think why because he was an absolute bastard to live with, but without him we wouldn't be here, would we?'

'I think not. Life has a way of making you take stock, doesn't it? We have to be grateful to Ben and so does Cambridge.'

I smiled ruefully. 'Well, I'm not sure everybody would agree with that but I certainly do.' I raised my glass and Sean chinked his against it.

'How about dinner this evening?' He said.

I blinked; although not totally surprised because I'd grown accustomed to his constant badgering to meet outside the work place. 'What I ought to do is go home and sober up.' I said.

'Oh, don't do that, I like you much better as you are. And don't forget you always have your bolt hole.'

How could I forget? I'd completely refurbished it, out of my own pocket, and now it was lovingly filled with my choice of furniture, my selected treasures and the colours everywhere were after my own heart. I didn't stay often overnight but every now and then felt the need for a break. I have to say my love life was zilch. Non-existent.

'Is that a yes?'

'Where will we eat?'

'How about I come to your place and cook you a nice steak? How does that sound?'

I smiled. 'Sean, it sounds pretty amazing but where will you buy the steak?'

'Why?'

'I'm very fussy. I only like fillet.'

'Let me worry about that. Okay?'

'As my daughter would say, h'okay.'

'So did you enjoy yourself, Natasha?' I asked.

She was five and a half years old and wise beyond her years. 'Yes. Although Aunt Jelly thought it was a fuss.'

'A *fuss?*'

Natasha's eyes lit up. For all the wrong reasons she saw she'd got my attention and I could see her mind ticking over as to what else she could say to keep it. She really was a Herriott-Greene and so like her aunt. 'We don't like fusses.'

I placed my hand on my daughter's hair and moved the pink slide over slightly. Why of why did Aunt Jelly place it bang in the middle of her head? 'Sometimes Aunt Jelly can be such a silly billy.'

'No she can't!'

I allowed my hand to wander further to my daughter's shoulder. I said softly. 'All right; she can't.' I'd adopted this attitude months ago. Make the point but if Natasha argued with it give in. How pathetic was I.

'Can I go home now?'

'If you like.'

Natasha looked me up and down, at my beautiful dress and jacket. It was midnight blue and the fabric a silk jersey. 'You look nice, mummy.'

I reached out and hugged her. 'Thank you, darling. What a lovely thing to say. And you look nice too.' I'd bought her a purple skirt and white satin blouse. She still loved her furry friend Purply, much to Aunt Jelly's chagrin.

'Actually, Aunt Jelly told me to say that.'

I was stumped momentarily. 'Well, wasn't that kind of Aunt Jelly? But what do you think?'

'I think you look nice too.'

'Thank you, darling. Thank you very much.'

'Can I go now?'

'Of course. See you later.'

She smiled. 'Alligator.'

I reflected as I watched my daughter run off and enter her safe world once more; a world where Aunt Jelly adored her. Aunt Jelly looked anxiously across the room at me and I knew I was summoned. I walked towards them. 'I think Natasha would like to go home.' She said.

'Of course; it's fine by me.'

'All this smoke is not good for her.'

'You're right. ...I might take off to London, you know, to see Camilla. You okay with that?'

'Of course.'

'You've got a taxi, have you?'

'No. Sean's giving us a lift.'

I looked across at Sean who raised his car keys. This was going to be interesting. No doubt he'd tell me all about it later when he was cooking my fillet steak.

'She's such a little bugger! I mean, I know she's having sex with all these blokes she sees and playing a dangerous game, but she's so bloody beautiful...' Sean looked at me. 'You do agree with that?'

'Oh yes, definitely.'

'The thing is; I don't know how to protect her.'

'Perhaps you can't.' I was speaking from my heart.

'But she's my daughter for God's sake!'

'Sometimes you have to let go. I've had to.'

Sean looked at me and then flipped the steaks over in the pan. 'With respect, your daughter is five and mine is nearly twenty.'

'All the more reason to let go!'

'These steaks are going to be ready in a minute. Have you got the plates?'

I produced them from the oven, suitably warm.

He put the steaks on the plates and I surrounded them with tomatoes, mushrooms and chips. We carried the meal through to the dining area of my flat. My beautiful Tiffany lamps glowed casting shadows around the room and through the vast expanse of windows Cambridge's lights beckoned in a gentle way. It all looked rather dramatic and I felt proud.

I'd set the table with my never been used before fine silver cutlery and two Royal Stuart crystal wine glasses gleamed lustrously. A solid silver candelabra with lit red candles was the centrepiece. 'You've certainly done wonders with this place.' Sean said.

'Thank you.'

'It's beautiful furniture - with a twist.'

I loved that comment. 'Thank you again. I've found this amazing cabinet maker and he'll do whatever I ask.'

Sean smiled. 'And you simply asked for this?' In a complimentary way he inclined his hand around the room.

'Sort of. Actually, yes. I knew what I wanted but he knew exactly how to interpret it. I like textures; I didn't just want wood, I wanted marble and glass and ironwork mixed in. He wasn't fazed and it all works so well together.'

'Like you and me?'

'Come to think of it, yes. Like you and me.'

Sean poured some red burgundy. 'I'll drink to that.'

I took a mouthful. '*Wow*. This is to die for. Where did you get it?'

'I have my secrets. Come on now, eat; before it gets cold.'

I had always thought of myself as naïve but there was a strong desire in my body that evening; I wanted intimacy. I sat opposite Sean talking about this and that and was sure that his intentions were to get me into bed. It excited me and in this enlightened seventies age I knew that to give in to him was allowed but when you are not in love isn't it tawdry to do so? I'd felt tawdry during sex for all of my married life so shouldn't I have some principles now?

Sean said; 'I don't want to go home.'

I couldn't help myself. 'You don't have to.'

'I want to sleep with you tonight. Is that against the ethics of H-G Properties?'

'What's ethics got to do with anything?'

'Nothing, except - I respect you and am afraid of blowing it.'

'If I said there was nothing to blow; that we keep this separate from our business relationship will that make you feel better?' There; I'd spelled it out.

He smiled knowingly. 'Impossible.'

Boldly, I stood up and held out my hand. 'In that case take a chance.'

He took my hand and followed me into the bedroom.

Sean lay across the bed fully clothed propping his head with one hand and watched me undress. I should have seen the adoration in his eyes but I was consumed by my own lust and when I was completely naked I lay beside him facing him. 'Your turn.' I said.

'You have a lovely body.' He caressed my face and kissed my neck. He sighed, 'Mine is no longer so lovely.'

'Who cares?' I rolled on to my back.

Sean smiled indulgently at my blithe manner and eased himself off the bed. As he started to remove his clothes he said, 'Do you know I've loved you from the first time I saw you.'

I was so surprised. 'When you came to pick up Ben? When you were going to California?'

'You stood there in your white trousers and pink jumper and I remember your hair was held away from your face with a large clip but wisps of it were escaping. You looked about the same age as my daughter and very vulnerable as though you were scared. I wanted to reach out and hug you. Ben came down and hardly looked at you before we left but your eyes stayed on him all the time. What an idiot the man was because I think you must have loved him deeply.'

'No - I didn't.'

Sean seemed surprised. 'Are you sure about that?'

'Very sure. When I first met him I was besotted and a virgin and for a while we had fantastic sex. After a few months it changed but it was too late because I was pregnant. He didn't want to marry me; he only did because I told him he was going to have a son. I trapped him but ended up being trapped myself.'

'But you wept about him in Meribel.'

'I was weeping because he had no respect for me and was screwing Bethany. And because his sister hates me and my daughter adores her. That's why I was weeping.'

In just his underpants Sean sat on the bed and then

removed them. He twisted round and lay beside me and I gently kissed his mouth. I also ran my hand down to his erection and felt excited at the prospect of our lovemaking. I whispered, 'And you made me feel so special. It was easy to pour out my heart to you.'

Sean caught his breath at my administrations. 'You know he warned me after that; told me to stay away. I wanted to ring you…'

I stopped what I was doing reminded about my hurt at the time. He didn't really love me because he would have rung whatever Ben said. 'It doesn't matter.' I kissed him again.

'I love you, Diana, it's important that you understand that.'

I was flippant. 'And there was me thinking you were only after my shares.'

He drew away as though stung. 'You don't really think that?' He started to climb off the bed and I panicked and grabbed his arm. He hesitated and looked at me with misery in his eyes. It reminded me so much of myself. How many times had I seen that look in my own eyes? Sean said, 'If you think that I should just go home.'

'Please don't. I'm sorry.' I pulled him closer. 'I want you, I really do.'

Sean relaxed beside me and I ran my hands over his body, stroking and caressing. Eventually he groaned before pulling me firmly into his arms.

'Stroke me - like this.' Sean held my hand and placed it so that I stroked his penis and caressed his testicles. Then he patiently replaced my hand. 'No; like this.' He showed me the way and I was so keen to learn.

I did as I was told thoroughly enjoying the experience, even more so his absolute enjoyment.

I asked, 'So, what did I do wrong?'

'Nothing - nothing at all.' But in his euphoria he added, 'Just too keen. Some things need to be slowed down.'

I quipped, 'Am I like that in business?'

He gave a lop-sided smile. 'Sometimes.'

I watched his face enjoying my control over him; just by a deftly placed stroke of the hand. 'Am I allowed to show you what I like?'

He looked at me in his way. 'I already know.'

I felt deflated. 'Tell me?'

'Power! Strength! And I agree but sometimes it's better flavoured with gentleness and - time.'

I considered this.

'It's not a race. This sort of pleasure is divine.'

I nuzzled up to him. 'Am I divine?'

He smiled. 'You are in my eyes.' He added, 'But divinity is a science and sex one of the ultimate pleasures.' He looked at me wisely, 'Don't you agree?'

I was an innocent. My experience of sex had been wham bam thank you mam for many years; previous to that I had been a teenager with hormones fizzing around like busy bees. How could I possibly know about ultimate pleasure?

Sean smiled and I realised it was a wise smile. 'Shall we learn together? I think I might like that.'

I warmed to him then; greatly. 'I think I might too. Shall we start now?'

He sighed as though I was an impatient child but I knew he liked me all the more for it.

1976

Agatha Christie died
L S Lowry died
Princess Margaret and Lord Snowdon separate
James Callaghan new labour Prime Minister
Howard Hughes died
Bjorn Borg wins Wimbledon
Montreal Olympics
Chairman Mao died
Jimmy Carter new USA President
Benjamin Britten died
Chelsea runners-up in Second Division

Burnt Orange

I was pleased with myself. I'd found the perfect house for my mother and Aunt Fi. It was in Newmarket down Black Bear Lane. The garden was small but that was what they wanted and it was a short walk into town. A lovely Victorian town house, spacious and smart and when I showed them round they were thrilled. Aunt Fi had been living with my mother for about a year now; her health was fragile and I think they liked each other's company. Both found great delight in criticising. I'd taken out a mortgage on the property and as and when I could afford it intended to pay it off. My salary was pretty healthy these days but I still owed Aunt Jelly a colossal amount of money and couldn't see my way clear to paying it off. I had thought of doing it in dribs and drabs but that would have taken forever. If only I could get my hands on the money in America! Camilla and I, Aunt Jelly and Natasha, my mother and Aunt Fi had had a holiday in the Cayman Islands earlier that year and I'd thoroughly checked out my account, which of course paid for the holiday, and it was accruing interest very nicely. Amazingly, the holiday was a great success and we all lived in the lap of luxury for three whole weeks. Even Aunt Jelly didn't complain.

Of course, I could sell some of the Cambridge properties but I continued to hang on. The block of flats in Fulham was now in the final phase and it was in the back of my mind that I could raise enough on that but Aunt Jelly wasn't exactly pestering me although she did give the occasional dig. I never threatened her with taking Natasha away though; it would have been pointless. She was now six and very much her own person; except it tended to replicate Aunt Jelly.

It had been a long hot summer. My relationship with Sean was good and he regularly told me he loved me although I never said I loved him; I didn't. But we had tremendous fun together; going to the theatre and eating out regularly. He was my escort at countless functions and he treated me very well. I wished I could reciprocate his feelings and every now and then thought perhaps I did. Had something inside me died? Was I not capable of love anymore?

I had promised Camilla to spend some time with her in London. She was becoming more and more famous among the celebrities of stage and screen and a new magazine called Cut It was doing an article on her and she had asked me if she could restyle and colour my hair. Together we would be on the front cover. At first I refused but she begged me. 'It will be good for you too, Diana! You're a business woman now and you're beautiful.'

'I am not!'

'You are. You've grown into yourself. You just don't see it.'

In the end I gave in; I was even looking forward to spending several days in London.

My hair was highlighted so that it was very blonde and I loved it! When Camilla had told me what she intended to do I was alarmed and protested but she calmed me. 'I'll put it straight back to your own boring mousy colour if you hate it!'

I pulled a face at her jibe. 'But you'll still ruin my hair.'

'No I won't and anyway you'll love it. I promise.'

And I did. But it was the cut that was most spectacular. It was a straight bob falling to just above my shoulders with a heavy fringe. Camilla giggled. 'You look about fifteen!'

I smiled and remembered Charlie.

The photo shoot went well and I was looking forward to seeing myself with Camilla on the front cover of Cut It. She and I had such fun and now it was my last evening; I was going home on the Sunday ready for work the following day. I had missed Natasha; of course I had, and was keen to see her reaction to mummy being featured in a magazine; I so wanted her to be proud of me.

It was a hot August Saturday evening and after supper we decided to go to Annabel's nightclub. This wasn't exactly my scene but Camilla assured me we'd have a great time.

It started off well enough apart from the fact that Camilla seemed to know everybody and she stopped and spoke to so many people that after a while I got bored and wandered off. I was quite drunk but ordered myself another champagne cocktail. Several blokes had asked me to dance and I had obliged but in my slinky red dress felt exposed somehow. I missed Sean's constant attention and when eventually I caught up with Camilla I explained that I was tired and thought I'd get a taxi back to her place.

She clucked her tongue. 'You really are a party pooper! Have you any idea how fantastic you look?

Everybody is giving you the eye. Why don't you just let go and have a blast?'

'I'm sorry, I can't.'

She sighed. 'Okay. We'll go. I'll get us a cab.'

'No! You needn't go too. I'm quite capable by myself.'

'Don't be daft. I can come here anytime. Of course I'll go with you.'

Without any further ado she went off to grab us a cab and I loved her all the more for it. I looked around once more thinking that perhaps at twenty-five and a half years-old I was past it.

I was standing in the entrance and Camilla was waving down a taxi. She turned and beckoned me and I started to walk towards her. Then I was swept aside! It was as though he came from no-where; grabbed my hand and pulled me to him. Charlie! My adorable Charlie! He was with a group of male friends and I can't tell you how he took my breath away; I'd completely forgotten those feelings. It was like a craving inside me erupting once more except he was now grown-up and even more desirable.

'Charlie! What are you doing here?'

I was aware of Camilla beckoning me frantically now.

'Came to watch Chelsea - Stamford Bridge.' He pointed to Annabel's. 'Are you going in?'

'No. …Just leaving.'

He looked absolutely devastated. 'But it's early! We could have caught up with each other. Stay, *please?*'

'I'm so sorry, Charlie, but I have to go.'

'Can't I persuade you?' His mouth, the way he smiled showing his delightful teeth made me want to press my lips against his; never to let go.

Camilla was sitting in the taxi now and I looked from her to Charlie. 'I have to go. I'm sorry.'

Holding both my shoulders he leaned towards me and kissed my mouth, tenderly yet seductively. 'You look amazing,' he whispered. 'I'd have recognised you anywhere.' He put his hand on his heart. 'I search for your face all the time.'

Before I had time to check myself I said, 'Ditto.'

Our hands held until the very last moment as I walked to the taxi. We let go and without looking back I climbed inside. 'Who was *that*?' Camilla demanded.

'No-one.'

'He didn't look like no-one! He's still staring.'

I turned and looked out of the back window of the taxi and he was. My captivating, bewitching Charlie was standing on the pavement watching our taxi drive off into the night. I couldn't bear it. If only I hadn't been so impatient to leave the club. Then I reminded myself that Charlie was still a very young man. What - eighteen? Disgraceful.

'We could go back?' said Camilla.

I looked at her. My timing had been all out again. Last time I'd missed him because I went to see my mother and now it was because I wanted to get back to Camilla's apartment. For a fleeting second I thought about agreeing with Camilla and turning back. But where would that take me? Into the arms of a boy? Again; disgraceful.

1979

Margaret Thatcher new Tory Prime Minister
John Wayne died
Sebastian Coe completes hat-trick of running records
Lord Mountbatten killed by IRA bomb
Mother Theresa wins Nobel Peace prize
Yorkshire Ripper claims 12th victim
Chelsea new manager – Geoff Hurst

Purple

I am twenty-eight years-old. My daughter is nine. It is a whole ten years since I met Ben Herriott-Greene and I have just repaid the biggest debt of my life! One inflicted on me; hanging over my head for five long years like the sword of Damocles. How did I do it? H-G Properties has prospered enormously well. Aunt Jelly could certainly not complain about her dividends, nor the rest of us. We've completed three building sites in London, and are about to start in the Docklands area, and all the flats have been sold. I benefited well, apart from more tax, and with a loan from dear Mr Chambers at the bank I gathered together enough to completely clear my debt with Aunt Jelly. I have also now repaid my debt to the bank. I can't tell you how wonderful it feels.

Natasha has moved on to St Mary's school in Cambridge and is doing very well. Aunt Jelly is still very much the prime figure in her life; it's interesting because when we go to the Christmas concerts and sports days I have to stand back and recognise Aunt Jelly's position. Of course, I do anyway; she has been the inspiration behind my daughter Natasha; her lifeline.

But where does that leave me?

I have Sean. He is constant. I now tell him that I love him because I do. Ever since my meeting with Charlie outside Annabel's I know that I am so capable of love it has become easy to tell Sean that I love him. But the love I feel for Sean cannot compare to my feelings for Charlie. I spend hours thinking this through. A boy that came to work in my garden; a fifteen year old? Someone I spent a scant few hours with; how does that figure in the scheme of anything?

It's not about thinking; it's about feeling.

Today is my mother's birthday. She is fifty-five and as fit as a flea. We have been invited to tea; that is me, Aunt Jelly and Natasha. After school Aunt Jelly and I will pick up Natasha and drive to Newmarket. I have the champagne in a cooler bag and a beautiful chocolate cake from Fitzbillies in Cambridge. There are five candles on it. Camilla suggested this. She said Aunt Fi was bound to say five five.

'Happy birthday!'
Within seconds of arriving at my mother's house Natasha positions herself very firmly in front of the television and pulls out her school books to start her homework. Aunt Jelly wanders off into the garden and my mother drags me aside and says, 'The Colonel's here, Diana!'

I've met the Colonel on several occasions. He is a staunch member of the golf club that my mother is now active in and although he left the army eons ago likes to be referred to as thus.

'And Fi is wearing a ridiculous yellow dress, and I swear it's just to attract his attention.'

Needless to say Aunt Fi does not belong to Newmarket Golf Club; she just enjoys the perks it provides; like suppers and dinners in the club house. My mother's mouth is pinched and she closes her eyes as though it's all too much to bear.

I glance from the kitchen into the sitting room and study my daughter as she writes and watches the television. This is all because of the ever indulgent Aunt

Jelly but somehow it works. Natasha continually does well at school and who am I to complain.

'He's asked me to the summer ball. She doesn't like that either.' My mother continues.

'Lovely. So when is it?'

My mother looks blank. 'Oh, in about a month's time, I think.' She runs a hand through her hair. 'It'll mean a new dress because I couldn't possibly wear the one I wore last time.'

She gives me that look; the one that means she will expect me to buy it. I already give my mother and Aunt Fi a healthy allowance but it's never enough. I ask, 'Is Aunt Fi going too?'

'Certainly not! Although she'd like to.'

I place the cool bag on the kitchen table and open it. 'Champagne!' I smile and think; thank God for champagne.

'That's nice, dear. You know where the glasses are.' With that she walks off and I smile again. How welcoming my mother is. I then open the cupboard where I know she keeps the glasses that I bought her and fill five champagne flutes.

I have to say I don't really like the Colonel. He has the most piercing blue eyes and when he looks at me I feel unnerved. I hand him a glass of champagne and his fat hairy fingers brush mine. Now I might be mistaken but I swear he thinks he's in with a chance. Yes, he disgusts me and not for the first time I wonder if he has sex with my mother. I can't help smirking at the thought and he notices.

'And what are you smiling about?' he asks.

Should I tell him?

Aunt Fi moves forward. 'Smiling about?'

'Oh, I'm just enjoying the occasion and thinking how nice it is to be invited.' Business speak; I'd grown so accustomed to it. Sometimes the lies just roll off my tongue.

At this point my mother calls us in for tea.

We are still sitting around the table having eaten ham salad and chocolate birthday cake and I will ring Camilla as soon as I get home because my mother said, 'Why only five candles?'

And Aunt Fi said, 'Five candles?'

I said, 'That makes two fives.' They all look at me as though I am stupid.

I decided that that was the right moment and handed my mother an envelope. She looks at it. 'What's this?'

'Your birthday present.'

She frowns and with a knife slits the envelope open. She withdraws the Deeds inside. My mother repeats, 'What's this?'

Perhaps I should have waited until we were on our own. 'The Deeds, mum, to this house.'

She unfolds them and pulls a disdainful face. I can feel my heart beating faster. Had I made some dreadful faux pas? Did she think she already had the Deeds?

'What do I need these for?' She looks at me curiously. 'Or are you just showing off again?'

I swallow hard and realise everyone is now looking at me as though I have committed some great crime. 'I've paid off the mortgage. I thought you might like to own the house.'

She shrugs. 'What difference does it make? I already live here. We're not all like you, Diana. We don't all want to own vast amounts of property.'

I am flabbergasted and don't know what to say.

She continues. 'I really thought you were going to give us a holiday. You've bought that place out in California and we've never seen it. Are you going to keep it all to yourself?'

I splutter. 'Of course not; I've only just bought it.'

'Airline tickets would have been a nice present. If you can afford to pay off this mortgage you can afford to buy some nice first class tickets.'

'Some?' I query.

'I don't want to go on my own.'

Aunt Fi parrots, 'On her own,' and shakes her head.

My mother looks at her sister and says, 'Fi will have to come.' In a far more indulgent way she also looks at Aunt Jelly and Natasha. 'And I'd like you two to come.' She smiled broadly at her granddaughter. 'Couldn't possibly go all that way without my treasure now could I?'

But it doesn't have the desired effect. I notice Natasha's eyes narrowing as she looks from my mother to me and then to Aunt Jelly. Not for the life of me can I guess what she's thinking. All I know is that she is enjoying this discomfiture.

I reach out my hand for the Deeds. 'I'll take them back then.'

She tosses them across the table and they land in the butter. I pick them up and wipe the butter off with the edge of the tablecloth.

'Don't do that with my best tablecloth! It'll stain.'

I did it on purpose. I put the Deeds back in the

envelope that my mother passes around the table and sip some of my champagne.

'Well?' My mother asks.

'Well?' Aunt Fi repeats.

'Tickets it is.' I say. 'But there's no furniture in the house yet. Do you mind?'

My mother looks at me in disgust. 'You really have grown too big for your boots, Diana, do you know that?'

'Know that?' Aunt Fi again.

I look at the Colonel and he is enjoying this too. I sit back and close my eyes. If Sean was here I'd ask him what to do. I really am flummoxed. What have I done to make these people so rude to me?

Aunt Jelly says, 'We need to have a chat when we get home, Diana.'

I look at her. She's disgusted too. 'What about?'

'Not here. When we get home.'

I wonder what on earth she means and it crosses my mind she is rich beyond most peoples' wildest dreams but will still accept me buying her an airline ticket.

She adds, 'You know your trouble, your timing is all out.'

I think at this point my mouth must have dropped open. Suddenly there is a chronic ache in my heart and I think of Charlie. How right she is.

Blunt Blue

'Have you made a Will?'

'Sorry?'

'For Natasha.' Aunt Jelly straightened her back. Natasha was in bed, long gone and asleep I hoped. 'Do you ever take time to think about your daughter?'

Now Aunt Jelly was someone I could let rip at. 'It might interest you to know that I think about my daughter nearly every hour of every day!'

'Do you now. Well that does surprise me.'

'Why?'

'Because there was me thinking you were far more interested in property!'

I was not. But what did she mean? 'What are you talking about?'

'I'm talking about you! For the last five years you've dedicated yourself to business. There's nothing wrong with that but you've totally neglected your daughter, and your mother too, and I think you need to take stock and certainly remember your daughter.'

'That is so unfair!'

'Is it?'

I took a deep breath. 'Get to the point.'

'What do you intend to leave her?'

'You mean, in my *Will?*'

'Yes! In your Will!'

'Does it matter? Aren't you rich enough?'

'Do you know, I thought you'd say that! I can provide for Natasha as I always have done and that lets you off the hook.'

This incensed me as she knew it would. 'No! I just

don't understand why this is an issue after all these years?'

'Don't you! Let me tell you, I've watched you go from being a mousey housewife to a perpetual business-woman who is now buying properties right, left and centre! It's the only thing that excites you, isn't it? Go on, admit it?'

I was stumped for words. Was she right? She continued. 'All this wealth you're amassing needs to go to its rightful owner and it won't if you don't make a Will!'

'Rightful owner?'

'Natasha! She's Ben's only flesh and blood. Don't look at me like that; if it wasn't for him you'd more than likely be living in some council house somewhere!'

How dare she say that to me? She was wicked. My hatred for this woman came flooding back. More to the point; did this mean her nastiness had returned? 'I work very hard, *Angelica.*'

Her eyes widened and it was all I needed to say. If she became nasty again she would no longer keep her supreme position as *Aunt Jelly.*

She swallowed hard and took a deep breath. In a kinder voice she said, 'Don't call me that; I'm only saying what has to be said.'

'So you're telling me to make a Will and leave everything to Natasha?'

'Wouldn't you do that anyway?'

'Actually, no. Other people have been very instrumental in building up H-G Properties to what it is today. I might like to leave some of my shares to them.' She opened her mouth to speak and I quickly added.

'And what about any future children I might have?'

Her beady eyes widened again. 'You'll *never* have anymore children.'

These words hit me like a ton of bricks. The woman was a witch. 'Why do you think that?'

'Because you're too busy with your buildings.'

'But I'm only twenty-eight!' I wanted to hurt her back. 'Not in my middle forties like you.'

She cringed as the words hit home; she hesitated but then repeated. 'I stand by what I said; you'll never have anymore children.'

I couldn't let it drop. Why didn't I just walk away? 'Ben certainly thought I would.'

She said softly and witheringly, 'What did Ben ever know about the real you? I'm the only one who knows that person.'

These words gripped my insides like a tourniquet and I turned and walked away.

I rang Camilla and between sobs and sips of brandy poured it all out to her. She listened and comforted me and assured me that none of it was true and that of course I'd have more children.

'The thing is I'm stuck in a situation that I can't get out of and always have been. These bloody *Herriott-Greens!*' I straightened myself and pulled my thoughts together. 'I only have myself to blame. That's true, isn't it?'

'Life is never that simple. You've had an amazing five years; done brilliantly well and she's jealous. She just wants it all to go to Natasha. Her whole life revolves around that child and she's bitter. Don't let your hatred for her make you bitter too.'

She was right. Of course she was. I was calmer now. 'What would I do without you? You've been my constant friend and never let me down. I love you so much.'

'Good. And would you like to hear my news?'

I sat upright. 'Yes.'

'I'm in love!'

Something shot through me like a bolt. 'In love? You?'

'Yes, me! She's wonderful, Diana, absolutely wonderful.'

Why was I so consumed with misgivings? What was wrong with me? I forced myself to sound happy. 'Who is she? Tell me all about her?'

'Her name is Rachel Turner and she's a psychologist. She runs her own business; you know, does all sorts of humane work. Honestly, she's amazing. I never ever in a million years thought I'd find somebody like her.'

'Fantastic. I'm so pleased for you. So when do I get to meet her?'

'Whenever you like; could you get down soon?'

'I certainly can. In fact I'm coming to London next week. What about Wednesday? Lunch?'

Camilla looked in her diary. 'Great! As long as Rachel is free. I'll get back to you, and *stop* worrying.'

'I will. I'm so pleased for you, so happy.'

'Me too. I keep pinching myself.'

We said our goodbyes and I went to refill my brandy glass.

Red Face Red

We were having supper at The Three Horseshoes in Madingley. I loved this ancient pub with its old world charm just outside Cambridge but for all that Sean was as miserable as I was.

'She's living in his house and looking after his bloody dog all day long and he treats her like a non-entity!'

I pushed my hand across the table and squeezed Sean's. For years now I'd been hearing about his precious daughter Mel and all her trials and tribulations but it had occurred to me on more than one occasion that she led rather an idle life and lived off her father. Having said that perhaps I had been too absorbed with my own life because I didn't recall any mention of Mel living with someone; where did this new chap pop up from?

'So how long has she been living with him?'

Sean shrugged. 'A few months now; he's never there, always away working. Apparently his grandmother left him the house. I have to say it's a lovely little cottage near the river; close to Midsummer Common, and very nicely furnished and for a while Mel seemed happy. I mean, he's respectable enough, but she should never have moved in with him.'

I smiled. 'People do that these days, Sean, hadn't you noticed?'

'But she's *beautiful!* Deserves much better than him!'

That again; Sean thought his daughter's beauty made her superior in every way. 'What does he do?'

'Some sort of jobbing gardener; works with his father.'

I think I froze. Sean didn't seem to notice because

he carried on talking. 'He's qualified and all that because she first met him at Cambridge Regional College; but he's so bloody selfish. Football mad and thinks nothing of buggering off to watch bloody Chelsea play at Stamford Bridge whenever he feels like it.'

I could feel myself sliding into my seat as though I wanted to disappear. I knew all about Chelsea; their fight to climb out of the second division; about the new manager Geoff Hurst; how could I not follow Charlie's team. My voice didn't sound like my own when I asked, 'What's his name?'

'Charlie. Charlie Stanford. Are you all right?'

I pulled myself up straight and tried to sound normal. 'Just that I think I know him. Ivor Stanford did our garden at Brooklands Avenue. His son Charlie used to help him out.'

'But that was years ago.'

'I know. He was only fifteen at the time.' But it didn't stop me loving him and the memory of those days stabbed at my heart.

'…Anyway, things are not looking too rosy for my poor Mel, bless her.'

I hesitated but had to ask. 'Is she in love with him?'

'Are you sure you're all right? You've gone very pale.'

'To be honest, I haven't been feeling too well. I had this row with Aunt Jelly about making a Will and - I wish they'd hurry up with our food.'

Sean smiled. 'And there was me going on about my daughter. Sorry, Diana. So tell me about this row?'

'Later.' I gulped some wine. How could I steer the conversation back to Charlie. I had to know everything. 'Are they engaged?'

Sean looked surprised. 'Mel and Charlie? No.' He looked up. 'Here comes our food. I'm starving too.'

I looked at my food; I had lied, my appetite had left me completely. I picked up my fork and started to toy with the rice around my chicken and pineapple. 'How old is he now?'

'Twenty-one, I think; a year or so younger than Mel. That's the trouble; she's anxious to settle down and Charlie doesn't look like the settling down kind.'

I remembered the look on his face outside Annabel's nightclub in London. Unless I was very mistaken he would have run away with me that night – and I him.

'I thought you were hungry?'

I put some rice into my mouth. 'Like I said, not feeling too good.'

Sean put down his steak knife and fork and took one of my hands. 'I'm sorry I've spoiled things this evening. I promise not to talk about Mel anymore - but you always seem to understand.' He grinned as though making a special point. 'And that's one of the reasons I've continued to love you in the way I have.'

I caught my breath. I couldn't stop thinking about Charlie with Mel! I said feebly, 'I'm always there for you. I've pounded your eardrums enough times about Natasha.' So now *please* tell me *everything*.

He smiled as though enlightened. 'You know what we should do?'

I smiled too thinking he was going to say build another block of flats or something.

'Get married.'

I think I stared at him unable to take in those two words. I know I couldn't speak.

'Okay, don't get too excited; just an idea.'

'Sean, you know what a mess I made of my marriage. It's not something I'm keen to try again.'

He nodded thoughtfully and took a mouthful of steak. Then he took a mouthful of red wine. 'It's not because of my vasectomy, is it?'

His eyes were filled with love and worry; a mixture of both. I had to be kind to him even though I never wanted to marry him. But Sean had looked after me all these years and been a friend in every sense of the word. I could not have coped without him.

'No.' In fact his vasectomy had been a bonus; made our sex life very uncomplicated.

'Because you see I was reading about it only the other day. You can have it reversed and it's quite successful. You're young and if you want more children I could do that.' He looked at me hopefully. Then he said, 'You don't know how much I regret having that bloody operation. Six months later my wife left me! Diana, I'd love to have a baby with you.' The words came from his heart.

If only he hadn't told me about Charlie I knew I'd now be thinking I could knock Aunt Jelly off her high-horse in one foul swoop if I married Sean and became pregnant. 'Please don't worry about having another operation. I'm sorry, but I don't want to get married.'

'So what do you want to do?'

'What do you mean?'

'Just - where do we go from here? It eats me up not being able to be with you all the time.'

'We're together more than most husbands and wives.'

He looked stern. 'You're not worried that I'm after your money, are you?'

I stared at him in an amazed way. 'That thought never crossed my mind.'

'Are you sure? Because I don't want a penny.'

'This isn't about money.'

'You said you loved me. Are you now saying that you don't?'

'I do love you. I just don't want to get married.'

'Don't you want more children?'

I swallowed hard. This was all too much to take in. First he tells me Charlie is his daughter's boyfriend and then he asks me to marry him and then do I want more children. Of course I want more children. 'I think I do but I'm not sure how it will work out.' Probably it will never work out like Aunt Jelly said.

His face hardened and he threw down his knife and fork and slouched heavily into his chair. 'What you're telling me is that I'm not in the frame?'

What could I say? I took a deep breath. 'How can I answer that when I don't even know what the frame is?'

'Clever answer but not from your heart. I know you well so please don't spare my feelings. I'd respect you a whole lot more if you told me the truth.'

Oh, you wouldn't. 'I have told you the truth. I don't want to get married but I do love you and can't imagine life without you.'

'I'm not uncle material. Not to your future children.' He stood up scraping back his chair. Everyone in the restaurant looked at him. 'I'll pay the bill and meet you outside.'

My face at this point had gone from pasty pale to beetroot red and I felt I was in the blackest hole. But it was no good arguing; I'd seen Sean in this sort of mood before. I had no choice but to follow him.

We drove home in silence. Sean pulled up outside the house in Brooklands Avenue which was sad because we had planned to spend the night together at the flat.

I said softly, 'I won't see you tomorrow. I'm going to London.'

He hugged the steering wheel and said, 'I think I might look for another job. I can't stomach this; not anymore. I know I couldn't bear what the future might hold.'

'That's utterly ridiculous! How could I cope without you?'

He faced me very angrily. 'You'll bloody have to.'

'Please don't be like this. Forgive me. Please. If you love me forgive me.'

'No. You can't have it all your own way.'

'Okay, so when will you leave?'

'When I find another job.' He climbed out of the car and came round to my side to open the door. I stepped out and went into the house. Neither of us said another word.

Murky Grey

I was meeting Camilla and Rachel in a small Italian restaurant in Chelsea and took a taxi from Kings Cross to the restaurant. I had dressed as trendily as possible, straight belted red and green striped dress with a long matching cardigan, knowing how Camilla always looked as though she'd stepped out of Vogue magazine but my mood was the murkiest grey ever. It was July and the weather was wonderful but in a few short days,

151

since my mother's birthday, everything had been turned upside down. I had taught myself to stop thinking about Charlie; no, that's a lie, I never stopped thinking about him but when I did it was as a cherished young man who'd lightened up my life. But when Sean said he was with Mel I felt as though my world had come to an end. The feelings overwhelmed me; a bit the same as my feelings for Aunt Jelly when she said I would never have anymore children.

The waiter showed me to the table and they were already there. As I approached I was aware of the dark penetrating eyes of my best friend's companion. Consequently my mood darkened even further. I kissed Camilla who looked fabulous in the palest pink lightweight jersey trouser suit and with a huge smile held out my hand to her lover. Rachel's handshake was weak but not the accompanying smile which surprised me. I sat down and the waiter poured me a glass of wine. I stole another look at Rachel who was older than I'd expected; middle forties, say; at her long nose and rosebud mouth; at the way her thick fringe almost touched her heavy lidded eyes; and the rest of her hair which was long and straight and a very shiny blackish brown. She was heavily made up and resembled a chubby Cleopatra. She was attractive.

'How did the birthday go?' Camilla asked.

I cringed. 'Not very well. I gave mother the Deeds to her house and she threw them back at me.'

Camilla blinked. 'Why?'

'She was expecting a holiday and as she already lives in the house didn't see the point of owning it.'

Rachel grinned at me while sipping her wine and said wisely, 'We don't all need to own things, you know.'

I agreed with her but Camilla butted in. 'Rachel, you have no idea what Deborah is like! If Diana stood on her hands and clapped her feet together she'd say her knickers were the wrong colour!'

We all laughed but Rachel continued in the same vein. 'I understand you own a lot of properties.'

I smiled warmly. 'I am a shareholder in H-G Properties. It's what we do.'

'Perhaps she was trying to tell you something.' Rachel's eyes held mine.

She was saying all these things in the friendliest manner but I really hadn't expected a psychology lesson for lunch, especially one that hit a raw nerve. 'Perhaps she was. There again, she's been trying to tell me something forever.'

Camilla very gently covered Rachel's hand with hers. 'When you meet Deborah you'll understand exactly what we mean.'

Rachel melted before her eyes. 'I have a lot to learn.' She looked at me and was candid. 'Camilla's told me so much about you. I suppose you could say I'm nervous of your position in her life.'

I was taken aback by her honesty and said, 'There's no need. I hardly pose a threat.'

'So tell me, what exactly do you do? I mean, I know you're terribly rich and all that, but what do you fill your day with. Camilla's never been clear about that.' She looked at me in an open way so it was strange that it occurred to me she didn't like me.

And I hated such questions. 'I'm part of a team.

There's me, Sean the accountant, and Tom the architect. Then there's the builders and plumbers and electricians…' I smiled for fun, '…And the candlestick makers. We keep a lot of people in work and provide housing for a lot more.' I looked at Camilla and then again at Rachel and just caught a sinister flicker in her eye. I added, 'I'm quite proud of what I do.'

Rachel leaned towards me. 'But what *do* you do?'

Camilla took a deep breath and touched her lover's shoulder. 'Lighten up, Rach, don't scare the poor mite off.'

Rachel backed off immediately. 'Sorry, but you know me, inclined to be nosy where you're concerned.'

'I keep control. I know what's going on. I find new sites and together with Sean we keep the bank happy. Don't worry, Rachel, I do have a fulfilling life.'

'And your daughter?'

I looked at Camilla whose face was quite red. What had she been telling her? 'My daughter is very well, thank you.' I asked quickly, 'And what exactly do you do?'

She laughed out loud. 'I'm just a lowly paid psychoanalyst.'

A *psychoanalyst*; I looked at Camilla who quickly said, 'Rachel's really sorted out my demons.'

'Your demons?'

She lowered her eyes and Rachel spoke for her. 'It was tough on Cam. She carries a lot of baggage, not least because of the appalling death of her parents. And let's face it she didn't have the most protreptic family life thereafter, did she?'

''Sorry, what does that mean?'

Rachel was effusive. 'Helpful; you know, instructive.'

She beamed at me wisely again.

I was offended; I don't know why. I mean, she was no doubt speaking the truth but I considered it thoroughly unprofessional for her to say it to me. Camilla, however, now appeared to be lapping it all up. I realised that I'd never really known her; just used her to tell my troubles to.

Camilla caught my eye. 'I'm sorry. You didn't come all the way down here to listen to this.'

'Of course I did. I'm just sorry I never realised. You always seem so together; your life in order. I envied you.'

She squeezed my hand. 'And I envied you.'

I shrank back. 'What?'

Rachel butted in. 'You never realised this because Camilla is very good at hiding her unhappiness.'

I took her point. I wasn't.

Camilla sipped some of her wine. 'Facing all this, well …' she giggled, 'was apocalyptic.'

Not knowing what else to say I asked flippantly, 'So are you suggesting we all go into therapy?'

Rachel protested. 'Nothing of the sort because each of us must live our lives as we choose. But it is enlightening when one sees things clearly, at least, it has been for Camilla.'

I picked up the menu in the hope that the conversation would be changed.

Camilla rubbed my shoulder. 'We've both through the mill.'

I smiled and said simply, 'I think I'll have the lemon sole.'

155

'What do you think?' Camilla asked anxiously when Rachel took herself off to the ladies room.

What could I say? That I thought this woman was bad news. 'I'm so sorry I never realised how unhappy you've been.'

She shook her head. 'It hasn't been that bad. I've had a great life. If you must know it was one of my client's who put me on to Rachel; she's hot news in the biz. I only went out of curiosity and somehow she managed to worm all this information out of me. It would do you the world of good. She'd sort you out in the flash.'

'Or screw me up even further.'

Camilla sat back in her chair as though stung. 'She hasn't screwed me up.'

'Because you're steady as a rock. Don't be upset with me, I couldn't bear it.'

'Is everything all right?'

I put my hands on the table. 'I have to stop pouring out my troubles to you. Rachel wouldn't like it.'

'Oh, don't be daft. Tell me?'

'Sean asked me to marry him.'

Camilla beamed. 'That's great, isn't it?'

Rachel chose this moment to return and sat down latching on to the conversation straight away. She must have elephant ears. 'What's great?' She asked me this before smiling lovingly at Camilla and saying, 'Before I forget, darling, that colour does nothing for your skin tone.'

Camilla was shocked and so was I. Camilla looked absolutely stunning in the pale pink; gorgeous.

'I disagree.' I said before I had time to check myself.

Rachel ignored me and stroked Camilla's arm. 'Best that I tell you the truth.'

'Of course,' Camilla said.

'So, what's great?' asked Rachel again.

'Diana's boyfriend has asked her to marry him!' Camilla said enthusiastically.

'Sean?' Rachel asked.

I looked at Camilla and wondered if she'd told Rachel everything about me. 'Yes, Sean.'

'And you said yes?'

'No. I said no.'

Rachel looked appalled; as though I'd committed a crime. 'For goodness sake why?'

I looked at Camilla for help but she just carried on as though she agreed with Rachel.

'Because I don't think I love him enough.'

Rachel sat back in her seat and tapped the table with a credit card. 'You're in denial. I can tell by looking at you. Your life has been out of sync; it's time you reconciled yourself.'

'Reconciled myself?'

She was in her element now and leaned forward to deliver her pearls of wisdom. 'You can't see the wood for the trees.' She touched my forehead between my eyes with her thumb and then pressed hard. I could smell her perfume; it was nice. 'You're out of step, Diana, just let go.'

'Of what?'

'The past, silly.'

Camilla giggled like a schoolgirl then nudged me. 'See, I told you she'd sort you out. You got all that for nothing.'

Rachel looked at her watch. 'And talking about nothing it's time I was on my way. I'll be late for my shelter clinic.' She stood up and after placing a lingering kiss on Camilla's mouth said, 'This is on me. I'll pay!' She held up the credit card and waved it at me. We watched her go.

Camilla said lovingly. 'She does this clinic every Wednesday for women in sheltered accommodation. They get her counselling totally free. She's pretty amazing.'

'Yes, she certainly is.' I looked at my dearest friend. 'But what was all that about?'

She squeezed my hand. 'It's not such a bad idea. Sean's a great guy. They don't grow on trees you know.'

'Not that; the out of sync bit. Am I?'

Camilla shrugged. 'You tell me? All I can say is Rachel normally hits the button. She's renowned for it.'

I took a deep breath. This was the time when I'd have liked to say to Camilla, come on, let's go back to your place and sink another bottle of wine but I knew I couldn't do that anymore.

'The truth now, what do you really think of Rachel?' Camilla looked me in the eye waiting for my reply.

'I think she looks at you as though she absolutely adores you.'

Camilla sat back and clapped her hands together. 'Really?' She sat forward and took one of my hands in hers. 'I've always envied you the way Sean looks at you. It's as though he can't bear you out of his sight. If Rachel feels the same way about me I am one lucky lady.'

'That's how Sean looks at me?'

'As though he idolises you. You should marry him.' She paused and added hesitantly. 'You're not still pining for that *boy*, are you?'

I said quickly, 'No! Not at all.'

'That's good.'

I pulled my hand away and changed the subject. 'This does change things between us. I won't be able to stay over with you anymore.' I was hoping she would say, of course you can, Rachel wasn't living with her.

'Not straight away, but we're looking for somewhere bigger and then you can.'

'That will be nice.' I looked at my watch. 'And now I must go.' I picked up my handbag. 'How kind of Rachel to pay for lunch, I was going to do that.'

Camilla grabbed my arm. 'There'll be plenty of other times. This isn't the end of our friendship; it's the beginning of Rachel being part of our friendship.'

'Yes, that's true. Why hadn't I thought of it like that?'

Sky Blue Pink

I dressed very carefully the following morning taking time with my hair; putting it up held together with a clip the way Sean liked it and I rehearsed what I was going to say to him.

He was already in his office when I arrived and I tapped gently on the door before entering. Then he took me by surprise because he jumped out of his seat and walked round the desk.

'Diana! I'm so pleased to see you.' He looked as though he hadn't slept for a week but he smiled lovingly at me taking both my hands in his. 'I've been such a frigging arsehole; I'm so sorry. Can you ever forgive me?'

I too smiled but mine was in amusement. 'For what?'

He inclined his hand around the room. 'Threatening to leave here and behaving like a spoiled boy because you don't want to marry me.' He rolled his eyes. 'About time I grew up.'

I moved in and kissed his mouth. 'You're forgiven and I accept.'

He held his breath then blinked and stared at me. 'I beg your pardon?'

I beamed and kissed him again. 'I accept your proposal of marriage. The sooner the better; you can whisk me off anytime you like and I'll pledge my troth.'

He was stunned. 'You're joking! Are you sure?'

'Absolutely.'

He made a whooping sound before picking me up off the floor and kissing me hard on the mouth. 'Diana Herriott-Greene, you've made me the happiest man in the world!' He put me down again and said, 'You'll never regret this. I'll make you the best husband ever.'

I hugged him. 'I think you will.'

He took a deep breath and sat on the edge of the desk pulling me towards him. 'Why did you change your mind?'

'I didn't change my mind; I made up my mind.' I sighed. 'I've been such an idiot thinking I'd be trapped again because you're not Ben; you're very different.'

He pushed me aside gently and paced the floor. Sean folded his arms and enthused, 'We must do this properly. Have a big party!' He poked me with one forefinger. 'I want you to look the works, and so will I. Natasha can be a bridesmaid…'

'Hang on! I don't want a church wedding.'

'No, not church, but we can still have a great reception.'

'That all takes time to arrange.'

'What about next spring?'

'But that's months away. I thought you wanted to marry me now.'

He looked at me apologetically; as though I was made of porcelain and he'd just accidentally broken a piece off. 'Of course I do, darling, but I also want to do this properly. I must have that bloody operation to reverse my vasectomy and we need a house! That'll all take time.' He poked me again. 'But we can buy an engagement ring straight away.'

'Great! Diamonds please. ...Are you sure you want all that palaver. I'd much rather just go to the registry office and have done with it.'

He stroked my face. 'You'll look absolutely amazing in a wedding dress.'

'I am not decking myself out in a wedding dress! Perish the thought.'

'But a lovely gown - something stunning; something I'll want to rip off you.'

He threw back his head and laughed. It was infectious; happiness is like that; I felt happy because I'd made him so happy.

'If that's what you want then a big do it'll be. But I'd like to set a date.' I breathed in. 'I need to say a specific date to Aunt Jelly and Natasha.'

'Shall we tell them together?'

'I'd like to do that on my own.'

'Sure. And I'll tell Mel.'

A shiver ran through me. 'How is she?'

He shrugged. 'Same as ever; haven't seen her lately. She rings and moans but Mel has always done that.'

I suddenly had a picture in my mind of Mel at our big do with Charlie beside her. That could happen. I took a deep breath; I'd made my decision. As the oracle Rachel had said, let go of the past. I was determined to.

Unearthly Green

'Hello, darling, how are you?' I held out my arms to my daughter. She moved into them in a robotic fashion; she was nine now and big girls like Natasha don't do cuddles and kisses. I wasn't the only one; I noticed that Aunt Jelly didn't get any either.

'I bought you a present from London.' This did raise a smile.

She took the parcel from me and impatiently ripped it open. These days she liked my presents because I took a lot of time finding out what was trendy with young people. Aunt Jelly was too set in her ways to do that; especially with clothes.

Her face lit up at the long shorts and polka dot T-shirt. 'Oh, mummy, they're really ace. Thank you.' Before she had time to think she hugged me. I saw the look on Aunt Jelly's face.

I handed her an envelope. 'And this is for you.'

Grudgingly she gave me a thin-lipped smile. 'What's this?'

'Open it and see.'

She did and removed two first-class airline tickets to

San Diego. Her eyes widened. 'Only two?'

'Yes; just you and Natasha; and mum and Aunt Fi, of course. If you want to go, that is?'

'What about the house out there? Is it furnished?'

'Yes. I've sorted all that out. I'm quite sure it will be very comfortable.'

'So where is it exactly?'

'Oceanside. Only about half an hour from San Diego. It's fabulous there; the original surfing paradise; very unspoiled and the house faces on to the ocean and is really spacious. You'll have a wonderful time; maid service, a cook and a chauffeur. I've booked two days at Disneyland in Los Angeles and a trip to Universal Studios. I think I've sorted everything down to the very last detail.'

Aunt Jelly looked at Natasha. 'What do you think?'

How ungrateful can you get? No thank you; just a maybe.

Natasha came up trumps. 'Yes please! I can tell all the girls at school when I go back. They always go on ace holidays and we never go anywhere.'

Aunt Jelly sucked in her cheeks in indignation. Serves you right.

'In that case…' She looked at me, 'We accept.'

'Aren't you coming?' Asked Natasha. I took a deep breath because I could not think of anything I would like less than two weeks with my mother, Aunt Fi and Aunt Jelly. 'I can't, but I will make sure you have a fantastic time.'

'So what's so important that you can't spare the time to join us?' Aunt Jelly asked.

'Sean is going into hospital. Nothing serious but I have to be around.'

'What's wrong with him?'

'Nothing is exactly wrong; it's a bit personal. Anyway that brings me to my other news. Guess what? We're getting married!'

Aunt Jelly's face was a picture! She was aghast at this news. 'Married? What on earth for?'

'Because we want to.' I looked at Natasha who'd lost interest and was looking at the television. 'What do you think, Natasha?'

She looked at me with disinterest. 'He's all right, I suppose.'

'When?' Asked Aunt Jelly.

'In the spring. 23 April, actually.'

She eyed me suspiciously. 'He won't be fathering any babies, you know.'

I was stunned by her blatantsy. 'Why?'

'Because I know for a fact that he's had a vasectomy.'

Natasha raised her head. 'What's a vasectomy?'

I looked at Aunt Jelly. She could answer that query. She said simply, 'It's when a man doesn't want any more children.' Natasha returned her attention to the screen and I had to admire such a rapid reply.

'How do you know this?' I asked.

'Ben told me.'

'Why on earth would Ben tell you that?'

'We were close, you know, Diana; Ben and I. Very close actually.'

I decided to continue as though her words had no effect on me. 'Anyway, Sean's keen to have a big party and there's lots to arrange.'

'Where will you live?' Aunt Jelly followed this with, 'What about Natasha?'

I looked at my daughter. 'She can share her time.' I looked at my sister-in-law, 'Between this place and wherever we live.'

'That's ridiculous! Natasha lives here.'

'I know that but I'm sure she'd like to spend some time with us and you are always welcome too.'

Aunt Jelly softened ever so slightly at this. 'I just don't want her unsettled. She's doing well at school and it's not good to move her around like a piece of luggage.'

'I wouldn't do that.' I looked at my daughter. 'You don't mind, do you?'

'Mind what?'

'Me marrying Sean.'

'Mummy, you're hardly ever here. Why should I mind?'

I was taken aback by her words. 'Is that what you think? That I'm hardly ever here?'

Natasha looked at me. 'Yes, actually.'

'Well I'm sorry.'

She shrugged, looked at Aunt Jelly and continued to watch the television.

I decided to leave them at this point but there was a yawning gap in my heart for the love of my daughter. How had I managed to mess things up so thoroughly?

Aunt Jelly sought me out after Natasha had gone to bed. I was about to pick up the telephone to speak to Camilla; tell her the news about Sean and me.

Aunt Jelly cleared her throat. 'Have you thought anymore about your Will?'

'I haven't made a Will.'

'You must. This is most important.'

'Why?'

'You know, you can be very vague when you want to be.'

'I'm not being vague, I just don't agree. It's not exactly life-threatening and Natasha is hardly going to be poor whatever I do.'

'That's not the point! This is Ben's money we're talking about. I'm damned if it's going to go to the likes of Sean's daughter!'

I gaped at my sister-in-law. 'Do you have any idea how you sound? You really are the archetypal prophet of doom.'

She didn't like that one bit. 'I just want to know that my niece is going to get what she is entitled to.

'*Angelica,* your niece is my daughter. It would pay you to remember that.'

She glared at me. 'I do. When you're here!'

I gulped because our lives had moved on to the point where I didn't have priority over my daughter anymore. But I was not going to be bamboozled into making Natasha my soul heir. 'You always forget that I have feelings - and integrity - but I take your point and maybe the best thing is that I move out while you're away. Sean and I are looking for a place to live anyway.'

She was surprised; it wasn't what she wanted to hear. 'What about your Will?'

I smiled at this bitter wretched woman whom I hated so very much; who was the master of my one and only child and who had always done her utmost to make me miserable. 'That's my business and contrary to what you may think it's also my money to do with as I wish. You might own my daughter but you don't own me.'

I walked away before she had time to reply.

I rang Camilla; I was consumed with rage and anxious to speak to my dear friend. The telephone was picked up by Rachel. 'Oh, hello, there. I'm awfully sorry but we're in the middle of preparing supper. Tell you what, I'll get Camilla to ring you back; it probably won't be tonight; tomorrow maybe.'

I opened my mouth to speak and she replaced the receiver. I was amazed at her insolence. What sort of three-way friendship was this going to be?

Sea Green

I poured it all out to Sean the following day. He listened with patience assuring me that Aunt Jelly was a harmless silly middle-aged woman who would surely get her come-uppance one day – most probably from Natasha. For some reason that didn't make me feel any better because I wanted Natasha to be secure.

He put his hand on mine and changed the subject. He said wistfully, 'I'm going into the Evelyn in three weeks time. Just an overnight stay. ...Painful, so let's hope it does the trick.'

The Evelyn was a private hospital in Cambridge. I squeezed his hand. 'You really don't have to do this.'

'I do! I want us to have children.'

'I want us to be happy.'

'We will be.'

'Which brings me to more important issues. When I was in London the other day I saw this amazing site in Battersea. We have to check it out. It's exactly right for us; position wise. We need to get down there.'

He squeezed my hand. 'Good 'ole Diana; always on to the next deal.'

'I have to do something to stop myself going mad.'

He looked in his diary. 'Next week, Tuesday?'

'Tuesday it is.'

He leaned towards me. 'I love you.'

I smiled. 'I love you too.'

Whitish Beige

'This is incredible! A great position. Won't be cheap.'

'Stop doing your accountancy bit!'

'What do you mean?'

I pulled a face and mimicked, 'Won't be cheap.' I shrugged defiantly. 'Who cares; we've got loads of money.'

He poked me. 'Thank God you've got me! You'd buy the whole of bloody Great Britain, you would.'

'Not at all.' I looked around. 'Just think about it; apartments in three storey town houses along the perimeter; the ground level having small gardens and then in the middle of the site lovely mews houses with the prettiest most picturesque gardens.'

Sean considered this. 'Hmm. Could work.' He added indulgently, 'I do love your imagination. Without it our lives would be very dull, I think.'

I threaded my arm through his. 'We'd never be dull.'

He took a deep breath. 'It could still break us.'

'It won't.'

Sean said sweetly, 'I love your chutzpah.'

'What's that?'

'I read about it somewhere and thought it definitely applied to you and I remember thinking that's why I love you.'

'Let's get on with it then. Go and see the agent.'

'Do you ever change?'

'No.'

'Good.'

'But on the way home I want to call in on Camilla.'

'She won't be there.'

'Maybe not, but I can leave a note through the door. I've rung hundreds of times and left loads of messages on her answer machine.'

'She's all right, you know.

'You really think so?'

'Of course she is. Silly.'

'Do you know how good that makes me feel? I couldn't bear to think that she was unhappy.'

'Why should she be unhappy?'

'I've told you all about Rachel.'

'I've met your sister on lots of occasions and she's some lady. Whoever this Rachel is I can't think that she'll pull the wool over Camilla's eyes.'

I loved the fact that he called Camilla my sister. 'It depends how vulnerable she is.'

'She's not vulnerable. That's rubbish.'

'She is vulnerable. We all are.'

He put his hand on mine. 'Well, you've got me now.'

Yes. My life was falling into place.

She answered the door! I was so pleased to see Camilla but her eyes were red and she looked as though the last thing she wanted was visitors. 'Come in, come in,' she said in her usual way but it wasn't the same.

'I've tried to ring but as we were in the area we thought we'd drop by. Are you okay?'

'Of course. I had a cancellation; that's why I'm here. What can I get you? Coffee, tea, wine?'

Sean stood behind me and I wished he was a million miles away. Camilla and I had so much history but we never opened up to each other when other people were around. I turned round and looked at him. He held out his hands. 'Go and make a cup of tea or something.'

Poor Sean went off as though he didn't belong and I felt strangely sad.

'You look tired, Camilla.'

'Do I? I'm not.'

'We've been looking at a site in Battersea - ripe for development. I've got loads of ideas floating around in my head; not just your average block of flats but something classy; smart living space.'

She smiled; a flicker of the old Camilla shining through. 'Great.'

'I didn't expect you to be home. We called on the off chance to give you our news.'

She looked at me as though having trouble taking in what I was saying. Camilla rubbed her forehead. 'A drink?'

'Sean's doing it. Guess what? We're getting married; next spring, 23 April.'

Her expression was blank. Was it only a fortnight ago that she had told me it was the thing to do.

As quickly her face broke into a smile. 'I'm so pleased.'

I moved towards her and she backed off. 'Camilla?'

Her ears pricked. We both turned and watched; me in dismay, as Rachel entered the apartment looking very glamorous. She strode up to us. 'How lovely to see you! You should have rung!'

Rachel's face showed only sheer delight as she flicked her glossy hair away from her face and gave Camilla a bunch of white chrysanthemums. 'Aren't they beautiful! They'll last forever, darling. Find a vase. They'll look lovely on that table over there.'

Camilla took the flowers as though she was a servant anxious to please. I could tell they weren't a gift of which she was pleased. Red roses might have done the trick.

I watched as she went off to find a vase. Sean appeared from the kitchen with two cups of tea. Rachel beamed with pleasure. 'Ah, you must be Sean! How wonderful to meet you at last. I've heard so much about you.'

And he beamed at her, flattered; rightfully so. I took one of the cups of tea and sipped it. Rachel put her copious bags and cases onto an available surface and removed her beautifully cut designer jacket. Running a hand through her hair she looked at Sean and me. 'So what brings you both here?'

'A site in Battersea; ripe for property development.' I said. Better to get it out straight away and await her criticism.

But Rachel was obviously on her very best behaviour. 'How wonderful! What are you planning?'

Sean spoke lovingly. 'Diana has ideas;' He looked heavenwards. 'The sky's the limit.'

Rachel looked behind me to see what Camilla was doing. She said, 'If you'd rung we could have organised something; as it is we're a bit busy, aren't we, Camilla?'

Before Camilla had time to answer I said, 'Actually I have rung lots of times and I've left messages. That's another reason we called.'

I saw the steely glint in Rachel's eyes once more. 'I do remember getting rid of a few messages by mistake the other day. I'm so sorry if they happened to be yours, Diana, how unfortunate.'

Camilla put the flowers on a small table next to the television. 'Not there, darling.' Rachel pointed to another table. 'Over there would be much better.' She beamed at Camilla. 'Don't you agree?'

Camilla nodded like some sort of zombie. What's happening to you, I thought. She's taken over your life. My best friend replaced the flowers then moved towards us saying, 'Diana's decided to get married.' She touched my hand and smiled enthusiastically at Sean. 'You've got yourself a great wife.'

'I know that.' Sean said with satisfaction.

Rachel made a point of touching my arm. 'I managed to persuade you after all.'

I glared at her and put down my cup of tea. Had she deliberately said that to antagonise me?

Sean looked at me. '*She* managed to persuade you?' I cringed.

Rachel eyes switched from friendly to assertive. 'Yes and I hope you know what you're letting yourself in for, Sean?'

He looked absolutely blank. 'I beg your pardon?'

Rachel pointed at me but kept her eyes on Sean's face. 'You do realise that Diana has a fractured psyche.' Her eyes were now hard and unforgiving.

Sean backed away; he didn't like her manner at all. '*What?*'

Rachel looked at a very embarrassed Camilla. 'We've talked about this, haven't we, Cam?'

'Rachel, *please.*' Insisted Camilla.

Rachel's eyes softened and she reached out and tapped Sean's arm. 'But I'm sure you're man enough to take her on.'

He surprised me then and I adored him for it. 'Take her on? What are you talking about? I thought it was your job to help people, not undermine them.'

Rachel's demeanour froze; she was incensed by Sean's comment and her eyes blazed; it was as though she lost control. 'I *do* help people.'

Camilla was retreating now as Rachel hissed at Sean, 'You're just prejudiced- like your fiancé!'

Sean moved in. '*Prejudiced?* What's that supposed to mean?' He smiled as though the truth had dawned. 'Rachel, I think you're a fake. You like scoring points over people you feel threatened by. Isn't that a gross misuse of your training?'

Camilla held out both hands defensively. 'Please, *please*, don't.'

Rachel looked at her. 'Calm down, Camilla. I can handle this without your interference.'

'I am not interfering! Please don't talk to me like that in front of my friends.'

Rachel backed off immediately. 'I'm so sorry, darling.'

She faced Sean and me with a beaming smile. 'I suppose I do get a bit carried away every now and again; especially when it's a subject close to my heart.' She looked directly at Sean. 'I do assure you I have everyone's best interest at heart.'

Quite calmly he said, 'I don't believe you. I've met people like you before.' He looked at me. 'Let's go home.'

I reached out towards Camilla. 'We shouldn't have come. I'm sorry. I was concerned about you never answering the phone and not returning my calls.'

She looked at Rachel who was seething at Sean's last remark. 'It wasn't intentional, Diana. Please don't worry because I'm absolutely fine.'

Rachel reached out and grabbed Camilla's arm. 'Why don't you tell them the truth?'

'The truth?'

'Yes, how you can't keep your appointments; how you're letting people down all the time. You're having some sort of crisis and you know it.'

'I'm not! How dare you talk to me like that?' With that Camilla rushed off.

Rachel faced us both. 'And now I insist that you both leave. I think you've made your thoughts perfectly clear but you know nothing about the truth.'

Sean took my hand and we started to walk towards the front door. He looked back over his shoulder. 'It won't last, lady. She's not stupid and sooner or later she's going to see you for what you really are. A mind bender.'

Rachel rushed forward and practically pushed us both out of the door before closing it firmly behind us.

'And did she persuade you to agree to marry me?'

I knew he was going to ask me that. 'There were lots of reasons why I want to marry you and I can assure you from the bottom of my heart that any influence coming from her was inconsequential. *Now* do you understand why I'm so worried about Camilla?'

'Yes, yes I do.'

'How do I help?'

'You don't. She'll be all right. Camilla's sharp.' He looked at me as he drove the car. 'Just be there for her when the time comes.'

'I will. I just hope you're right.'

Burnt Orange

And then my life changed forever.

I rang Camilla from the office the very next day. She answered the phone and seemed positive and happy. 'Rachel's says to apologise. She had a bad day; nothing to worry about.'

'I do worry. Are you sure you're all right?'

'Of course I am. This is all very silly, Diana. I'm sure you have tiffs with Sean and that's all that's happened. In some ways it was a good thing you both called round because it's enabled Rachel and me to clear a few misunderstandings up. Now please don't worry because I am perfectly all right. I must dash, got three appointments today. I'll be in touch, I promise. So pleased with your news.'

She was gone. My heart lifted except I didn't believe a word of it.

'Mel! Whatever's the matter?'

I had taken a cup of tea into Sean's office when the phone rang. I watched the alarm on his face as he spoke to his daughter.

'Sweetie, calm down. Take a deep breath; calm yourself, sweetie. Now tell me what's the matter?'

He listened and I could hear Mel's high pitched voice down the phone. I suppose at that point I should have felt some sort of panic but I didn't. At that point I was more concerned about Sean.

When he finally replaced the receiver he put his head between his hands. 'The bastard!'

I did panic now. 'What's happened?'

'Charlie has asked Mel to move out by the end of next week!'

'Why?'

'You tell me? I couldn't make head nor tail of what she was saying; except he's gone away and wants her out by the time he gets back.' Sean's face hardened. 'He really is a prize shit. She can stay until then because of his stupid dog! The poor kid is distraught!'

'So what is she going to do?'

Sean scraped back his chair. 'I'm going over there. She should leave straight away. Why should a daughter of mine be made to stay because of a bloody dog?'

'Sean, perhaps she wants to stay. This could just be a quarrel and when Charlie comes back it will have blown over and they'll make it up.'

'It doesn't sound like it. And why should he keep putting her through all this misery. She doesn't deserve it; she's much too good for the likes of him!'

Sean took my hand as he walked round the desk.

'Will you come with me?'

'Whatever for?'

'To persuade her to leave, of course.'

'What about the dog?'

Sean rolled his eyes. 'We'll sort something out. He must have some neighbours. Are you coming?'

'You sure he's not there?'

'Of course I am! He's in bloody Glasgow of all places. Apparently he and his father have two weeks work up there.'

'I'll come but I'm not sure what good it will do.'

Sean winked. 'Moral support; isn't that what a future wife is for?'

I duly followed him and we drove to Charlie's house.

It was a picturesque little terrace house near the river in Cambridge; Midsummer Common was a stone's throw away. The garden was beautiful with lots of geraniums in pots and roses round the door. 'Did you say Charlie's grandmother left him this house?' I asked.

'Yes, and the dog by all accounts.'

Sean knocked on the door and it was opened by a tearful Mel. Even in her heartbroken state she still looked beautiful with her long dark hair tumbling down her back. She rushed into her father's arms as a child might and he clung to her. Then Mel looked at me.

'Has daddy told you?' Tears welled into her eyes.

'He has. I'm so sorry.'

She put her right hand beneath her left breast. 'Charlie was everything to me, *everything*. And he said I was spoiled rotten and needed to be taught a lesson!'

Sean placed a tender arm around her shoulders. 'Come on, sweetie, don't upset yourself like this, not for the likes of him.'

'I thought he adored me and was going to look after me forever.'

Sean cooed in Mel's ear. 'Well, he's lost his chance now. Come on, don't cry.' He added persuasively. 'I think you should come home and have done with all this.'

She softened beneath his touch then put her hand to her mouth. 'I can't, Daddy, there's Hettie to think about. He thinks more of Hettie than me and you can have no idea how that makes me feel.'

'So why didn't he take Hettie with him?' I asked.

'Because the site won't allow dogs. He's doing some sort of tree demolition. I mean, why they have to go all the way up there I don't know.'

'So where is Hettie?' I asked.

'In there.' Mel pointed to a small room off the kitchen. It was like a scullery and I walked through and there lay Hettie in a cosy little dog bed. She was cowering as though she knew she was about to be left to starve. I knelt down and stroked her and she looked up at me with the most imploring darkest brown eyes that simply broke my heart. She was Charlie's dog; my beloved Charlie and I knew she must be the nicest little dog in the world. 'What is she?' I asked.

'I think she's some sort of terrier; he calls her a bitsa.'

'What's a bitsa?'

'Bits of this; bits of that.'

I smiled and Hettie rolled onto her back for me to stroke her tummy. She was a tan colour with velvety ears that flopped over at the tips. I fell in love with her there and then.

Sean was insistent. 'I want you to come home with me, Mel. I'm not taking no for an answer.'

'What about Hettie?'

'I suppose she'll have to come too.'

Before I had time to think of what I was saying the words were out. 'I could look after her. She'd be all right at Brooklands Avenue. Aunt Jelly and Natasha are going on holiday next week but she'll be all right with me.'

'No, I'll keep her.' Insisted Mel. 'She knows me.'

I was so disappointed. I wanted to take Hettie home with me and give her lots of love. She didn't look as though she'd been given much by Mel.

'And then when Charlie comes back he'll just have to come looking for her, won't he?' Mel said confidently. She didn't want Hettie; just Charlie to come looking for her.

While Mel went to get her stuff together I looked around the house. It had been prettily furnished with a colonial style table, chairs and a lovely dresser. I don't suppose it was Charlie's taste; more his late grandmothers but it was cheerful and there were photographs around. None, I noticed, of Charlie with Mel but certainly several of Charlie at Chelsea's football ground. I smiled at that.

'Come on, sweetie,' said Sean in his fatherly way. 'Let's get you out of this awful place.'

I frowned; even with his precious daughter hurt and dejected he couldn't honestly think that this house was an awful place.

Mel allowed herself to be assisted to her father's car. I walked behind with Hettie on her lead and carrying her doggie bed.

'I've decided to go to Spain! Some of my friends are in Barcelona and they say it's wonderful there. I really am in desperate need of a holiday.'

Sean looked adoringly at Mel. 'So when are you thinking of going?'

I'd invited them both to Sunday lunch at Brooklands Avenue having waved off on holiday Aunt Jelly and Natasha the day before. Hettie was in the garden; I was keeping my eye on her intermittently and was more than pleased to see her enjoying the space to roam. But now she was lying in the sun on the terrace.

'Actually as soon as possible. No point in hanging around. I'd have thought Charlie would have been in touch; he always checks to see that Hettie is all right and sometimes sends his friend Pete round. He'll know I've left and am staying with you, Daddy.' She smirked. 'And I could have left Hettie in his pokey little house!'

Sean patted her arm. 'But you didn't.'

'Of course not.'

'He knows that, sweetie.'

'Sometimes I wonder if he knows anything about me at all.'

'You know what - you've had a lucky escape. You're out of his league, far too good; you must remember that.'

Mel was chewing her hair as this conversation was going on. I watched her face and tried to imagine how she really felt; did she love Charlie. Had his magic worked on her?

I asked. 'When you say as soon as possible what exactly do you mean?'

Mel looked sheepish. 'There's a seat on British Airways tomorrow morning - I have to confirm as soon as possible. Please, daddy. *Please?'*

He looked indulgently at his daughter. 'Go and book it. I'll pay.'

'Daddy! I love you so much! Thank you!' She rushed off to the telephone in the hall.

Sean looked at me; his face showing all the signs of a father who'd hit exactly the right note. I suppose he had except I adored Charlie. He couldn't possibly be this person that Mel was painting. Could he?

'What about the dog?' I asked looking at Hettie basking in the sun on the terrace.

'I'll sort something out.' Sean said dismissively. 'Fortunately the cad will be back before I go into the Evelyn.'

'Why don't you just leave Hettie here? She'll be fine with me.'

He smiled. 'Why do I get the feeling you like Hettie?'

'That's easy. I do.'

The flicker of a frown crossed Sean's face. 'Didn't know you were a dog lover.'

'I'm not a dog lover; I just like animals.' I pointed to Hettie. 'And you have to admit she's a sweetheart.'

He looked at her too. 'No actually; I see her as a factor in Mel's unhappiness.'

I studied Sean's face and wondered if he really did see his daughter as the perfect specimen he constantly pushed. It crossed my mind how I was going to feel about this when we were married. Might I become fed up with it all?

'In that case I'd better look after her because you might accidentally lose her on some motorway.' I smiled.

He smiled too. 'How right you are. You look after her

then. But if you bring her into the office can you please make sure she complies with our strict dress code.'

I laughed and was going to say something witty when Sean shocked me. 'Is there more to all this than you're letting on?'

I paused for thought feeling my face colour. 'What do you mean?'

'Every time Charlie's name is mentioned you become very - well, twitchy. You didn't have a thing with his father, did you?'

I was stunned; lost for words. Did Sean really see me as so much older than I actually was? Had he forgotten I was only twenty-eight?

'See - you're doing it again. Clamming up! Something happened, didn't it?'

I crossed my hands over my heart. '*Nothing* happened between Ivor Stanford and me. This is ridiculous, just because I don't always agree with you.'

He was immediately defensive. 'What don't you agree with?'

'The way you think your daughter can do no wrong! The way you talk about Charlie as though he's a second-class citizen just because he's a gardener!' I stopped as I saw the look on Sean's face and realised I'd gone too far; we were about to have our first real argument.

'The fact that Charlie's a gardener has absolutely nothing whatsoever to do with anything! He's an appalling specimen of a young man; that's what's relevant. In case you've forgotten he's broken my daughter's heart and that bloody dog out there is thought more highly of than her. So tell me what I can possibly have got wrong?'

I stood up and started to walk away. Sean called

after me. 'Is this what you always do when you don't like what's being said?'

I faced him once more. 'Yes, because you wouldn't like what I have to say.'

He stood up and came close to me. 'Say it, please.'

I looked behind Sean at Mel. She stood in the doorway. 'What on earth are you two bickering about?'

Sean turned round quickly and moved towards his daughter placing placating hands on hers. 'It's nothing, sweetie, nothing at all.'

Mel looked at me and then back at her father. 'It didn't sound like nothing. You were shouting. It's about me, isn't it?' She looked at me again. 'I want to know. Say what you're arguing about?'

I took a deep breath and my curiosity got the better of me. 'Just - if Charlie treated you so badly why did you love him so much?'

She blinked. Sean robustly turned towards me. 'What sort of question is that?'

'You've both just told me to say it and that's *it.*'

Sean put his arm around Mel. 'You don't have to answer. Come on, it's time we went home.'

'I want to!' She said with tears springing into her eyes.

Sean gave me a filthy look and I really wished I hadn't started any of this. Why after all this time hadn't I learned that with my fractured psyche I should keep my heartfelt thoughts hidden.

'I loved him because he was different; I could never get enough of him. I always tired of the others eventually.'

'He was different all right!' Sean scoffed.

'And he treated me badly. …I didn't deserve it.'

Sean faced me. 'Anymore questions?'

I was contrite. 'Just an apology; I'm truly sorry I've upset you both; it wasn't my intention.' I smiled at Sean. 'See, Rachel was right. I do have a fractured psyche after all.'

He smiled too but made no comment.

They both left shortly after that and I took Hettie for a long walk. I talked to her about her owner Charlie all the way. If only she could have answered my questions.

Sweetest Orange

Mel left for Barcelona and Sean and I got over our difference of opinion. I think he saw my apology as an admission that I had been in the wrong; not that I was fearful of the upset I'd created. I wondered if Sean ever thought that his daughter was anything other than perfect and this worried me. In the past we'd been able to commiserate with each other about our daughters but now Sean held Mel up as the epitome of perfection.

I said to him one morning in the office; Hettie lay at my feet, 'When are we going to buy this engagement ring?'

'I know; I'm sorry about that but what with one thing and another. Shall we say after I've had my op. Is that okay?'

'Fine.' I felt like saying; I'll pay for it myself if you can't afford it.

He leaned across my desk. 'We can get it today if you really want to?'

'No. After your op is fine.' I looked down at Hettie who'd really settled with me. 'So do we take Hettie back to Charlie? Isn't he home by now?'

Sean shrugged. 'He can bloody well come and find her. Why should we go chasing after him?'

I didn't answer. I didn't want to lose Hettie; she was my dog now.

Still no sign of Charlie; I wondered if he was all right. I'd rung my mother in Oceanside and they were all having a wonderful time; I'd even spoken to Natasha who excitedly told me about Disneyland. Sean went into the Evelyn for the reversal of his vasectomy and after making sure he'd settled in I went back to my flat with Hettie. We alternated between Brooklands Avenue and the flat because I was gradually moving my stuff out. Hettie didn't mind. I took her for lots of walks around Cambridge and she seemed to be a very happy dog.

It was the middle of the morning when my doorbell rang and I remember rushing to answer it before Hettie started barking. She'd only just started doing that; the cowering dog in the kitchen had come out of her shell.

So I opened the front door impatiently; who was it? Immediately my heart flew into my mouth. He was standing with his back to me and his arms were folded; his body had filled out so that there was no mistaking his manhood. Charlie turned and looked at me with a very stern expression on his face. Even so I noticed that his blond hair was attractively unkempt, his skin had cleared to perfection and looked deliciously clean and his magical hazel eyes stayed on my face. He was older, all of twenty-one; no longer the boy of yesterday. And then Hettie shot out from nowhere and scampered round his feet yipping and yapping in absolute delight.

'You *are* here.' Charlie bent down and fussed his dog and she rolled on to her back and was beside herself with joy.

He stood up. 'Have you any idea the trouble I've had trying to find my dog?'

I could imagine. 'Come in.' I beckoned him inside and after I'd closed the door said. 'Mel was upset. She couldn't stay at yours anymore. We had to bring Hettie with us.'

'She could have taken her to my mother.'

I was surprised. 'Did you suggest that?'

'We discussed it all before I left for Glasgow but Mel wanted to stay 'til I got back. Where is she? Is she all right?'

'Do you care?'

He frowned. 'Of course I care.'

'She's in Barcelona.'

'Barcelona?'

'She needed a holiday.' I glanced at Hettie who was now settling herself on the sofa. 'And I've got Hettie.'

Charlie looked at his dog and smiled; the first time since he'd arrived. 'Lucky Hettie. She's certainly made herself at home.'

'She's an adorable dog. I love her to bits.'

He looked at me, his eyes staying on my face and it was as though he was reminding himself of who I was and a shiver went through me. I realised then that nothing had changed; we were still the same people outside Annabel's nightclub.

His stance softened completely as he said, 'I love her too.' He paused thoughtfully; 'Mel never said that *you* worked with her father. …His secretary sent me to Brooklands Avenue and when you weren't there she sent me here.' He added distastefully, 'And he's your fiancé? Bit old isn't he?'

And you're too young; I averted my eyes. 'We've been together a while. Are you going to make it up with Mel?'

Momentarily he was stumped before holding up his hands. 'I don't know what she's told you…'

'…You broke her heart.'

He hesitated. 'Broke her heart?'

'Yes.'

'She does have one then?'

'That's unkind. She adores you and you treated her badly; just expected her to look after your dog.'

Charlie laughed; he really laughed showing his adorable teeth and I imagined them close to mine. 'Mel moved in on the understanding she looked after Hettie because I can't always take her to work.'

'Is that really true?'

'Yes. What's she been telling you?'

'A different story.'

He bit his lip. In fascination I watched him do it. 'She thinks all men are going to fall at her feet.' He added, 'I didn't.'

'No?'

'No.' His eyes held mine; I was captivated. He took a few steps closer and ran one forefinger over my mouth. How dare he?! All the same it sent a shiver down my spine and I quickly licked my lips. Defiantly he whispered, 'Mel's not the one for me and maybe I did use her a bit but I never made any promises. How could I? It's you I love.'

'*Charlie.*' I swallowed hard; his boldness really took my breath away. 'You're a baby and much too young for me.'

He took a step even closer and I could smell the soap on his skin. It was a delicious combination of citrus and musk, or perhaps it was cologne. I was mesmerised but still aware that he was by far overstepping the mark. I remembered Natasha; how I was always weak against the will of Angelica. Was this not the same? No, I decided this was different; definitely different. So I didn't move back and Charlie leaned towards me and kissed me very gently on my mouth. This was our third tentative kiss and I remonstrated with myself not to respond. 'I'm not too young,' he whispered. 'And no way are you too old.'

Shame overwhelmed me. 'This really can't happen.'

'It already has happened.' He looked upwards. 'How many years ago was it?' His eyes rested on mine once more. 'Or should I tell you in hours and minutes?'

I had to get a grip. 'You were fifteen. I should have known better.'

But his eyes lit up. 'I've got a picture of you; I keep it safe next to my bed. You were on the cover of some magazine and I saw it and bought it.' He smiled in his disarming way. 'It was the only copy in the newsagents and I fought with some woman to have it.'

His face was now full of passion and I remembered, 'That was when my friend Camilla did my hair; when you and I met outside Annabel's.'

He frowned. 'I didn't even know your husband had

died. They told me that as well at your office.'

'Who told you?'

He shrugged. 'Sean's secretary.'

'What else did she tell you?'

He took a quick intake of breath. 'Only that you're going to marry him.'

I lowered my eyes.

He said with a determination in his voice. 'Don't.'

I looked at him and his face was consumed with love. I knew it was love; had I not seen it in my own reflection when thinking of him? I had to turn away; I walked towards Hettie and stroked her. 'You'll be taking her away?'

'Not if you don't want me to.'

I faced him once more. 'Aren't you working today?'

He smiled. 'Yes. I'm late.'

I said firmly. 'You should go.'

'Yes, I should.' He looked around the flat. 'Amazing place. I like it.'

'Thank you. It's my bolt-hole.'

'Where's your daughter? Natasha is it?'

'She's on holiday in California.'

'With that awful aunt?'

'Yes; with that awful aunt.'

Charlie walked towards Hettie and fondled her ears. 'I'll leave you here, baby. You've got a new carer.' He looked at me. 'Do I get visiting rights?'

I hesitated, but not for long. 'I suppose so.'

He left then; looking back once as I stood in the doorway watching him go. He mouthed I love you. I smiled and closed the door.

Much later I went to see Sean in the Evelyn. He was drowsy from the anaesthetic and feeling very sore. I sat next to his bed feeling thoroughly totally guilty. 'It went well they told me.' He smiled in a sleepy way. 'Have you heard from Mel?'

I wanted to lie; but I hadn't heard from Mel. 'Sean, darling, she needs this holiday.'

'I know.' He sighed. 'Diana, I've been thinking. I've got it all wrong. Mel's; well, Mel. You were right when you asked her why she loved Charlie. She probably is totally selfish. Oh, I don't know; all I know is that I love you. ...Darling, you are the most important thing in my life.'

He took a deep breath. 'Forget my bloody daughter, it's you I need and want; and love.' He had obviously been thinking a lot about this. 'I'm so sorry how I behaved towards you the other day because you can have no idea how much I really do need you.' He added contritely, 'And we'll get that ring as soon as I leave here.'

I remember touching his arm; sqeezing it; saying all the right things. What I did eventually whisper was the truth. 'I love you.' I can't tell you how much I loved Sean. He was the touchstone in my life; my very best friend; the person who had taught me most about business; the person who had backed me while I went off on a roll about so many stupid projects. But love is a varied thing. I'm afraid it doesn't work in quite the way it should. Sometimes it grabs you; enthrals you. It makes you feel as though you can't live without it.

I'd left Hettie in the flat and was anxious to get back to her. So I went back to my bolt-hole thinking I was strong. Thinking that because of Sean's words I was safe.

But what is safety? Is it the love of a good man or is it that cloud in the sky? The one you watch as it passes by with the light behind it creating zillions of colours; the one that you want to beam yourself up to forever.

As the lift doors opened I saw them. A hundred red roses at least! He'd been back and they were propped up against the front door. I felt sick at heart because I'd missed him. Bad timing again because I got the feeling that I'd only just missed him.

I picked up the flowers and took them inside. Hettie was thrilled to see me. I smelled the roses; their scent was wonderful; I don't know where he'd found them because they weren't shop bought hybrids; they were naturally grown. That meant all the more to me. I temporarily put them in the sink and filled it with water then took Hettie off for a walk.

I arrived back at the flat and the phone was ringing. I fumbled with my key then raced inside to answer it.

'Hello, darling. You arrived home safely?' It was Sean and disappointment and guilt overwhelmed me.

'Sean, yes, safely back. I've just taken Hettie for a walk.' The words were out before I had time to think.

Sean grunted down the phone. 'About time he picked that bloody thing up!'

'How are you feeling?' I was keen to change the subject.

'Much better. Anyway, I just wanted to say goodnight and that I love you. I do hope this bloody operation works. If it does how many shall we have?'

I laughed. 'Oh, at least three.'

'You think so?'

'It doesn't matter, Sean. Let's see what happens.'

He told me he loved me again and I said I loved him. I looked at Hettie as I replaced the receiver. 'Oh, dear, Hettie. What sort of game am I playing?'

Hettie just wagged her tail and made herself comfortable on the sofa.

I looked at the phone willing it to ring again. No way could I ring Charlie even though I wanted to thank him for the flowers. That would be like succumbing to his advances and I was engaged to be married; committed to Sean. I could not behave so recklessly. It would never do. I just wanted him to ring me so that I could hear his voice.

But he didn't ring and I felt a sort of relief. This was a young man and at my age I should know better. I took the flowers from the kitchen sink and arranged them in various vases and containers all around the apartment; they looked wonderful because I'd cut down the stems and made them into posies.

So at about ten o'clock I decided to have a bath. I was actually soaking in it when I heard the doorbell. Well, I didn't hear it at first; just Hettie barking. I scrambled out of the bath and wrapped myself in a white towelling robe. I looked briefly in the mirror; at my hair randomly held up in a bulldog clip; no make-up; just a shiny face. As I stared at myself I knew it was him; this is where a sensible lady would not answer the door.

But of course I did.

He was wearing an open necked pale blue long sleeved shirt with the cuffs rolled back twice above his wrists and his thumbs were hooked into the pockets of beige chinos. He looked shy; especially when he was presented with me in a bathrobe.

'Thank you for the roses.'

'You liked them?'

'Where were they from?'

'Just a few gardens here and there.'

'Charlie, you must have ravaged those gardens.'

'I suppose I did.'

I stepped back as though it was the most natural thing in the world to do and Charlie stepped forward. We were now standing in the sitting room and Hettie, having been totally surprised by Charlie's presence had finally settled down.

'I wasn't expecting you.'

He took his thumbs out of his trousers and nervously tapped them together. Charlie's hands were one of his most erotic features; especially when watching him crumbling soil between his fingers. He said unsurely, 'I didn't know if *he* might be here so I took a risk.' Charlie swallowed hard. 'Hettie could have been my excuse.'

'Actually he's in hospital.'

I swear he looked hopeful. 'Is he ill?'

'No no. He's fine. He'll be out tomorrow. So you dropped off the flowers and went home, then came back?'

'Yes, but I hung around a bit.'

'I took Hettie for a walk earlier; I didn't see you.'

'I dropped off the flowers then went home for a bath.' Charlie smiled in an unsure way. 'I came straight back but it took a while to pluck up courage to come up here. I had to see you, Diana, and you look wonderful.'

'I've just got out of the bath. I don't look wonderful.'

'You do; always. Have you any idea how you make me feel; how you've always made me feel.' He held out one hand and touched my face and I could feel a mixture of soft and hard skin and it was sensual.

He dropped his hand and moved in and I took several steps back. He reached out and took my hands in his. 'Don't fight this, please. It was always going to happen; I knew you'd come back into my life.'

'This can't take us anywhere. I'm engaged to be married and you're much too young for me.'

'I'm *not* too young and *he's* much too old!' He hesitated and squeezed my hands. 'This is no ordinary feeling; age doesn't count.'

'But you don't know me.'

He smiled in his way. 'I bet I do. The only surprises will be good ones. I watched you constantly when we worked in your garden and dreamt about you every night. At that time it was just that; a dream, but when I saw you outside Annabel's I knew you felt the same way. Don't you?'

I struggled to find the right words. 'You're very special but I'm scared.'

'Of what?'

'Getting hurt; hurting people. And the whole of my instincts tell me this can't possibly work.'

'The whole of my instincts tell me this is for real and if I let you slip through my fingers I'll regret it for evermore.'

I pulled my hands out of his and boldly cupped his face. I kissed him very gently and the taste of his mouth, the softness and the wetness was bliss. He moved in wrapping his arms around me and it was thrilling; like coming alive.

'We're in full view of the window here.' I whispered.

'Let's move.'

I took his hand and walked towards the bedroom listening to the wise voice in my head telling me to stop now; this was provocative behaviour. Charlie was still the boy that his father had warned me off.

The blind was drawn in the bedroom but I could see my face in a mirror that covered nearly the whole of the opposite wall; it was flushed; hot even. Charlie's stood behind me; he too looked in the mirror and smiled. I still held one of his hands in mine and looked down at it turning it over and wondering how hands can be so erotic; his squared off fingers with clean fingernails clipped short and the odd bits of rough skin from his labours. He slipped it away from me and touched my shoulders trying to turn me round but I stood my ground keeping my back to him. I brought my hands to my face and closed my eyes. I no longer wanted to see myself in the mirror.

Then I heard it; the sound of this young man removing his clothing. Wasn't that what I wanted; wasn't that why I'd brought him in here? For one fleeting second I panicked and turned but he just took my face in his hands and kissed me and this kiss was so different; his tongue filled my mouth and I weakened. My robe simply fell from my shoulders and Charlie pushed me so that I lay half across the bed with my feet still touching the carpet. He groaned in pleasure as his eyes wandered over my body; then he sank to his knees and buried his head in my vulva; licking so gently; caressing me with his tongue; driving me crazy. I felt wanton; lascivious and stretched my arms behind my head in sheer abandonment. As I did so I remembered Ben's seduction technique but I didn't care; Charlie was adept and it was superb and I was overwhelmed by his prowess. He raised himself and smiled; my own secretions quite visible around his mouth. I was the child now and lifted myself to look at his genitals; at his size and erection and our eyes met in mutual satisfaction as he pushed me back down again and I watched him slide his penis inside me. With his hands supporting his body he pushed and withdrew; pushed and withdrew and I wanted it to last forever.

His eyes stayed on mine as though watching my response and then as his pace quickened my excitement raced and because of his deep penetration and the angle we lay I felt the first tantalising and elusive rush of orgasm but there was no let down here; it easily reached its peak and stayed and stayed and had Charlie been able to keep going then I'm quite sure so would I.

He stayed with me that night and we talked about his work; his plans for their landscape gardening business. I asked about the tree felling in Glasgow; actually it was near Loch Lomand but Mel never listened to details; and he said there was a lot of money made from felling, thinning and trimming back overgrown trees and although his father wasn't keen he loved climbing up in a harness and sawing off branches. But he also loved laying terraces, creating flower beds and growing vegetables; and pond life and all aspects of their thriving business. He said it was very hard work but he loved being outdoors even when it was freezing cold.

'So you met Mel at Cambridge Regional College?'

'Yes. She's two years older than me and was finishing up her course as I started mine so we didn't really get to know each other then; it was later. She just always seemed to be there wherever I went and she came back to my place one night with a load of others and never left. You could say she seduced me.'

'I'm sure you were a willing partner.'

'I was at first but she's such a lazy cow; correction; a selfish lazy cow.'

'I might be.'

'I know you're not! You're like me, a worker.'

'I've made a mess of my life, Charlie. Totally cocked up my relationship with my daughter; Aunt Jelly is her mother, not me. I suppose you could say I deserve that because Ben only married me because I was pregnant and I tricked him by saying the baby was going to be a boy. He was desperate for a son. And lo and behold it turned out to be a girl who looked just like his dreadful sister and I couldn't bond with her at all.' I drew breath. 'You know, before we married Ben tried to pay me off; persuade me to have an abortion and I threw the money back at him. That's the other reason he married me; nobody had ever thrown his wretched money back at him before.'

'I bet he did love you deep down.'

'He didn't. Well, perhaps a bit at the end when I looked after him; he had a horrible death; I wouldn't wish that on anyone.'

'So how come you work with Sean?'

I considered the question and wondered whether to tell him the truth about my inheritance. Not yet, I decided. That could wait a while. 'H-G Properties was my husband's company. I like working there actually. I'm quite good at finding and securing sites to build on. We've built some great houses and flats in Cambridge and London.'

Charlie looked at me with intelligent eyes. 'You own it, don't you?'

'Some of it.'

'He left it to you? Your husband, I mean.'

'Yes.'

'You see, he did love you.'

'Believe me, Charlie, Ben didn't understand love. He only understood pounds and pence and he wanted me tied down so that his sister could look after his daughter.'

Charlie's eyes stayed on my face. 'I can't imagine anyone not loving you. If they know you they must love you.'

'That's *definitely* not so. I've already been told; I have a fractured psyche.'

Charlie laughed then; a gentle laugh but genuine nonetheless. 'What a load of tosh!'

'It's not! I do. You don't understand. You're far too young.'

He rolled over in bed and took my face in his hands. 'I wasn't born yesterday. You've obviously been spending too much time with people who like to expound stupid views. And what in God's name is a fractured psyche? I mean, if it exists then we must all have one.'

I had to agree. 'The person who told me about mine certainly does.'

'Yes, and I bet it was someone who's insanely jealous of you.'

'No. She's a control freak.' I loved talking like this with Charlie. Would I ever get enough of him? He spoke my language; the language that my father had spoken. Funny that; both gardeners. 'You know, you're wise beyond your years.'

'Because I don't go in for bullshit, you mean?'

'No. Because you listen; so many of the important people in my life don't and I get out of step with them.'

'We're kindred spirits.'

'On borrowed time; this can't possibly last.'

He sat up and said quite fiercely, 'After *this* you'd walk away from me?'

I stroked his face. 'There are too many other people in my life who have a strong hold over me; what am I supposed to do? Say I've fallen in love with Charlie Stanford so I'm off now?'

'You have then?'

'What?'

'Fallen in love with me?'

'Haven't I said so a thousand times over the last few hours?'

'Endearments; if it's true how can you turn your back on us?'

I looked at his adoring eyes, his tousled hair and sensuous mouth. 'I can't.'

'Marry me?'

'Charlie!'

'I'd marry you tomorrow.'

'I'm supposed to be marrying somebody else.'

'But you don't love him. You wouldn't be here with me now if you did.'

'I *do* love him. Just not like this. And sadly this is wrong.'

Charlie whispered in my ear. 'It can't be. Have you no faith?'

I took a sharp intake of breath. 'My father used to say that!'

'Good, because you have to have faith in your own feelings.'

'Who taught you to think like this?'

'My gran; she was a wise old bird and bloody good with money.'

'She's the one who left you your lovely house?'

'Have your seen it?' I could see the pride on Charlie's face and I loved him all the more for it.

'I went with Sean when we picked up Mel, and Hettie, of course. I liked your home. It was filled with personality.'

His face was animated. 'She used to polish that furniture like there was no tomorrow and left it all to me. I'm some lucky chap, don't you think?'

'You've got a super home.'

'She had good investments too. Sometimes it pays to be the only grandchild.' He smiled.

'So where do your mum and dad live?'

'Grantchester; near the river; a cracking house. They paid a pittance for it twenty years ago; an absolute wreck it was and gradually they did it up. We didn't have much money so we lived on what was practically a building site for years. People thought we were mad but I never knew any different and loved all the piles of rubble and camping under a leaky roof. Now it's worth a bloody fortune and people think we weren't quite so mad after all.'

'And your gardening business really pays well?'

'Hard work does. You have to put the effort in to achieve.'

'Did Gran teach you that?'

'Most definitely.'

'I love her.'

'She would have loved you too.'

I looked at my watch. 'It's six-thirty! What time do you have to be at work?'

'Half an hour ago!'

'You're joking!'

He pulled me to him. 'I am.'

'We haven't slept. You'll never be able to work.'

'I think I will as long as you promise you won't walk away from this?'

He looked at me; his eyes searching. But how could I promise such a thing? 'I promise.' I said.

Cloudy Grey

I picked Sean up from the Evelyn that afternoon and I could hardly look him in the eye. He was cheerful; still sore but in a positive mood. Charlie and I had parted without discussion about where we went from here and I thought we both knew that breathing space was what was needed now.

'Shall I take you home?' I asked.

'No. I think I'd like to come back to your place; if it's okay with you?'

Panic hit me but I said blithely, 'Of course.'

Sean patted my hand. 'I need some tender loving care.'

'I'll do my best.' It was then I remembered Hettie. Oh, God, what was he going to say about the dog?

'She's still here!' He exclaimed. 'What the hell is he playing at? Doesn't he care about his damned dog at all?'

Hettie ran to me but backed off pretty sharpish at Sean's harsh words.

'It's okay. Charlie's been in touch. He's still very busy and I said Hettie was okay with me.'

Sean scowled at me. 'Now you see the treatment my daughter got! He's using you, Diana. You should tell him to pick the frigging dog up!'

I looked at this man that I'd promised to marry. 'Calm down, Sean. It's no big deal. I really don't mind.'

'I do! It makes me mad as hell.'

I sighed. 'What can I get you? How about something cool and soothing?' This did bring a bit of a smile to Sean's face. He pulled me closer. 'You're cool and soothing.' He kissed my mouth and I thought how different his kiss was from Charlie's. Charlie's mouth was softer. 'But as you've asked a cold beer wouldn't go amiss.'

I slid from his arms and went to fetch the beer. I had it in mind to pour myself a large glass of wine to settle my own nerves.

What I dreaded most happened. Charlie called round after he'd finished work. I raced to answer the door and Hettie went mad when she saw her master. He looked dusty and dishevelled but it just added to my desire; I wanted him so much. Even so I mouthed in the most juvenile manner, 'Sean's here.'

I really would have expected Charlie to back off but

he calmly bent down and petted Hettie and as he raised himself his eyes held mine and told me that he was not going to creep away like a scared boy and I recognised his strength of character. I was proud.

He moved towards me and I swear he was going to kiss me; I backed off with no choice but to let him in. As he did so his hand caught mine sending a shiver through me; he passed over a small package. I looked at it wondering what on earth it could be. I quickly put it in the pocket of my loose white trousers and together we went through to the sitting room to face Sean.

I said. 'Charlie's here, Sean.' I looked at Charlie. 'Can I offer you a drink?'

He shook his head. 'No thank you.'

With some discomfort Sean stood up and glared at Charlie. 'Come to pick up your dog, have you?'

I looked at Sean. 'I've already told you, Hettie's staying here.'

Charlie eyes caught mine and held for several seconds. 'Thank you. I appreciate what you're doing for me.'

Sean scowled. 'You, boy, have got one almighty nerve! Now you've finished manipulating my daughter you think you can manipulate my fiancé. Well, you're wrong. Take your dog and go!' He pointed to the front door.

I was incensed. 'This is my home. I make the decisions here.'

He looked at me furiously. 'Can't you see what he's doing?'

I swallowed hard. 'Charlie is not the villain you're making him out to be.'

Charlie then backed off and I could see that he was

angry. 'I'll go.' He looked at me his eyes a mixture of love and confusion. 'Do you want me to take Hettie?'

'No!'

Charlie looked relieved and walked towards the front door.

Sean called after him. 'I don't know what your game is, boy, but don't think you're going to win.'

Charlie looked back at him. 'Win what? I think I've already got what I want.'

I could feel my heart beating rapidly and was very relieved when Charlie disappeared out of the front door. Sean glared at me. 'What was that supposed to mean?'

'It means, Sean, that you're making an absolute prat of yourself over a dog that I happen to like. You don't own me and please don't think you can order me about.'

I really thought Sean was then going to ask me if there was something going on between Charlie and myself and I would have told him the truth but he didn't. Sean walked into the kitchen and poured himself another beer and I knew then that the thought had not crossed his mind. Charlie was nothing more than a boy in his eyes and I was very much a woman.

Acid Green

I opened the small package that Charlie had given me and inside was a ring. It was a plaited gold band with three stones; an opal, a diamond and a ruby. The stones were twisted into the plait and I knew he'd bought this ring from a specialist shop and probably paid a fortune for it. Needless to say I adored it. It fitted the third finger of my left hand perfectly and I put it on. Up until this stage I'd continued to wear my wedding band but this was now replaced with Charlie's ring.

Also, needless to say, Sean didn't notice.

You must know what craving, yearning and hungering for someone is like; Charlie came up to see Hettie and I ached for him; he filled my mind; made me dizzy with desire. I *wanted* him. But it wasn't enough. Charlie wasn't content.

'You don't sleep with him anymore, do you?'

I didn't like to say that Sean was still getting over his operation; but I wouldn't have had sex with him anyway. I'd have made every excuse known to woman.

Natasha, Aunt Jelly, my mother and Aunt Fi returned from California. They'd had a wonderful time; Natasha was brimming with all the exciting trips they'd been on and her conversation was littered with American twang; she couldn't wait to go back to school to tell all her friends about it.

Charlie and I had been together for three whole weeks when he asked me to spend the following Saturday night and Sunday with him. 'Make some excuse, *please*. We could take Hettie to Holkham Bay.'

My brain was in some sort of tangle. I loved this young man; wanted him; imagined spending the rest of my life with him but he was twenty-one for God's sake; he was an infant in all the people's eyes around me.

'I'm going to London on Saturday to get Camilla to do my hair.' I said to Sean when he came into my office on Thursday morning.

He gave me a cursory look. 'Hair looks all right to me.'

I smiled. 'That's because I look after it. Anyway, she's asked me to stay over and spend Sunday with her. Rachel is on some course somewhere.' The lies just rolled off my tongue.

Sean's eyes stayed on my face quizzically. 'So you're allowed back in the fold again, are you? This is news to me.'

'I rang her…'

Sean interrupted. 'You actually got through?'

I smiled again. 'Eventually; I wouldn't be invited if Rachel was around and I don't doubt Camilla will forget to tell her I'm there.'

Sean tutted. 'How bloody ridiculous. I really am surprised those two are still together. I thought Camilla had more sense.'

'But you don't mind?'

He shrugged. 'Would it matter if I did?'

Since our argument over Charlie and Hettie things had not been the same between Sean and me. For the first time in my life I was steeped in guilt. Yes, I'd felt guilty over Natasha and, I suppose, guilty over contriving to get Ben to marry me but it was nothing like the shameful stomach churning guilt I felt now.

'I'm sorry if you think that. I don't want to make you unhappy.'

'Oh, I'm not unhappy; just bloody confused.' He leaned on my desk. 'So tell me, Diana, what are you going to do about Hettie this weekend?'

I blinked and looked down at Hettie who was lying contentedly at my feet. 'She'll be with Charlie.'

Sean shook his head. 'This I find very hard to take.'

And I was saved by the bell! The telephone rang and it was a very tearful Mel on the line and could she speak to Daddy. I passed over the phone to him and breathed a very temporary sigh of relief.

I watched as Sean listened to his daughter with a frown on his face. I could still hear her high-pitched whining voice down the other end of the phone. He said, 'Sweetie, calm down. So who is this person who's causing all this trouble?' Very briefly he looked at me and rolled his eyes. Then he said, 'Mel, why don't you just come home.' He continued to listen. 'Okay, okay. Yes, yes. A flight on Sunday. Yes, I'll pay. You come home, sweetie. I'll pick you up at the airport.'

He replaced the receiver and rubbed his face with both hands. Poor Sean, he didn't deserve this sort of treatment from neither his daughter nor me. He sighed and half smiled; all previous conversation totally forgotten. 'I don't know what it is about my daughter but she certainly has a habit of upsetting people.'

I reached across the desk and squeezed his hands. 'Poor, Sean. You don't deserve all this.'

He glanced at our hands clasped together and then looked puzzled; withdrew his hands and said, 'Where did you get that?' He was looking at the ring Charlie had bought me.

Another lie. 'Natasha bought it back from California.' I twisted the ring on my finger. 'It's rather nice, don't you think? She got it from Disneyland.'

Sean gave a thin-lipped smiled. 'Why are you wearing it on that finger?'

'Because it seems appropriate somehow. I've

removed my wedding ring but I don't like not to have a ring on that finger.'

Sean tutted again. 'It that a dig at me?'

'No.'

He stood up and walked towards the door. 'Like I said, Diana, you really do behave in some odd ways sometimes.'

'Well perhaps I've found it odd that you haven't bothered to buy me a ring?'

'It's just a frigging ring! What difference does it make?'

I looked at Charlie's ring. 'A lot, actually.'

Sean left then slamming the door as he did so.

Later on he apologized assuring me he intended to buy me a wonderful engagement ring; 'We should go to London.' he said and quickly added, 'Perhaps I should come up with you on Saturday; then I could go straight to the airport on Sunday to pick Mel up.' Before I could draw breath he added. 'Surely you could find time before or after having your hair done to come with me to Hatton Gardens?'

For a few seconds I couldn't think of the right lie. 'Sean; this is catch-up time for Camilla and me. If I swan off to buy an engagement ring it could look as though she's not important enough; if you get my drift?'

He studied my face for several seconds and I could feel myself going redder and redder. I took a deep breath and decided to say no more. I felt as though I was digging an enormous hole for myself. It crossed my mind; just tell him the truth.

'The ring's not that important then?'

I grinned. 'It's only a frigging ring.'
He walked away shaking his head.

Warm Orange

For early September the weather was wonderful. Charlie was working on Saturday so I visited Natasha and Aunt Jelly. Natasha was preparing to go back to school and seemed happy. It occurred to me that she and I could have a good relationship living apart. She didn't seem to mind at all; Aunt Jelly was mother to her; not me and it didn't hurt quite so much anymore; perhaps it was because of Charlie.

I'd had no more contact from Sean and was glad. My biggest fear was that he would try to get in touch with me at Camilla's but now that he was picking Mel up from the airport that was unlikely. We had never lived in each other's pockets; always had our independence.

So I prepared supper that evening for Charlie and me. I knew he liked fish so I'd bought halibut to grill and would serve it with fried potatoes, courgettes and broad beans. For someone so young Charlie had an educated palate. His family had always grown their own vegetables and he'd been brought up on fresh produce. We had talked for hours about our likes and dislikes and I couldn't get enough of listening to him. Our union wasn't just about sex.

I'd already taken Hettie for a walk looking over my shoulder all the time lest Sean should appear from nowhere. I then showered and changed into a simple button-through red dress. I washed my hair and wore it down.

He arrived dusty and tired but greeted me with an enormous smile; telling me I looked beautiful. He cuddled Hettie and then went straight through to have a bath; Charlie liked to bathe; and as he cleaned the days grime from his hair and body I sat on the loo talking to him.

'So you've been trimming branches off trees all day?' I asked.

'And taking some down completely; there's a huge amount to do.'

'So where is it?'

'A private stud farm this side of Newmarket; owned by some Irish millionaire called McGraedy.' He looked lovingly at me. 'And this guy is really rich, I can tell you.'

I saw the glint in his eye and wondered at this point whether to tell Charlie about my own personal wealth but the moment passed and I didn't.

He continued. 'He's revamping the whole place and he's right to do so as loads of the trees are practically dead stopping the younger ones growing properly. He's got a huge planting project for us as well. You should come out sometime and see it. I'll show you what I do. Dad calls me Tarzan.'

I smiled. 'I'd love to.'

'I'd love you to too.'

I took a deep breath. 'But what will your father say?'

Charlie stood up in the bath and I gazed at his wonderful body glistening with water before I handed him a towel. 'I've kind of told him.'

My eyes widened. 'About us?'

Charlie rubbed the towel through his hair and

down his body. 'Not everything; he doesn't know you're engaged to Sean Jackson but he's not too bothered about the rest.'

'The rest?'

Charlie kissed my mouth. 'I'm not a teenager anymore and he doesn't mind that you're older.' He kissed me again. 'I only mention that because I know it worries you.'

'Does it not worry you even a little bit?'

He kissed me again. 'Not even a tincy wincy little bit.'

'It might do when we're older.'

'It won't.'

I followed him out of the bathroom to the bedroom where he pulled on jeans and a t-shirt. He looked at me. 'I'm hungry.'

'I'll go and get it ready. Do you fancy a drink?'

'Glass of white wine would be great.'

I gazed at him lovingly. 'You're far too grown up, you know. Most twenty-one year olds would want a beer.'

'I'm not a beer fan - but I would like to watch Match of the Day later. First time I've missed a Chelsea match in ages.' He held up one hand. 'And don't tell me the score.'

'I don't know the score and I'd love to watch it with you.'

As I walked through to the kitchen to pour the wine and start cooking I felt that everything was slipping into place; I had to take my chances with Charlie; I had no choice.

We ate supper which he gave me full marks for and then curled up together to watch the match. Sadly Chelsea lost and I think I was as disappointed as he was.

It wasn't long after that we went to bed and by the time I'd finished in the bathroom Charlie had fallen asleep. I climbed in beside him and lay as close as I could without waking him. I was quite content; no wonder he was exhausted. It wasn't long before I fell asleep as well.

When I opened my eyes the next morning Charlie was already caressing me and I was aroused. 'What a way to wake up.' I whispered.

'I've been longing for you to wake.' He started to kiss me and I was aware of this fresh young man first thing in the morning; I didn't feel fresh.

'Can I at least clean my teeth and go to the loo?' I asked.

He didn't stop. 'Only if you have to because I like you just the way you are.'

I didn't have to so I let go and wallowed in Charlie's touch. I whispered, 'Who taught you? Who taught you how to make love?'

He whispered back, 'Nobody taught me and you do have the most delicious divine zone.'

'Do I?' I felt guilty; divine zone was Sean speak for the genital area and I'd passed it on to Charlie.

He laughed softly in my ear. 'You sound as though you've had some lousy lovers?'

'No.' I was defensive of Sean. Except, in the four weeks I'd been intimate with Charlie he had aroused feelings within me I didn't know existed. I added,

'Anyway, I've only had two.'

'I'll kill them both.' He was serious.

'One's already gone.'

Charlie said bitterly, 'And the other I can't bear to think of you with.'

I remembered only too well my feelings about Mel. 'It's the same for me, Charlie. But we don't own each other.'

'I want to own you, Diana. I never want to let you go.' He buried his face in my neck before shifting on top of me and pushing himself inside me in a masterful way but the sadness in his eyes made me want to protect him forever.

I responded to his rhythm and was pleased when the sadness was replaced by lust.

Hettie was scratching and whining at the door. We were now relaxed and more than content lying close to each other talking about the day ahead and this and that. Reluctantly Charlie climbed out of bed. 'I'll take her.' He pulled on some clothes and called out, 'It's okay, baby, Daddy's coming.' He turned round and grinned at me and I saw the boy in the man.

While he was gone I showered and went through to the kitchen to make sandwiches for our trip to Holkham Bay. My favourite: egg; his favourite: ham, mustard and lettuce and both our second choice; cheese and tomato. I also packed apples and bananas, a large bar of fruit and nut chocolate and two bottles of chilled Chablis; a flask of coffee as well, and water for Hettie. I placed most of it in a cool box and went off to find a blanket.

Holkham Bay is two-miles west of Wells-next-the-Sea on the Norfolk coast and Charlie was more than happy to drive; especially in my new Mercedes Sports. He asked, 'So is this a company car?'

I smiled. 'Sort of.' I was glad he didn't query any further.

Hettie sat at my feet and we drove via Kings Lynn and Burnham Market and parked close to Holkham Hall which was a magnificent eighteenth century Palladian building. Charlie mentioned that it was owned by the Coke family and built by Thomas Coke, the first Earl of Leicester.

We parked along a grass verge and then walked for about five minutes to the most stupendous beach I'd ever seen. It completely took my breath away. 'This is gorgeous.'

Ten miles, apparently, of pine fringed splendour with masses of dunes to hide away in and a maze of creeks. I asked in wonder, 'How did you find this place?' I was also curious about Charlie's knowledge of the place.

'My parents brought me here as a child. I loved it then and love it even more now.'

'You have good parents; you're very lucky.'

Carrying the cool box he squeezed me. 'I'm the luckiest person in the world because I'm with you.'

Charlie didn't just say things like that; it was as though he really meant them. 'And I'm the luckiest person too.'

Hettie raced on ahead enjoying all the thrills and spills and smells around her. The weather was breezy; quite chilly but sunny and we found a suitable dune to dump our lunch so that we could go for a long walk. We both slipped off our shoes and rolled up our jeans and set off arm in arm towards the sea. I touched my camera in my pocket thinking I must take some photographs of this place and in the whole of my life cannot remember feeling so happy. The sea blew saltiness in our faces and felt cold on our feet but we walked along the edge never leaving each other's side. I think I could have walked like this forever; especially with Hettie scampering ahead like a puppy with four tails. We didn't speak much just enjoyed the vast expanse of sand and the commanding and somewhat choppy green-blue sea; and being together. How could I not treasure this memory forever.

When we decided we'd gone far enough we turned round to head back to our chosen dune for lunch. 'We'll never find it.' I said.

'I'm good at finding.'

'Are you?'

He stopped and brushed my lips with his. I could taste the salt on his mouth and it filled me with longing. 'I found you again. I knew I would.'

He carried on then purposefully looking ahead and I couldn't help stealing the odd glance at his face noting the passion there and I realised I had never experienced such feelings before. This was ideal. *We* were ideal; my thoughts crystallized - I had to take my chances with Charlie.

There weren't many people around and he stopped and told me to put my hands over my eyes and not to peep. On my life I must not peep. I stood there for what seemed ages and then he said, 'You can open them now.'

He's drawn a large heart in the sand near the water's edge with an arrow through it. Inside the heart he'd written a D and a C. He took my hand and stepping carefully not to spoil his artwork we both stood as close as possible to where the arrow went through the heart. He kissed me gently and lovingly and when he stopped I was aware of an older couple watching us.

Then he did the most amazing thing. Charlie got down on one knee and with a dazzling smile and adoring eyes said, 'Will you marry me, Dan?' Sometimes he called me Dan. 'One day I'm going to make you so proud of me.'

For a few seconds I gazed at his gorgeous face before dropping to my knees. I cupped his face with my hands and kissed him whispering, 'I'm already proud of you and I will marry you.'

The old couple were still watching. I quickly stood up and took my camera out of my pocket. I went over to them and offered it to the woman because she was smiling. 'Will you take a picture of us please?'

She was more than happy to oblige and as I stepped back into the heart Charlie and I hugged each other and a complete stranger took a photograph of us. Charlie then scooped me up into his arms and whirled me round and round. I felt dizzy with joy and we both laughed relentlessly with the stupidity of our actions until he set me down again. The amused couple handed back the camera and we all went on our way but I was so pleased because I knew that Hettie had been in the frame as well.

As we walked back to our dune I said, 'I wonder

what will happen to our heart.'

'It will be pulled into the sea.' He stole a look at me and I caught an earnest expression. 'I like the thought of that because the sea goes on and on forever just like you and me.'

'You are an idealist. The most romantic person I've ever known.'

He squeezed me tightly. 'I've got news for you; I've never been romantic in my life until now. If you asked anyone they'd agree. But you bring out something so totally different in me; you always have.'

'That's a lovely thing to say. Thank you.'

'No need. Thank *you.*'

It took us a while to return to our dune but just as Charlie had said he found it easily enough and we were ravenous. We greedily ate our lunch and drank one of the bottles of wine and Hettie lapped her water and enjoyed a few titbits; then we lay back on the blanket huddled together with Hettie by Charlie's side.

I was sleepy but aware of Charlie touching me; tender caresses that felt wickedly wonderful. To my surprise he removed his jeans and underpants and then started to remove mine. 'We can't.' I said weakly.

'Yes, we can. Nobody's around.' He yanked my jeans down and a little more gently removed my knickers.

'But the sand - it'll get inside me.'

'No it won't.' Quite powerfully he pulled me on top of him so that I straddled him and could see over the dune and I was grateful that there was no-one around. As he carefully repositioned me and pushed himself inside me he said lustfully, '*I want you.*'

We had this rhythm, Charlie and I, so maybe our

bodies were meant to fit together as they did. It did feel salaciously wanton having sex on the beach like this but at the same time it was the most natural thing in the world for us to do.

Much later I took photographs of Charlie with Hettie; the sea in the background and he did the same with me. Then we drank the second bottle of wine as the sun began to set on the horizon. By this time the sky was licked with a myriad of oranges and reds and really quite majestic in its splendour. I finished the film in the camera and hoped that I had captured forever such colours because it would be paramount in how I would remember this most wonderful day.

On the way home Charlie said, 'I want to get married soon.' Taking his eyes off the road he looked at me. 'You haven't changed your mind?'

I reached over and kissed his cheek. 'No.'

'We could go to Shire Hall tomorrow.'

I was amazed at his impatience. 'When are you thinking of getting married?'

'As soon as possible.' He caught his breath as though he'd blundered. 'Unless you want one of those does?'

I laughed. 'I most certainly do not want one of those does.'

He patted my hand in relief. 'Phew. Neither do I.'

'So when exactly are you thinking of?'

He smiled and stole another look at me. 'Tomorrow?'

'You really are impossible.'

'Let's go and see how long it takes.'

I could live with that. 'Yes.'

'Tell you what, tomorrow come to the stud and I can show you the work we do then we could go to Shire Hall.'

'But it would have to be before they close.'

'Lunchtime; I can take the afternoon off. I'll catch up the following day. Dad won't mind.' Charlie added, 'And how about us paying them a visit on the way home?'

'Your parents?' I felt panic-stricken.

'I'd love you to meet mum and tell them our plans.'

'Your mum might be horrified.'

He glanced at me and shook his head. 'She'll love you.'

I hoped so.

Their house was outstanding. With the September nights drawing in it was getting quite dark when we arrived back in Cambridge but I could still see that the garden alone was a work of art with its clever paving and exotically planted borders. Inside this lovingly restored cream plastered and oak timbered late nineteenth-century house there was a wealth of photographs on well polished tables; landscape watercolours on the walls and well chosen traditional furniture adorning every room. I suddenly got a measure of Charlie's refined tastes. He'd been brought up to appreciate care and attention; this was so different from anything I'd ever experienced in my life; apart from my late-father that is.

Charlie's mum was called Winnie and she was delightful. She had Charlie's nose and was slight in her build and an attractive woman; about forty-five, I would say. Angelica's age, and yet Winnie was very different

Chrissa Mills

from Angelica; Charlie was absolutely right because she welcomed me warmly and scurried off to make coffee. When she returned with a tray laden with sandwiches and slices of Dundee cake I realised how hungry I was. Charlie and I glanced at each other with a sneaky smile as we tucked in once more to sandwiches.

'We're getting married.' Charlie said between mouthfuls of Dundee cake.

I could see Winnie gulp and Ivor looked at me in surprise.

'A bit sudden,' he said.

I lowered my eyes shamefully. Did they think I was snaffling their baby? Was I?

Charlie said, 'If I don't marry Diana the rest of my life will be pointless.'

Ivor blinked and reached over to squeeze his son's shoulder. 'Strong words, boy.'

Winnie faced me. 'What about you, Diana?'

This was where I always ran away; a difficult question. I decided to tell the truth. 'From the first time I saw Charlie I fell for him; completely.'

'But you're older and wiser.'

Charlie heaved a sigh of exasperation at his mother's words and she hastily added, 'What I mean is: don't hurt him.'

I caught my breath. 'I won't, ever.'

Charlie rose from his chair and came over and sat beside me. He squeezed my hand and it made me feel secure in his love. He said, 'I was brought up with real love.' He looked at his parents, 'And that's what this is - and I've done all the chasing. So, please, we'd like your blessing.'

220

Winnie looked at her husband; they both smiled; they knew they had no choice and said in unison. 'You have it, Charlie.'

He squeezed my hand again and then asked his father in a manner I so admired. 'May I have tomorrow afternoon off? I'll make the time up, promise.'

Ivor laughed; a real throaty laugh. 'I sometimes wonder who works for whom in our business.'

Charlie was quick. 'I work for you, dad.'

'Hmmm.' Ivor winked at me. 'May I ask why?'

Charlie answered. 'We're going to Shire Hall to book a date. We want the least possible palaver. You two can be there though.'

'But I was planning to wear a hat at your wedding?' Winnie said.

'You can. I have no problem with that.'

She looked at me. 'What about you? Don't you want a proper do?'

'No. I just want Charlie.'

I knew I'd said exactly the right words as soon as they left my mouth. Ivor and Winnie nodded wisely and I was overwhelmed with their generosity of spirit.

Believe it or not it was only on our drive back to my flat that I thought about Sean. Guilt ran through me.

It was as though Charlie could read my mind. 'When are you going to tell him?'

'Tomorrow; first thing.'

'Promise?'

'I promise.'

Charlie breathed a sigh of relief.

Angry Red

We fell into bed almost as soon as we got home. It was a mixture of euphoria and exhaustion; even Hettie went straight to her bed. But our bliss was soon to change dramatically with an incessant ringing of the front door bell.

I sat up with a jolt. 'Who on earth is that?' But I knew immediately who it was. Like lightning I grabbed a robe and ran a hand through my dishevelled hair and the ringing continued. 'What time is it?'

Charlie looked at the bedside clock. 'Ten past eleven. Let me see who it is.'

I looked at him sternly. 'Stay there. Please.'

I saw a flicker of anger cross his face but I had to go. I closed the bedroom door and moved swiftly to the front door. I opened it and an enraged Sean stood before me with a tearful Mel behind him.

Sean barged past me and she followed. I stood there with my mouth open. 'Sean…' I muttered.

'Yes,' he said sarcastically. 'Sean. You remember who I am then? Your *fiancé?*'

I caught my breath and my heart felt as though it couldn't beat any faster. With his finger pointing at me he started. 'Or perhaps you've conveniently forgotten? Like all the other things you've forgotten and lied about.'

I looked from him to Mel who was catching sobs in the back of her throat. Hettie appeared and then disappeared when she saw Mel. 'I'm sorry, Sean. I was going to speak to you tomorrow.'

'Oh, I'm sure you were. And how's Camilla?' He tapped the side of his head, 'But no, there was no

Camilla this weekend, was there? Funny that. I just happened to ring on the way to the airport and who should answer the phone but Doctor Rachel and she soon put me right about you.'

'I can explain…'

'I think Mel's the one who's done the explaining. Straight away she latched on to the fact. Charlie boy would not leave his dog here unless it was beneficial to him. So tell me, it's boys in short trousers now, is it?'

Before I had time to answer I watched Mel pick up Charlie's sweater thrown over the back of the sofa. She caught another sob and looked at me with absolute loathing in her eyes. 'You *have* stolen him from me.'

I gasped in protest but I didn't need to put right her monumental exaggeration because Charlie appeared. He was fully dressed and looked very angry.

Flashes of red and silvery white now appeared before my eyes because Sean cried out in disgust and lunged forward with his fist about to smash into Charlie's face. Without effort Charlie blocked him; holding his arm so that Sean couldn't move. I realised how strong he was. Sean couldn't move but Mel could and she came at Charlie from the other side and scratched his face pulling at the skin from just below his eye to his mouth in a deliberate and spiteful way. I was immediately reminded of Natasha. Charlie let go of Sean's arm and put his hand to his bleeding face and Sean took the opportunity to smack his other cheek as hard as he could. I was screaming at them to stop and now trying to drag Sean away.

Charlie just took control. He pushed Sean hard so that he staggered backwards and then faced Mel holding out his hand bloody from his face. He said calmly, 'Still using your fingernails.'

'You deserve it! You think you can treat me like shit and get away with it?' Mel was screeching like a spoiled brat and she pointed at me. 'She's my dad's fiancé! What on earth do you see in an older woman like her?'

Charlie laughed and looked at Mel in amazement. 'Dan's only a few years older than you and her age has *nothing* to do with it.'

Sean was distraught. 'How could you behave like this, Diana? You meant everything to me. I loved you with all of my heart and trusted you. Is this how you repay me? Shack up with my daughter's boyfriend. You absolutely *disgust* me.'

Charlie was beside me now; one arm wrapped tightly around me. 'I am not your daughter's boyfriend and never really have been. She's the liar around here. I've never come close to loving her.'

Mel screamed at him, 'You said you loved me loads of times!'

I could feel Charlie's body tighten as he fought to control his anger. Still clinging on to him I looked at Sean. I took a deep breath to calm myself before saying, 'I'm sorry. I never wanted all this but my feelings for Charlie are different, Sean. Always have been.'

Sean stared at me as though stumped for words. He then said pitifully, 'He's too young for you.'

'No!' Charlie hit back. 'It's you who's too old for her. She's only twenty-eight for God's sake.'

Sean braced himself. 'So that's that.' He indicated at Charlie with disgust but looked at me. 'We go down the pan because of some kid who chops down trees for a living?'

'*Yes.*' Charlie said. 'This kid who chops down trees for a living loves Diana and she loves me.'

Mel caught another sob and headed towards the door. Hettie was now cowering beside the sofa; obviously frightened but intrigued by what was going on and as Mel passed she deliberately kicked her. Hettie scuttled off whimpering and Charlie moved like a thunderbolt, grabbing one of Mel's arms. He then smacked her round the face. I could see the shock of his actions in Mel's eyes. 'You are one nasty bitch, Mel Jackson. Don't you dare treat my dog like that *ever.*'

Sean did nothing. I think he too was shocked by what Mel had done. She looked at her father in little-girl fashion; quite subdued now. 'Daddy, are you going to let him do that to me?'

Sean closed his eyes as though in agony before walking forward and taking his daughter's hand brusquely. 'Come on, time for us to go.' He pulled her towards the front door and they left slamming it firmly behind them.

I looked at the bleeding welt on one side of Charlie's face and the bruise on the other and held out my arms to him. He moved into them and we held each other tightly hardly able to fathom what had just happened.

Later, as I bathed the deep scratch down the left side of Charlie's face I asked if Mel had ever scratched him before.

'Not me, but I've seen her lash out at other people. She's got a screw loose.'

'I think she's just spoiled rotten by her father.'

I applied antiseptic to the wound and kissed his mouth. 'You'll mend. Can't have you not looking your best at our wedding.'

Charlie looked at me closely. 'Does what happened affect your job with Sean?'

I took a deep breath. 'Not really.'

'I never wanted to mess up your life.'

'You haven't.'

He kissed me and tasting of antiseptic whispered, 'I'll never let you down.'

I believed him.

Black

Ivor picked Charlie up at seven the following morning and I decided to take Hettie to the vet's to get her checked out. Charlie and I were reasonably sure that nothing serious had occurred but the kick was nasty. On the way to the vet's I posted off the roll of film I'd taken the previous day knowing it would return within ten days. I couldn't wait to see what the photographs looked like.

I was meeting Charlie at two o'clock and had no intention of going to the office. My head was still buzzing with Sean and Mel's behaviour the night before; some space was needed now. When I returned from the vet's, Hettie having been given the all-clear, I tried to ring Camilla and with no surprise got the answer machine. I left a message saying I urgently needed to talk to her and I sent my love. Surely Rachel wouldn't block me again. I hoped not. I missed my friend so much.

I was actually preparing to leave the flat to go and meet Charlie when the front door bell went. I felt irritated because I didn't want to be late so I opened it impatiently. Sean stood before me and he didn't look too happy. This was all I needed.

'Sean.'

'Can I come in?' He then proceeded to enter.

'Actually, I'm just going out and I'm late as it is.'

'It's important; something you need to know.'

I closed the front door and looked at Sean who I have to say appeared very haggard and drawn and I felt an enormous stab of guilt for what I'd put him through.

He began. 'I think you ought to know that Charlie Stanford likes nice things in life.' He laughed sarcastically, 'In case you hadn't already realised.'

I frowned. 'What's that supposed to mean?'

'It means, Diana, that you can provide those nice things.'

Anger overwhelmed me and I took a deep breath. 'What are you talking about?'

'Just something Mel said about him and you.'

'What exactly?'

'He's after your money; you should be aware.'

I laughed. 'He knows nothing about my so called money and I really don't see how this is any of your business anymore.' I wanted him to leave and went to open the door again but he grabbed my arm.

'Don't make an idiot of yourself. Of course he knows about your money. I keep telling you, he's no-good.'

'I don't believe a word of what you're saying. You're just trying to make trouble.'

'Mel told me.'

'Told you what?'

'Told me that he called you that rich widow from Brooklands Avenue!'

There was a pause and to say I was flabbergasted was an understatement. I blurted out, 'Charlie never said that.'

'Why would Mel lie?'

Because she lies about everything; Charlie had told me he didn't know I was widowed. 'When? When exactly did he say that?'

Sean shrugged. 'I didn't ask but it must have been when they were living together in his house. For God's sake, let the scales fall from your eyes. He's a kid and he thinks he's on to a good thing. Face facts, it won't last; it can't last. When he's in his late twenties you'll be pushing forty! And he'll probably have gone through most of your money like frigging wildfire.'

At this point I covered my ears with my hands. 'Go now, please. I really don't want to hear anymore of this.'

'The truth, you mean?' He came close to me and lifted my chin with one hand. 'It hurts, doesn't it? The truth often does. When I learned the truth about you it hurt me too.' Sean dropped his hand away from my face and went out of the door. I stared at that door for several seconds after he'd gone hardly able to believe what had just been said.

I was really late now; it was already two o'clock. I drove as fast as I could when all I really wanted to do was cry. Sean's words had certainly hit the spot and I racked my brain to think if there could possibly be any truth in them. I would ask Charlie; straight away. It didn't make sense; none of it did. Why would he lie to me; that rich widow from Brooklands Avenue didn't sound like Charlie speak. And I planned to tell him everything about my inheritance eventually, probably after we were married but I was sure he knew nothing now. Then I remembered something and it hit me like a meteor. All those years ago; he'd bought the hairdressing magazine with my picture on the cover. Inside the magazine were more pictures of Camilla doing my hair and, I racked my brain again, what did it say about me? Did it talk about me being a successful business woman as Camilla had described me at the time? Did the article say I was widowed and wealthy? I simply could not remember.

I followed Charlie's instructions on how to find the stud where he and his father were working. As I drove through the enormous gates at the entrance I could see what looked like a brand new white van parked on a concrete area. On the side it said Stanford Landscape Gardeners. A bit different from the battered old van they'd driven when they did my garden.

I carried on driving as Charlie had instructed me to do and I could see Ivor ahead. There was a belt of Leylandi trees; I noticed that about half had been chopped down to, say, ten feet high. Ivor was looking up. That's when I saw Charlie in all his gear; a bright red and green harness wrapped tightly around him and he was wearing thick protective gloves. The harness appeared to be secured on to the adjacent uncut tree and Charlie had a chainsaw in his hand. He saw me immediately and beamed with pleasure. I parked close by and with a heavy heart walked over to Ivor.

Charlie shouted out, 'What kept you? You're late!'

'I know,' I called back. 'I got held up. Tell you about it later.'

Charlie nodded; I swear he noticed that I was upset.

Even from a distance his face showed disquiet; I loved him all the more for it. How could a person who picks up vibes from such a distance be an out and out gold-digger as Sean had implied?

He started the chainsaw up again and branches began to fall to the ground. It was obviously Ivor's job to drag them away into the huge pile close by.

Ivor said, 'He thought he might as well do a bit more when you weren't here at two. Won't take long.'

I watched Charlie noting his adeptness; how he almost abseiled around the tree. 'Looks pretty dangerous to me.' I said anxiously and I was aware that my beloved young man was performing; showing me his art.

'It is if you don't know what you're doing. Charlie does and he enjoys it and I have to say it pays really well.' He smiled and nudged me. 'For all the nice things in life that he likes.'

I looked at Ivor and could hear my pathetic thin voice ask, 'He does, does he?'

Ivor glanced at me with the flicker of a frown on his forehead. 'You know he does.'

'Of course,' I muttered.

Ivor was now watching Charlie and I looked at the admiration on his face. I thought back to last night at their house in Grantchester. They were thoroughly nice people; how could they have possibly produced a con-man?

He glanced at me. 'Bit of a tussle last night?'

I stared at Ivor. 'Last night?'

'Charlie's face. Lucky escape he had from her, I must say.'

I remembered then, Charlie's face. It wasn't so visible

down here with him way up in the tree but how could I have forgotten so easily? I wondered what exactly Charlie had told his father; whether he'd mentioned Sean; my relationship with Sean. It was all such a mess and I stumbled over my words, '….She's very spiteful; …Mel.'

'You can say that again. How's Hettie? I hear she kicked her.'

'Hettie's fine. I got her checked out. She's absolutely fine.' My voice became choked with emotion. 'I love her so much.'

Ivor smiled and his attention went back to his beloved son. I took a deep breath; I so wanted Charlie to come down from the tree and comfort me.

I looked at Ivor; he was such a decent man. I appraised him; and that was the point when his expression changed. I continued to stare, watching and studying and because of my train of thought it took several seconds before I registered the sheer alarm in Ivor's eyes.

'Oh, my God!' he said in a ghastly low voice. Then he shouted out, bellowed even, 'Throw out the chainsaw, Charlie! Quick! Just do it!'

My eyes moved to Charlie and I couldn't see anything untoward and he seemed confused; he looked at his father.

'Do it!' Ivor roared. 'The bloody harness is giving way!' Ivor roared even louder. 'For Christ sake hold on!' He moved closer to the tree his body rigid with fear and his fists clenched on either side of his stocky frame.

I was helpless; all I could do was look up at the man I loved; in fact loved with every fibre of my body and it was then that I saw it; the harness webbing secured to the next tree slithering away like a treacherous snake.

Charlie threw out the chainsaw and appeared to be holding on tightly quite secure within the remaining branches of the tree. I was standing next to Ivor but don't remember moving there because my body was leaden with fear. I saw the utter confusion on Charlie's face; he couldn't see the harness loosening because it was behind him but the chainsaw plummeted to the ground and I felt enormous relief. That thing was lethal.

'Hold on, Charlie!'

Ivor's fists were beating either side of his thighs now as he swore and hissed beneath his breath, 'That fucking harness has snapped!' He shouted out once more, 'Don't let go of that branch, boy, and for Christ sake get a firm foothold!' Ivor's voice was breaking with the sort of emotion you never want to hear and I was terrified.

'Shit!' Charlie uttered as his foot slipped. 'Oh, *bloody shit!'* There was a blood curdling tremor in his voice; my big and so strong Charlie seemed chillingly vulnerable and for the first time in our relationship I knew he was scared stiff and I wanted to claw my way up the tree and grab him as a mother might. I felt myself lurching forward and remember Ivor pulling me back as we both watched as Charlie struggled to get a grip and a firm foothold - and he did! He steadied himself and Ivor's wretched gasps signalled relief and my fingernails tore at my face as I bit down hard on my bottom lip tasting blood.

'Thank God.' Ivor rasped at me.

'That's my boy!' He shouted more calmly now. 'Just keep hold. Just keep hold!'

Ivor hissed at me. 'Look at that fucking harness.'

He bawled out to Charlie. 'Is there anyway you can unclip the harness?'

Suddenly the harness webbing whipped away from the other tree like lightning and thrashed against the branches of Charlie's tree; then it stopped abruptly as it was caught within the dense foliage. Once more we breathed a sigh of relief.

Charlie was fumbling with his harness and cursing, really cursing and it was harrowing to listen to his profanities. He finally unleashed it and tried to shake it off but in doing so lost his foothold and was hanging on by his hands while his feet were flailing around as he desperately tried to secure another foothold. With the harness half-on and half-off he groaned as the gloves he was wearing lost their grip and he started to fall but he tenuously caught hold again and all the while his face was showing the sheer terror he was feeling. Ivor and I held our breath as Charlie gained another secure foothold.

'Get rid of the gloves! …Steady now!'

Almost angrily Charlie pulled off his gloves and then tried to shrug off the harness.

'You're doing great, boy, you'll climb down that tree easy!'

Charlie was now free of the harness! It was going to be all right. Then catastrophe! It was as though my sweet darling boy lost his nerve and didn't know what to do with his feet nor his hands and he just slipped. We screamed and shrieked but could only watch as he plummeted downwards battered and tossed about by the lower branches of the Leylandi tree. I could see the horror in his eyes as he pitifully tried to claw hold of anything to stop his fall. I felt sick; I thought I was going to be sick.

Charlie cried out in the most appalling way as one of the branches struck his stomach and he didn't struggle anymore after that and eventually landed in a crumpled heap at the bottom. We raced towards him.

'Charlie!' I knelt beside him; his eyes were open and he was still alive. Relief overwhelmed me.

'We need an ambulance.' Ivor said. 'There's a house further up. We need to use their phone.'

'You go! You know where it is. Here…' I gave him the keys, 'take my car.'

'Yes - yes. I'll be as quick as I can.'

Charlie's eyes were steadfastly on my face and I didn't know what to do because I hardly dare touch him. He was lying on his back but his legs were twisted sideways and one arm was beneath him. 'It's going to be all right; your dad's gone for help. Just hang on, my darling, I promise you, it's going to be all right.'

Then he groaned; a wounded groan and his eyes flickered. He struggled to speak and in the end just whispered, '…Dan.'

I put my face as close as I dare to his. 'I'm here, Charlie. I'll always be here.'

His eyes flickered again and I was so afraid. 'Don't die on me, Charlie! *Don't!*'

But my heart lurched as I watched his eyes lose their life; the wondrous light that had captivated me from day one faded and they simply became blank in a way that I remembered when Ben died; but I clung on; he wasn't gone; he couldn't be. I crouched there staring at his eyes willing him back even though he didn't see me anymore and I wondered what in God's name I could do. It was then that I placed my mouth on his and breathed into it; if I could have given him my life's breath I would have done so. But there was no response so I doggedly kept going breathing and breathing into Charlie's warm mouth tasting the blood from my own where I had bitten down hard on it earlier and I continued to do this for what seemed an eternity before Ivor returned. He tried to pull me away but I clung on as though if I let go Charlie really would die. 'The ambulance is on its way.' Ivor said and I released my mouth from Charlie's. I was really weeping now, sobbing uncontrollably and I watched as the colour drained from Ivor's face and he fell to the ground and put his ear to his son's chest and then frantically felt for his pulse. *'No!'* He keened and then even more pitifully said, *'No,* this can't be happening.' He shook Charlie's shoulders. 'I can't lose you, son, I can't lose you!'

We both sat there wailing and talking to Charlie; urging him to be alive. Both of us refused to believe that he was not.

Eventually the ambulance arrived with blaring lights and an ear deafening siren. Two men jumped out and ran towards us. Don't ask me what they looked like; I'd never remember in a hundred years but they knelt beside Charlie and did all the necessary procedures that you would expect of experienced ambulance men - and then they shook their heads in what can only be assumed as commiseration and sympathy. Gently they closed his eyes and respectfully placed him on a stretcher; he was totally lifeless.

'Can I come with you?' I begged. It was only at this point that I noticed other people milling around. Inquisitive eyes were on us and on my darling Charlie. I wanted to scream at them to stop staring and go away.

The ambulance men saw my distress. One of them said, 'You can, love, of course.'

Ivor was ashen. 'Are you coming?' I asked him.

'Perhaps I should follow in your car?'

'…Yes.'

So I sat in the back of the ambulance next to the stretcher as one of the ambulance men sat opposite me.Charlie lay there sleeping and I held his hand. His body was straighter now and I stroked his face; I stroked where Mel had scratched him and apart from that scratch and the bruise from Sean's smack there was not another mark on his face. I kissed his warm soft lips; lips that had caressed every single zone of my body and I whispered endearments in both of his ears. The ambulance man just watched; he didn't say a word.

'I love you, Charlie,' I kept saying over and over again. 'I'll love you forever.'

Mourning Grey

At about five-thirty Ivor and I left Charlie in the Chapel of Rest at Addenbrookes hospital. He'd died from multiple internal injuries and we were numb with grief and mentally exhausted but somehow still managed to speak about funeral directors; visiting Shire Hall to register his death, and then about Winnie. She didn't know that her son had died that afternoon because Ivor had been unable to get through to her on the telephone. It was constantly engaged. Ivor said that she had an unintentional habit of leaving the phone off the hook and he was both anxious to tell her the terrible news and dreading going home to do so.

When we climbed into my car and I was about to take him home, he asked me, 'Do you want to come in with me?'

'I think you need to be on your own with Winnie and besides I have to get back to Hettie. Poor baby, she's been locked up in that flat for hours.'

I was driving and Ivor touched my arm. 'You shouldn't be on your own, you know, not at a time like this. You need your family.'

'I'll be all right,' I said feebly but I could feel sobs bubbling up again in my throat as I realised there was no-one I could turn to, except Camilla and I could never get through to her.

Ivor said softly. 'He really loved you. He was cock-a-hoop that you'd agreed to marry him and when you didn't arrive at two o'clock he was peering around and worried sick that you might have lost your way.'

I blurted out, 'And if I hadn't been late he wouldn't be dead!' The tears were falling prolifically again now.

'Diana!' Ivor put a firm hand on my shoulder. 'No, no! That's not true. That harness could have snapped at anytime and in no way is it your fault. You must never think that.'

'But I do think it! My timing is always so bloody out but never like this before. I'll never forgive myself, *not ever.*'

Ivor gave a huge sigh. 'You will, my dear.' He handed me his handkerchief and I rubbed it against my eyes. 'Because Charlie would never have wanted you to blame yourself for this. He knew the risks he was taking.'

'Well I hope you're going to sue that blasted firm who makes those harnesses!'

Ivor made a rude noise in the back of his throat. 'And what good will that do? It certainly won't bring Charlie back.'

'Oh, Ivor, what am I going to do without him?'

'The same as me and Winnie, somehow we'll survive.'

I shuddered as another sob escaped me. 'I really don't see how. This is just too terrible for words.'

Ivor didn't answer. There was no answer.

I rang Camilla and Rachel answered the phone. I begged her to let me speak to Camilla but the cow wouldn't listen to a word. When I said that I'd just lost Charlie, that he'd died, she remained implacable. Was she made of stone?

So I took Hettie for a walk but I can't remember where. On our return I fed the sweet love and then took to my bed. I left the bedroom door open and Hettie crept in as I knew she would. She jumped up on to the bed, sniffed around; I'm sure it was because of Charlie's scent; then she curled up beside me. It was strangely comforting as I cried myself to sleep.

I don't know how I got through the next few days. I continually rang Camilla and either left a message on the answer machine or spoke to a very rude Rachel. Stop pestering us, she told me. In the end I did.

As for my mother, I simply couldn't face her.

Natasha. She was my daughter; she'd somehow give

me the comfort I craved so I went to see her after school even though I was an absolute wreck.

I used my key and it occurred to me that my status in this house had changed dramatically by my association with Charlie. Don't ask me why I felt like that; I just did. I walked through to the sitting room where I expected to find Natasha in front of the television doing her homework and I was right. She briefly raised her head to me but didn't speak just carried on with her homework.

I moved forward and sunk on to my hands and knees crawling across the carpet towards her desperate to take her into my arms for comfort. 'How are you, darling? I've missed you.'

She raised her eyes to mine again and said sulkily, 'Where've you been?' I saw the flicker of caring as she added. 'Have you been crying?'

I could feel more sobs welling up and struggled to suppress them. 'Yes. I've lost somebody I loved very much.'

'Who?' Her eyes were questioning but in a cold way.

'Do you remember Charlie? He did our garden and trod on Jakie?'

Natasha screwed her face up wrinkling her young brow. 'The one I smacked?'

I swallowed hard. Memories; even ones like that hurt so much. 'Yes, the one you smacked.'

'Where's he gone?'

I said simply, 'He died. He fell from a very tall tree and - died.' Tears were streaming down my face now.

She studied me; even putting her pencil in her mouth. 'Are you very very sad?' She asked.

'Yes, very sad.'

'I'm sad sometimes.' She sniffed. 'Aunt Jelly makes me better.'

I sat back on my heels cut to the quick. Was this my daughter's way of saying; don't expect any sympathy from me? 'You love Aunt Jelly very much.' I said pathetically.

Natasha's face looked blank as though she didn't understand love, only sadness. She carried on with the homework and didn't answer.

'It's you,' Aunt Jelly said and I turned to see her standing in the doorway. 'So you remember where we live?'

I stood up and wiped away my tears with the tips of my fingers.

She looked at me curiously. 'What's the matter?'

'Someone has died who I loved very much.' And before either of us had a chance to say anything my daughter stood up and stomped out of the room. Her departing words were. 'Horrid Charlie - who cares about him.'

Aunt Jelly watched my daughter's behaviour with a smirk on her face. 'If you came here for sympathy you'll not be getting any from Natasha.' She added, 'You neglect your daughter for what? Sex?' She scoffed, 'Natasha and I; we know what you're like.'

My heart was breaking. I should not have come. I walked out of the sitting room towards the front door. As I opened it to leave Natasha, apparently sitting on the stairs, said, 'I think you're horrid too.'

I faced her knowing that this wasn't just about neglect. Aunt Jelly had actively encouraged me to stay away on numerous occasions. 'Why?'

She pinched her mouth together. 'Because Aunt Jelly says so.'

I wanted so much to find the right words. 'Whatever Aunt Jelly says I'll always love you, Natasha. Please remember that.'

And then I simply closed the front door behind me.

When Sean found out about Charlie; it was in the Cambridge Evening News and the Newmarket Journal, he rang me. I couldn't speak to him. I just put the phone down. After myself I blamed him for Charlie's death; he was the one who'd held me up.

The only people I kept in constant touch with were Ivor and Winnie. In hindsight it was shared pain but they looked after me so well; fed me and consoled me when there was no-one else in the world to do so.

Charlie was cremated. Apparently he had always said that was his preferred choice. Cambridge Crematorium was packed! I walked with Ivor and Winnie behind his coffin, on which I'd placed one hundred red roses, into a sea of young and older faces. Ivor and Winnie had asked people to wear a blue ribbon in honour of Charlie's love of Chelsea football club. Nearly everybody had obliged. I had mine tied in my hair.

It was only as we gathered outside after the service that I noticed Sean and Mel. I would have liked to run away but Sean stopped me in my tracks. Mel didn't come near and I was glad. She'd lied to Sean; hadn't she?

'Diana, I never wanted this, you must know that.'

'I don't know anything, Sean. I don't even want to think about it.'

'I'm just so sorry for the extra pain I've caused you and if there is anything; *anything* at all that I can do to make some sort of amends I will.'

It occurred to me then that there was something he could do for me; something that I hadn't the strength for.

'Anything?' I asked.

'Yes, anything.'

'Go and see Camilla. I've tried and tried to get through to her on the phone and that ghastly Rachel won't let me speak to her and won't pass on messages. Something's really wrong. God knows how you'll do it, Sean, but find some way of seeing her and please tell her I need her *so much*. Will you do that for me?'

He smiled in a slightly cynical way. 'Of course.'

'Promise?'

'I promise.'

'Soon?'

'Now, if you like.'

I nodded. 'I like.'

He went back to his daughter and they both left shortly afterwards. I noticed that Mel had a tear-stained face. I didn't. My tears had all been shed.

Grey Blue

The doorbell rang. Hettie started to bark; I looked at the time, eight-fifteen. I went to the door and opened it and a very weary Camilla simply fell into my arms and the tears I thought I'd completely shed fell from my eyes once more like rain. 'Camilla! It can't be! Thank God. Oh, Camilla, you don't know how glad I am to see you.'

She said nothing, just clung to me like there was no tomorrow. I looked through my tears at Sean who was standing behind us next to a large suitcase. He raised his hand to leave but I stopped him. With Camilla still clinging to me I said, 'How did you do it?'

He guffawed. 'With great difficulty! In the end I waited 'til the grisly witchdoctor went out on some appointment or other and then banged on the door until Camilla eventually answered it.'

I held Camilla away from me slightly and looked at her wretched face and what seemed like a thousand tiny lines interwoven within its contours. 'What's happened to you?' I asked.

'I think I'm a wreck,' she whimpered. 'But I'm so glad you sent Sean for me. I wanted so much to get out of that place but I've never had the strength until now.'

'What on earth did she do to you?'

Sean moved forward and placed Camilla's suitcase inside the front door. Then he held up his hand. 'I really must go. I'll speak to you later.'

I nodded and he left. I closed the front door and Camilla and I went over to the sofa and sat down. I repeated, 'What on earth did she do to you?'

Camilla shook her head. 'Nothing that I can explain; at least, I don't think so. She just wormed her way into my head and controlled me. I can't operate anymore; I've lost all of my clients and I can't do a bloody thing.' She quickly put both hands to her mouth and said apologetically, 'Rachel looks after me in her way, she pays for everything and all that, but she says I've had a breakdown, and yet whenever I try to rally myself she tells me I need more time to recover. I'm on about four different pills every day and most of the time I feel like a zombie.'

'I've rung a hundred times. So why would she never let me speak to you?'

'You're negative energy; bad for me.' Camilla looked upwards pathetically, 'And I allowed myself to believe her. How daft am I.'

'Not daft. She's brainwashed you.'

She covered her face with her hands then raked them through her unwashed hair. 'I know it all sounds stupid and pathetic but when Sean barged his way in and said you needed me; that you'd lost Charlie and was devastated I had a reason to leave.' She reached out and took my hands in hers. 'I'm so sorry for your loss, Diana. I had no idea you loved him so much.'

'Who told you that?'

'Sean, of course.'

I took a deep breath. 'I'm grateful to him then.'

Camilla rested her head against my shoulder. 'What if she comes after me?'

I pictured in my mind Rachel coming here and demanding that Camilla went back with her. Somehow I knew she wouldn't. 'She'll get the same treatment she gave me.'

'But she's very clever.'

'I know. But she's also very wicked.'

'No, no, not wicked. She really does mean well. She does an awful lot of good deeds.'

'Awful being the operative word!' I studied my friend. 'Camilla, you're not still in love with her?'

She blinked. 'How can you love someone who imprisons you?'

'Precisely.' I took a deep breath and made an attempt to smile; I hadn't done that in a while. 'Shall we have a drink?'

'Alcohol?' Camilla looked amazed.

'Just a glass of wine.'

'But I'm not allowed, not with my medication.'

'Stop the medication then. Come on; start to live in the real world again.' I stood up and went off to fetch two glasses of wine. As I poured them in the kitchen I realised that although the pain of Charlie's death was in no way diminished it was going to be a whole lot easier to bear with Camilla by my side because I had a reason to live; I had to pull her together again.

We shared my bed that night. Camilla was frightened to be on her own. I had changed the sheets that morning because hard as I tried I could no longer smell Charlie on them; even Hettie didn't bother to sniff them anymore. I made Camilla take a long luxurious bath and as I washed her hair I began to tell her the story of Charlie and me.

Finally she asked, 'Why did you never tell me you were madly in love with him?'

'I was ashamed.'

Through the soapsuds she remembered. 'That time; outside Annabel's; I could see he was crazy about you but I really did think you were just, well, flattered.'

I latched on to her words. 'You thought he was crazy about me?'

'The way he looked at you. The way he watched us drive away.' She took a deep breath. 'He was gorgeous, for a man, I'll give you that.'

Leaning on the side of the bath I could feel the tears well up again. 'I loved him with every fibre of my mind and body. I'm sure he felt the same way.'

Camilla grabbed my hands and squeezed them. 'Of course he did.'

I had to ask. 'That time, outside Annabel's; you did my hair for the cover and the article in Cut It magazine. Do you remember what was said about me?'

Camilla's eyes widened. 'What do you mean?'

'Did it say I was widowed? Did it say I was successful and rich?'

She shrugged. 'Can't remember. Probably; you are, aren't you?'

My heart plummeted. 'Yes, but Charlie never knew that, or rather I thought he didn't.'

She frowned. 'How can he not have known?'

'I just never told him. It was nearly six weeks ago when he turned up here for Hettie and he said he didn't even know I was widowed; nor that I worked with Mel's father.' I touched my forehead. 'And I just never got round to telling him the truth.'

Camilla was stumped for words. I could see she didn't know what to say and didn't want to say the wrong thing so I continued.

'Sean said he was just after my money. He said Mel told him Charlie called me that rich widow from Brooklands Avenue.'

Camilla took a deep positive breath. 'Don't believe a word of it! Sean's madly in love with you and insanely jealous. And I never liked that daughter of his. She's a spoiled bitch!'

'That's what Charlie said!' I grabbed one of Camilla's

hands. 'I love you. Thank you.'

'And *he* loved you.' She sighed. 'Don't be silly, Diana. Don't let gossip ruin what you had.'

'I won't.' …Positive words.

The following morning we both took Hettie for a walk. No way would Camilla stay in the flat on her own in case the witch, as we'd started to call Rachel, came knocking on the door. And during breakfast of tea and toast Camilla explained about herself; she reflected upon life with the *witch* as though trapped in an ever decreasing circle and every time she tried to escape something always knocked her back. She messed up clients' hair, or the new kid on the block produced trendier hairstyles, or she wore the wrong clothes, or she ate the wrong food or drank too much wine. Also her hair products stopped selling. She told me that Rachel gave away all her pretty colourful clothes to the women's refuge and when Camilla objected she called her selfish and opinionated and that her judgement in clothes was sadly in need of a makeover; she was much better suited to greys and browns. Eventually she lost all her confidence and clients cancelled appointments and never re-made them.

'Camilla, you are beautiful and very talented. Believe me. And please don't ever ignore me again.'

She grabbed my hands as though they secured her future. 'I won't! Not ever.'

I sighed and with my mind reeling from my dear friend's situation I rose out of my chair. 'I need to do something.' I went over to a small table near the front door and picked up Charlie's keys. I held them as though they were prized. 'I want to go to his house, check things out. He told me he had the cover picture from Cut It beside his bed.' I hung my head. I hoped Camilla understood. I looked at her. 'The rest of the magazine might be there too.'

Camilla walked towards me. 'Don't! That's not a good thing to do.'

'But I have to. If I'm disappointed, I'm disappointed.'

'Why put yourself through it.'

'Regardless of the results I need to know if Charlie knew the truth about my wealth. If he did I'll live with it; if he didn't, I can't tell you, I'll be so relieved.'

'Diana, believe me, it's best not to know.'

'No!'

Camilla raised herself and came towards me. 'Okay. I'm with you. All I ask is that you don't leave me behind.'

'You know I won't. You can stick to me like glue for as long as it takes.'

She took a deep breath and nodded, 'Thanks.'

Hettie wasn't too keen to be back at Charlie's cottage. I think there might have been too many memories of Mel. She kept close to my heels as I walked up the path and unlocked the front door. So did Camilla.

'What a pretty house!' She exclaimed.

'He was left it by his grandmother three years ago. Apparently she was a wise old bird.'

I unlocked the door and stepped inside immediately breathing in the smell of Charlie and nostalgia overwhelmed me and I wanted to run away and something told me to do just that. Camilla had been right; I could

248

end up with even more of a broken heart.

But doggedly I continued. Camilla was looking at photographs around the place. 'I'm just popping upstairs,' I said. 'Do you want to come?'

She smiled. 'I think I'm safe enough down here with Hettie.' She bent down and patted my beloved dog. 'Aren't we, Hettie?'

I was relieved and went up the stairs slowly dreading that Charlie had told me a lie; dreading the thought that maybe our whole relationship was a sham.

There were three bedrooms and a bathroom. I assumed that Charlie slept in the larger one with the double bed. I stood inside the doorway looking at the bed and imagining him in it with Mel. I shook my head to dispel such memories. I wondered which side he had slept. There were bedside chests on either side with drawers. I decided to opt for the right hand side and walked towards the three drawer chest. I opened the top drawer and inside was loose change, receipts, nail clippers, condoms and rubbishy bits. This had obviously been Charlie's side of the bed. I closed the top drawer and opened the middle one. This was stuffed with underpants and socks. I pulled out a pair of underpants and sniffed them. They smelled of Charlie. I wondered if Mel had washed them for him. Was his scent washing powder or cologne or a mixture of both? There was so much about Charlie that I hadn't had time to find out.

I closed the middle drawer and opened the third. This was full of documents; a driving licence and a passport. I picked them out; I'd keep them. But there was no magazine and certainly no picture of me. Perhaps he'd lied. I closed the drawer.

I walked round to the other side of the bed and opened the top drawer. It was empty as were the other two drawers. Mel had taken all her stuff with her.

I walked towards the door and glanced back one more time to get a feel of Charlie being in this room and that was when I noticed that the chests were on castors and slightly off the ground. I bobbed down and crawled back to the right hand chest pushing my hand beneath it. I withdrew what I'd been looking for. Within a plastic sleeve was the picture of me from the cover of Cut It. I couldn't help smiling because even I had to admit I looked great. Camilla was in the background with a tail comb in her hand. My smile widened because Charlie had taken the time to preserve this picture within a plastic sleeve. But that's all it was; just the front cover picture. I pushed my hand beneath the chest again but there was nothing there. I stood up and pulled the chest away from the wall and lo and behold the rest of the magazine was lodged behind. It was rolled up and ragged and obviously forgotten about. I picked it up and sat on the bed straightening it out.

My heart was beating rapidly now as I turned the pages until I came to the article about Camilla and me. I started to read and at the very beginning it described me as a Cambridge mother of six year-old Natasha and the memory came flooding back. Yes! That had been so important to me then. That was my most essential role; being the mother of Natasha. I knew she and Aunt Jelly would read this and I was making a point.

I read the whole article which described in detail how Camilla had coloured and re-styled my hair. It talked about Camilla's numerous and famous clients and the only thing it said about me was that I was her very best friend. Nothing! NOTHING about me being a rich widow; I whooped with joy!

Camilla came racing up the stairs, as did Hettie. She stood in the doorway and couldn't help beaming at my tears of relief. 'It just says I'm a Cambridge mother of six year-old Natasha and your very best friend! It doesn't say I'm a rich business woman. Oh, Camilla, Mel was lying! Charlie didn't know anymore than he told me, I'm sure of it now.'

Camilla sat beside me and hugged me. Then she looked at the article and I could see tears welling into her eyes. 'Was that person really me?' She added sadly. 'I was very different then.'

I squeezed her. 'And will be again.'

She looked at me. 'Do you really think so?'

'I know so.' I took a deep breath and stood up. 'Come on. I've got another visit to make before we go home.'

'Where's that?'

'Mel.'

Sean's house was in Bandon Road, Girton; a large Victorian semi and I knew she'd be there because she was such a lazy cow. It was only ten-thirty in the morning and Mel was more than likely still in bed. I was quite sure that Sean would be at the office and I hoped so. Camilla stayed in the car with Hettie; she was still looking at the old copy of Cut It which we'd brought away with us along with the front cover picture.

I rang the doorbell and waited. I was about to give up when it was answered by a bleary-eyed Mel. She looked aghast when she saw me standing there. 'Diana!'

'Can I come in, please?'

Wearing a robe with uncombed hair she allowed me to step inside. She still looked beautiful.

'Can I make you a cup of coffee or something?' She asked suppressing a yawn.

I followed her through to the kitchen. It was very untidy and dismal. Sean and I had spent hardly anytime in his house; he much preferred to come to me. I could see why. This place was sullen. 'No thank you. I just want one tiny piece of information but before I ask will you promise to tell the truth?'

She glared at me. 'I always tell the truth!'

That was the first lie. I had to word my question in a way that would trap her into the truth. 'Charlie's no longer with us, Mel, and you are the only one who can tell me the truth about something that has been said.' I put a smug expression on my face. 'When you lived together I realise you must have spoken about me a lot.'

Her eyes widened in indignation. 'We never spoke about you at all!'

I shrugged as though hurt. 'Not even me running H-G Properties?' I knew that would incense her; I was a side-kick in her eyes.

'Definitely not! I didn't even know he knew you.'

'So why tell your father he called me *that rich widow from Brooklands Avenue?*'

She shot me a spiteful look. 'Why are you interrogating me? You had him, didn't you?' She started to walk towards the door and opened it. 'Please go.'

I softened my voice. 'He left you something and I can't pass it on unless you tell me the truth.'

So greedy. 'What? What did he leave me?'

'You tell me the truth first.'

So *very* greedy. She sighed. 'I might have said to Daddy about the rich widow bit but it was only because we were both so hurt and angry.' She scowled. 'I don't know what you did to Charlie but he never looked at me the way he looked at you.' She sniffed. 'He knew he was on to a good thing.'

I swallowed hard and said simply. 'Thank you.'

I started to walk towards the door and Mel asked impatiently, 'What about my present?'

I looked back. 'You've already got it! We share it; the memory that he was an amazing guy - not a gold digger.'

She slammed the door behind me.

Hint of Orange

Camilla's pills consisted of two anti-depressants, a sleeping pill and a pick-me-up in the morning. We decided that she should not take the sleeping pill unless absolutely necessary and that she didn't need the uppers and the anti-drepressants should be more spaced out; one a day; then one every two days and so on.

So, anyway, there we sat in bed slurping red wine and talking about where we both go from here. The pain in my heart was constant and I had to remind myself that Camilla's pain was probably similar. We both kept bursting into tears; tears that I thought I'd shed. But she'd lost so much as well; having said that losing Charlie couldn't possibly compare to anything else.

Hettie was lying on the bed between us. We didn't mind. Hettie was allowed special rights now.

'You know, he always called Hettie baby.' I looked at Camilla. 'I do too now.'

Camilla fondled Hettie's ears. 'Baby,' she cooed.

I gulped and sat up with such a jolt that I spilled some of my wine. 'Camilla! My God!'

She sat up straight too. 'What is it? What's the matter?'

I put down my glass of wine and faced her. 'I'm pregnant! I must be.' I took a sharp intake of breath. 'I haven't had a period since I've been with Charlie.' I looked at my friend who appeared somewhat disbelieving but I was telling the truth. 'With everything that's been going on I didn't notice.'

'You mean, you just did it; didn't take any precautions?'

'I suppose we did. I think I forgot I could get pregnant.'

Camilla squeezed my arm. 'Diana, trauma does funny things. Just because you haven't had a period doesn't mean you're pregnant. Don't get your hopes up.'

'No! I am! I must be.'

'You can't be. I remember only too well your morning sickness.'

I pouted with the ghastly memory. 'Yes, but that means nothing.' I looked at my friend. 'I am. I know it.' I put my hands on my stomach. 'There's a baby in my tummy and it's Charlie's. Oh, Camilla, this simply has to be true.'

She looked very dubious. 'I just don't want you to be devastated.'

'I'll do a private test. It only takes twenty-four hours. I'll do it tomorrow. This is just wonderful. It has to be right.'

She took a hesitant breath and ran her hand down Hettie's back. 'I hope so.'

With my hands still on my stomach I tried to imagine what Charlie would have said. My face crumpled because he'd gone before his time and it was all my fault. If I hadn't been late on that day he'd still be here.

'Why so sad?'

I looked at Camilla. 'On the day he died we were supposed to be going to Shire Hall to book a date to get married. I was late getting to him and he decided to do some more work. You know, climb another tree and that's when the harness snapped. If I'd been on time they might have noticed that the harness was faulty before starting work the next day.'

'Or it could have been worse.'

'What do you mean?'

'He lost his life but he didn't suffer for a long while. He could have been brain-damaged, or taken his father with him. So many ifs and buts. It wasn't your fault; it was a fluke accident.'

I leaned over and put my head on her shoulder. 'Thank you.'

She said wisely. 'You're not the only nurse-maid round here. I need to look after you too.'

'You always have.'

'I've always wanted to.'

I picked up my wine and we both clinked to that.

Reflective Orange

Camilla said she'd stay in the car.

'Come in, they won't mind.'

She shook her head. 'No. I think you should tell them on your own. Tell you what - call me in when they know.'

'Okay. Do you mind if I take Hettie?'

Camilla looked at my dog and said reluctantly, 'If you must.'

Hettie jumped out and we walked up the path to Ivor and Winnie's house. It was early evening and I hoped they'd both be in. I knocked on the door and Ivor opened it and beamed with pleasure to see me standing there. 'Come in, come in. It's good to see you, Diana.'

I stepped over the threshold and Winnie came rushing through and hugged me. 'How have you been, my dear?'

'I'm all right. And you?'

She nodded. 'We're coping. Would you like a drink? Glass of wine?'

'I won't thank you. I actually came to give you some wonderful news.'

Ivor looked at me in a very startled fashion and I apologetically held out one hand. 'Sorry, that came out wrong. But I promise you will think it's wonderful.'

Winnie's eyes narrowed in a reflective way and she touched my shoulder. 'I can guess.'

I smiled and she continued. 'You're pregnant and it's Charlie's.' Ivor's countenance totally changed now; he looked overwhelmed and about to burst into tears. He grabbed both of my arms.

'You're sure? Charlie's baby?'

'Definitely Charlie's and I am sure.'

'Diana, you don't know how happy this has made me.' Ivor threw his arms around me and hugged me tightly. 'When did you find out?'

'Half an hour ago.'

Winnie was insistent now. 'You must come into the sitting room.'

I hesitated. 'I have my very best friend in the car. She's been through a terrible time herself; you could say we're commiserating with each other. Would you mind if she came in too?'

I knew they wouldn't mind. Both said simultaneously, 'Bring her in.'

As we were about to leave Ivor and Winnie blew me away. They handed me the most beautiful urn. 'We thought you'd like these.'

I took the urn into my hands and stared at it. 'Charlie?'

Ivor took a deep breath. 'We've thought and thought about what we can do with his ashes and then we decided that you'd know best.'

I was so moved; this proved they must have recognised our deep love. I remember hugging the urn tightly; this was still my Charlie. I saw Camilla's face in the background; the tears well in her eyes.

'I know exactly what I'd like to do with these precious ashes.' I looked across the room to Winnie and Ivor. 'And I hope you approve and I really want you both to be with me.' I looked at Camilla. 'You too.'

All their eyes lit up. Ivor said, 'You just say what it is and we'll be there.'

Camilla almost whispered. 'Me too if it's not an imposition?'

Ivor reached out a hand and squeezed one of Camilla's. He'd recognised her situation; he was such a lovely man. 'You're more than welcome.'

Cold Blue

I missed Natasha so much and had no choice but to brave the hostile atmosphere I would no doubt receive and visit my daughter. It was Saturday morning and Camilla didn't accompany me on this occasion; she went shopping instead and we arranged to meet in the Berni Inn for lunch. She still wouldn't stay in the flat on her own but I think she was getting some sort of perspective now on what had happened to her and fully realised what a tyrant Rachel had been. It was the first step, anyway.

After leaving Hettie with Winnie I drove to Brooklands Avenue and rang the doorbell which was strange; I had lived in this house for so many years but it seemed inappropriate somehow to use my key, especially after my last encounter with Aunt Jelly.

The door was answered by Natasha who actually smiled when she saw me standing there. This was quickly followed by a grimace as though she'd remembered our last encounter. 'It's you.' She said flatly.

'Hello, Natasha.' I stepped over the threshold and towards her but she backed off and lowered her face distastefully. I tried to cover my hurt by sounding jolly.'How are you? How's school?'

'Boring sometimes.'

I looked at my daughter noticing her pasty complexion and old fashioned hair unflatteringly scraped back off her face and tied with a large ribbon. She resembled Alice in Wonderland, except she was far more like Aunt Jelly. I studied her for several seconds wondering what she would eventually look like as a grown woman. Would she be attractive to men? Would she be warm and sexy or cold and dispassionate? I hoped it wouldn't be the latter.

She seemed so much older than her nine tender years as we walked through to the kitchen where Aunt Jelly was baking a cake. I saw the baking tin in the oven and said enthusiastically, 'Smells good in here.'

Aunt Jelly stopped her mixing of chocolate butter-cream and peered at me as though I was dirt beneath her feet. 'You're here again.'

'Of course.' I tried to sound positive.

Before I could say anything else Aunt Jelly proclaimed. 'We now know all about your behaviour with that gardening boy.' Her eyes flashed and she looked at Natasha as though encouraging my daughter to join in. Natasha, true to form, looked from one to the other of us and it really was as though she was enjoying my discomfiture.

I stuck up for myself. 'If you're referring to Charlie it would be reasonable of you to let me explain.'

Aunt Jelly was her usual spiteful self. 'I think you could explain 'til you're blue in the face and it would mean nothing to us.' She looked once more at Natasha who now had a slight smile on her face; I couldn't for the life of me think why the smile was there. What a strange child I'd produced. 'Pass me that spoon over there, will you, Natasha.'

Natasha did as she was told. She then sat down and put both elbows on the kitchen table and cupped her face with her hands obviously waiting for my reply.

I found it hard to draw my eyes away from my daughter and Ben's words came flooding back and hit me hard. Natasha was first and foremost a Herriott-fucking-Greene! I took a deep breath and said, 'I loved him and his death was horrible.'

Aunt Jelly carried on her mixing. 'But you loved Sean. Seems to me and Natasha that you'll love anyone that takes your fancy whatever age they are.' She clucked her tongue. 'Good job I'm here to look after your daughter.' She glared at me her watery blue eyes almost popping out of her head.

'You made sure of that!' I said bitterly. 'Personally, I wish you'd never laid eyes on her!'

She was shocked and looked at Natasha who shifted her position and put her hands in her lap. 'Now, where would *you* be if Aunt Jelly wasn't here to look after you?' My sister-in-law's eyes shifted beadily from my daughter to me.

'She'd be *normal* and happy!'

Natasha's eyes widened and for a while Aunt Jelly didn't reply. 'We bumped into Sean's daughter Mel.' Her tone was meddling. 'She told us how you stole the gardening boy from her and broke her father's heart.'

'*Rubbish!*'

'How they found you in bed with him!' I caught my breath as Angelica sidled closer to Natasha and placed a hand on her shoulder. Natasha looked at it and slid away.

I was appalled by Angelica's words and yet so glad Natasha had rejected her touch; what a mixture of feelings!

'How can you say such things in front of my daughter?'

'*Daughter!* Huh! I'm the mother around her and if you don't like what's being said you should have considered what sort of example you're setting.'

I looked at Natasha whose expression was fathomless. Did she understand all this? Like her precious aunt did she actually enjoy it?

'If I haven't been a good example you've been much worse!'

Angelica's eyes narrowed and through clenched teeth she uttered, 'We don't need you here!' She looked at Natasha. 'Do we?'

Natasha didn't reply and I wanted to whisk her up into my arms and take her away from this frightful situation. If I was anything remotely like a real mother I would do just that! What was stopping me? Nothing! Am I stupid? Ben's words were stopping me and that was *everything*. On his deathbed; 'You're a dreamer, Diana, and my daughter is nothing like you, she's a Herriott-*fucking*-Greene!' He'd claimed her then, for his wretched sister and set his Will up accordingly. And then the torturous aftermath; my struggle with a sobbing Natasha that I'd dared to take from her idolised Aunt Jelly; this all sprang fiercely into my head. - But I almost did.

'Why don't you just go?' Angelica hissed.

I hated her! Regardless of memories I would grab my daughter now! I reached out and Natasha recoiled. I was now so choked with emotion and so weakened by these two females in my life that I felt dizzy and grabbed the table to steady myself. I saw the look on Angelica's face as I stumbled over my next words. 'I …I have something to tell you.'

She stiffened as though momentarily confounded. She said spitefully, 'I hope it's that you've made a Will.'

'It's nothing to do with a Will!' I was exasperated.

Angelica took a deep resigned breath and resumed the beating of her chocolate butter cream as though she was now totally disinterested.

I braced myself and walked calmly towards Natasha who was sitting on the very end of the table. 'Natasha.' I grabbed her hand tightly before she had a chance to repel me. I said softly, 'You're going to have a brother - or a sister.' She jerked her hand away and I rushed on, 'I'm going to have a baby.'

Angelica broke off her administrations and glared at me. 'The *gardening* boy.'

'Yes.' I looked at my daughter and reached out again but she withdrew completely. I implored, 'But, Natasha, it will be good for you.'

Natasha wrenched herself from the table and stormed off with supposed indignation. I was ridiculously shocked! Why did I think that she could possibly be happy at the thought of having a brother or a sister?

Angelica leaned across the table her face red with rage. 'How dare you? How dare you come here and deliver such appalling news and expect your daughter to be glad! Let me tell you, lady, all you've ever been is trouble; that's how Ben once described you! And that thing – that *thing* in your belly is rotten to the core *just like you*.' She drew breath. I watched her miserable face twist as she prepared to deliver more damaging words.

'Ben knew what you were like and I bet he's turning in his grave! How is Natasha going to face her school friends? Have you even bothered to think about that? They'll poke fun at her and the teachers will loathe you even more than they already do.'

'No!' Momentarily I covered my ears with my hands. 'They won't! You're the rotten one! And eventually it's you they'll poke fun at!' I added vehemently, *'Angelica.'*

She screamed at me. 'My name is Aunt Jelly!' She patted her chest. 'I am *the* most important person in Natasha's life; *Aunt Jelly.'*

I laughed bitterly. *'Aunt Jelly!* Aunt Jelly sounds like something out of a children's horror story!'

It was as though I'd hit her! '*You* - are a common tart! Nothing better than a prostitute! Get out of here and don't you ever come back!'

I curled my top lip; I despised her so much and retreated in search of Natasha. Angelica dogged my footsteps her breathing ragged with fury. I was relieved to find my daughter in the sitting room.

'Natasha!' I blurted out. 'Come with me! Please? Come home with me?'

She looked so surprised; I hurried on, 'You'll love this new baby and we'll be a proper family; no way does it come between you and me.'

But her face became distorted and my daughter pointed at my stomach. 'That baby will never make me better because it'll be like you. Aunt Jelly says you're selfish and don't care about me at all.' She tilted her head to one side and added petulantly, 'And, anyway, I'm a Herriott-Greene and that's not.'

I was lost; more importantly I had now really lost my daughter. 'My name is definitely Herriott-Greene and this baby is going to be the same as us.'

Natasha's face was now red with confusion and anger before it crumpled forlornly. 'But you're not really, Aunt Jelly said so, and why should that have my name? And what about my *inheritance?*'

I couldn't believe my daughter's words. 'Natasha, what are you talking about?'

She flung herself towards me stopping short so that she could poke me in the stomach. 'It's my money, not *thats!* Daddy would have wanted me to have it.'

I steadied myself; feeling quite sick. I turned to Angelica. 'You fed her all this garbage. You've corrupted a nine-year old. Ben wouldn't have wanted this. No way should she be thinking about money at her age.'

Defensively Natasha looked at her aunt. 'I should, shouldn't I?'

Angelica stepped forward and put her arm around my daughter. 'Of course you should. It's your birthright.' She looked at me coldly. 'I'd like you to leave us, for good. You and your bastard.'

Sickened, I caught my breath before looking at my pitiful daughter. 'One day, Natasha, you'll realise what the real truth is and how I tried so hard to protect you. I'll be waiting.' I added, 'I'll never give up on you.'

I turned to Angelica. 'How do you live with yourself? How do you sleep at night? What happened to make you so vile; so withered inside?'

I saw the stunned look on her face before I left as quickly as I could.

'How did it turn out like this? How did I get into this situation? My own daughter despises me.'

Camilla reached across the restaurant table and squeezed my hands. 'It's not your fault. You must know that.'

'I don't know that! How can it not be my fault? I've obviously been a terrible mother.' I slumped back in my seat. 'I've deserved everything I've got.' I was thinking about Charlie.

Camilla smiled. I noticed that the lines on her face were beginning to fade. 'When this new baby is born you'll think differently about everything and so will Natasha.'

'I don't think so! I can't see how I'm ever going to get round this situation. Angelica does everything to make Natasha hate me and I am powerless to stop it.'

Camilla looked thoughtful. 'Then why don't you just accept it because as you've often said you're not going to change things. Try to push it to the back of your mind and get on with your own life. Natasha will be okay because Angelica is besotted with her.'

'But it's a divisive and unhealthy love. *Corruptive.*'

'And so was mine with Rachel! And I know that some things you can't fight. And you're pregnant again so let go of Natasha. Just let go.' She added, 'Wasn't that Ben's dying wish?'

Yes! It was. I listened to her words and they comforted me; moreover Camilla's pearls of wisdom were still there. I attempted a smile. 'Are you coming with me this afternoon to see mother and Aunt Fi?'

Camilla rolled her eyes. 'As long as you're prepared for the worst.'

I shuddered. 'How can something as wonderful as Charlie's baby cause so much havoc and vitriol?'

My friend nodded wisely. 'I think perhaps - jealousy.'

'You're lucky to catch us; we were just off to the supermarket.' My mother looked me up and down, as did Aunt Fi, and added, 'You know, Diana, you really ought not to wear black, it doesn't suit you at all.'

'At all.' Said Aunt Fi.

I took a deep breath as Camilla suppressed a giggle and nudged me. 'Actually I quite like me in black.'

My mother rolled her eyes in indignation. 'Anyone would think you were in mourning.'

Her words hit home and I gulped away the lump that appeared in my throat. But I wasn't wearing black because of mourning Charlie; if that were the case I would definitely be in Chelsea blue!

'And how are you Camilla?' My mother asked. 'Haven't seen you in a while.'

'In a while.' Aunt Fi repeated and I swear Camilla was about to laugh. She must be feeling better.

'I'm getting better.' Camilla said.

'Have you been ill?' My mother asked.

'Ill?' repeated Aunt Fi.

'A bad experience with a girlfriend.'

My mother peered at Camilla; she had no idea that her fostered daughter was gay. 'Did she steal from you?'

'Not at all.' I saw Camilla take a deep breath and I knew she was going to tell my mother and Aunt Fi the truth about her sexuality and I wanted to reach out and cover her mouth with my hand. Not because I had a problem with it, merely I did not want Camilla hurt any more. Instead I watched as she stumbled over her next words.

'I think you ought to know, Deborah - and Fi; I think it only right that you know the truth about me. You see…' She cleared her throat, 'I prefer women to men. … I'm gay.'

My mother was absolutely horrified and so was Aunt Fi. She turned her attention to me. 'Are *you* gay?'

'No, of course not. But Camilla is perfectly normal.'

'Normal! You call that sort of behaviour normal!'

'Normal' Repeated Aunt Fi.

'Yes, I do.' I put my arm around my beloved friend.

My mother tutted in indignation. 'Don't think you're going to get any sympathy from me.'

Camilla spoke softly. 'It's not sympathy I want, Deborah, it's acceptance.'

I saw my mother's implacable face; the way this whole situation was going and remembered her love of a wrangle. 'We didn't come here to talk about this. I've something very important to tell you.'

She put her hand to her head. 'Not more shocking news, I hope.'

I felt the impulse to laugh. 'You might think so.'

'What now? What on earth have you been up to, Diana?'

'Quite a lot. I'm going to have a baby.'

If my mother looked horrified at Camilla's news she now looked mortified at mine.

'But you're not married!'

I smiled. 'No, and I'm not going to be married.'

'Why? Has Sean left you?'

I shook my head. 'The baby is not Sean's. The father is a man called Charlie Stanford and sadly he died a couple of weeks ago. I loved him very much.'

'Charlie Stanford? Who on earth is he?'

'I just said, he's a man I loved with all of my heart and I'm now pregnant and please try to be happy for me because I am over the moon about it.'

'Over the moon!' My mother scoffed vehemently. 'I'm supposed to accept that?' She moved closer to me. 'I'm disgusted. You bring shame on this family.'

'Shame.' Repeated Aunt Fi.

I stared at my mother trying to fathom her reasoning and I remembered something my father once said. There's no rhyme nor reason with your mother. 'I haven't brought shame on this family, mum. How can you say that?'

'How can I go down the golf club and tell them that you're pregnant! You've put me in a dreadful situation.'

'Situation.'

'Oh, shut up, Fi!' Camilla glared at Aunt Fi who looked really hurt. 'For God's sake stop repeating the last words that Deborah says.'

'I don't do that!' Aunt Fi said indignantly.

'Yes you do!' This was my mother now.

Aunt Fi just burst into tears and scurried off.

My mother looked at me. 'See what you've done.'

'It wasn't Diana, it was me!' Camilla said quickly.

'Mum, please try to be happy for me. I loved Charlie and this baby is going to be so special.'

My mother cut me off. 'What about Natasha? What's that poor mite going to think to all this?'

I was stumped and couldn't think of an answer.

'She won't like it! Neither will Aunt Jelly! You've put us all in an impossible position and I think you should think very carefully about a termination.'

I lost it then. 'You are one very selfish old lady! I've looked after you and Aunt Fi for years and all you've done is moan and groan. How my father put up with you I'll never know.' I turned to Camilla and said. 'Let's go.'

She nodded and we both walked out of my mother's house and went home.

Memorable Orange

We picked up Hettie and drove back to the flat. I decided to check my mail box on the ground floor; I hadn't done it in a while because my heart just wasn't in it and, anyway, most of my mail still went to Brooklands Avenue or the office but some filtered through to here.

There was a package inside and my heart flipped in anticipation and dread because I knew it was the photographs that I'd taken at Holkham Bay. There was also a letter which I passed to Camilla. She gasped. 'Rachel.'

We took the lift to the penthouse neither of us saying a word. Only Hettie was noisy as she always was in the lift; impatient to be out.

As soon as we were inside the flat Camilla opened her letter and I watched as she read what seemed like reams of writing. I saw the expression on her face and realised she was not over Rachel.

When she'd finished reading she handed me the letter. I scanned it politely but really wasn't interested.

I gave it back. Camilla spoke anxiously. 'She says that I've come here for a quick fix; that you won't be able to make me better; I'm heading straight back to the fundamental problems in my life that will eventually get me.' Camilla hurried on obviously quoting her erstwhile lover word for word. 'I'd already hit rock bottom and recovery was well on the way but now I'll go into a never-ending spiral searching for my true-self and in the end be desolate because I've lost the one true love of my life.'

Camilla's face crumpled. All the lines that were fading were back. 'She says she loved me so much and was the only person who really cared about my well-being. What if she's right? What if I didn't trust her enough?'

I could think of only one word to say, *'Wrong!'*

Camilla touched her forehead and shook her head. 'I'm such a burden on you, Diana.'

I moved forward and took both of her hands in mine and this included the damned letter. 'You are never a burden.' I was aware that Camilla's eyes were not on my face. 'Look at me! Please. She's a witch, Camilla, and she's casting her spell. Somehow she managed to get inside your head, God knows how because you used to be such a tough cookie. But she did and it might take a while to get her out again. But you can make a start right now. You know what you should do with that letter?'

I'd got her attention now. Camilla raised her eyes to me. 'What?'

I took the letter and started to tear it into shreds. At first Camilla objected then she just accepted what I was doing and watched as though fascinated. When it was in tiny fragments I screwed it all up and went over to the window and threw it out. Naughty of me but I had to make my point and I certainly didn't want Camilla piecing the letter together again as I feared she might.

Camilla watched the remains of Rachel's letter being taken by the wind and land on the top of a small yew tree. It seemed to wedge itself firmly within its dense foliage and I suspected it would stay like that until it biodegraded. Only after I closed the window did she say, 'You are right. I do know that but I'm scared.'

'I know and if you loved Rachel you wouldn't be scared. Believe me, there's no mistaking real love.'

She blinked as though I'd made a profound point. 'Like you and Charlie?'

I nodded and remembered the photographs. I walked back to my package and opened it. Hesitantly I withdrew the twenty-four photographs that I'd taken on the day before Charlie died and the tears started to cascade down my face. Each one of Charlie looked so like the boy I'd fallen head-over-heels in love with when he was only fifteen. I passed them one by one to Camilla and she studied them too. Then my heart lifted when I came to the one of us both standing in the heart that he'd scored out in the sand. 'See,' I said, 'that's where he asked me to marry him.'

'What a romantic, and he's bloody gorgeous. No wonder you loved him.'

But it was the next two photographs that gripped my heart. Obviously the stranger, the lady whom I'd asked to take a photograph had decided that one wasn't enough. There was two more of me in Charlie's arms being swung around as though we were the happiest people alive. Hettie was standing beside us, tail erect and watching as though she understood completely our deep love. They were wonderful photographs and I knew I'd frame them and treasure them forever.

'Diana, how do you bear it?'

I took a deep breath. 'I don't know but one thing's for sure, you've helped me so much.'

Her face lit up. 'Is that the truth?'

'God's most honest.'

Camilla hugged me then and I hoped so much that she'd get over that insidious letter from Rachel.

Sky Blue Orange

'I'll just sit here if you don't mind.' Camilla plopped herself down on a hillock within the sand dunes of Holkham Bay.

'That's fine.' I said hugging Charlie's urn with a Chelsea blue ribbon tied round its neck. I also wore one in my hair and Ivor and Winnie wore blue ribbons on their jumpers as did Camilla. I said softly, 'You'll be okay.' Camilla nodded and I wanted to reassure her. 'But you can come with us if you'd prefer.'

'No. That wouldn't be right. I'll stay here.' Ivor and Winnie then went to great lengths to reassure Camilla that she was indeed very safe.

I looked towards the sea and further on. There was hardly a soul about; I wanted to try and find the spot where Charlie had asked me to marry him. Eventually we set off with Hettie at our heels. I turned and waved to Camilla. Huddled up in a blanket she waved back.

It was October and chilly but there was a chink in the clouds, it was feasible that the sun might come out.

So we walked and walked, Ivor and Winnie quite fit for our expedition. We chatted about Charlie; Winnie speaking of him as a sweet-natured child, Ivor mentioning with love and respect his talent as a gardener and me readily admitting that he'd stolen my heart the very first time I laid eyes on him.

'And you his.' Said Ivor. 'He calmed down a lot after you.'

I smiled and couldn't resist asking. 'He was no angel then?'

Winnie answered. 'He matured very early and teenage girls popped up everywhere.'

I could imagine; I felt a strange sort of pride.

As the sun started to peak through I realised we were approaching the right spot because I remembered the tree line and the formation of the dunes and even though I couldn't be precisely accurate it didn't really matter.

With an enormous lump in my throat, I said, 'I think this is about right.'

Ivor and Winnie looked at me; saw my tear-stained face and I saw theirs. 'It all goes out to the same sea.' I said. 'And that's what he said; our special heart would be pulled into the sea and go on and on forever.'

So the three of us and Hettie walked to the water's edge; the sea was icy and even though we'd removed our shoes and got used to the cold sand it still gave us a jolt. I started to unscrew the ornate lid on the urn and tossed it behind me on to the sand. I looked inside the urn at the body of ashes and couldn't help myself; sobs overwhelmed me; this was the remains of the man I thought I would spend the rest of my life with. Winnie and Ivor did their best to control their tears but all three of us were now wailing and I thought of other countries; how they mourned their lost ones and were unafraid to show their feelings. This was us now; opening weeping for Charlie. Taking the blue bow away I put my hand inside the urn and withdrew a handful of the ashes and I leaned forward and threw them out towards the sea. A gust of wind caught them and blew them straight back into our faces. It was the strangest, gentlest feeling and it made us laugh.

Ivor said, 'Charlie's farewell kiss!'

'Yes!' I agreed and a feeling of well-being overtook me. I put another hand into the urn and withdrew another handful throwing it out into the sea. Some came back, some floated out. Ivor and Winnie did the same and we carried on like this until all the ashes were gone. All three of us had Charlie's ashes on our clothes, our faces and in our hair, as did Hettie, but we didn't care because it all seemed so right somehow.

Finally we walked back to Camilla who was still sitting there huddled inside the blanket. She looked up at us and it raised a smile. We then looked back towards the sea and with our hands brushed away what ashes we could. The rest we'd take home. Charlie was always going to be everywhere anyway.

Ivor drove home and Camilla fell asleep against me on the back seat. But I couldn't sleep; I could only think of the day's events and the fact that only a short while ago I was leaving Holkham Bay in a very different state of mind. Then I was covered with the memory of the warmth of his body as he'd made love to me. Now I was covered in his ashes.

Conditional Orange

'There is another solution.' Sean said, one hand cupping his face. I sat opposite him in his office and was pleased to see he looked less ragged than he had the last time we'd met. Camilla was waiting in reception with Hettie; my sad friend didn't want to be far from my side at the moment and Hettie was a comfort to her.

'What's that?' I asked even though nothing could change my mind now.

Sean took his hand away from his face and using both hands gripped the edge of his desk. 'We could still get married.' He looked down at his hands as though studying them before raising his eyes to me. I could see the pain there and felt an impulse to walk round the desk and put my arms around him. I didn't.

'That would not be a good idea, Sean, and I think you know that.'

He leaned forward. 'I would be a good father to your child, I promise you that. And - it would give you respectability - and your baby.'

I felt the impulse to laugh but I didn't. 'It's not respectability I care about, it's the *future* of my child and that of Camilla.'

'Please, Diana, *please* think about it.'

'No, Sean. I'm not going to mess you about on this one. The answer is no.' I took a deep breath. 'But I still want to be involved here, I'll only be a telephone call away and we'll still see each other often.' I corrected myself, 'From a business point of view that is.'

He nodded cynically. 'Of course.'

I reached across the desk and he took my left hand in his. His fingers touched Charlie's precious ring and he looked at it. 'He gave you this, didn't he?'

I pulled my hand away. 'Yes.'

'You see, even that you lied about.'

'Only to save your feelings, but there'll be no more lies, not ever.'

'I hope not.' He took a deep breath and put both his hands behind his head. 'So what's the plan of action, boss?'

I also took a deep breath. 'First and foremost I want to give you ten percent of my shares.' I saw the look of astonishment on Sean's face and I felt he was about to protest. I held up both hands to stop him. 'Hear me out. You can do what you like with them, sell some to Tom maybe, but I feel I owe you at least that because you've been the best friend I've ever had, apart from Camilla that is, and you're my business partner and I won't be doing much business in the near future. Anyway, I want to give them to you, Sean, from the bottom of my heart.'

'Thank you.' His gratitude was obvious. 'I accept.'

I beamed him a smile. 'I thought perhaps you would.' I hurried on, 'You have complete power of attorney to run H-G Properties as you think fit as long as you keep me in the picture and it's important you understand that I trust you implicitly.' I saw him melt before my eyes and said quickly. 'And the other important thing I'd like you to do is sell Camilla's flat in Fulham, get what you can for it. As far as I'm aware Rachel is still living there; she has written to Camilla and really upset her again so this needs to be done without any intervention from Camilla whatsoever. Again, she's prepared to give you total control. We suspect Rachel will object, you know, put up obstacles, but with you in charge she'll get nowhere.' I saw the look of steel cross his face and was more than pleased because Sean liked a tussle. 'Would you be prepared to do that for me?'

He reached one hand across the desk and I took it with my right hand. We held each other's hands tightly. 'You must know I'd do anything for you.'

'Bless you. Yes, I do know that.' I gulped back the lump in my throat. 'Sean, we'll see lots of each other in the future. I'm not deserting you.'

'Too right. I'll never let you do that. Whatever tiny hold I have will never be let go of.'

I pulled my hand away. 'I'm so sorry about the operation. I wouldn't have put you through all that intentionally.'

He was philosophical. 'It was my idea and I'm glad I've had it done.' He shrugged. 'Might produce another child sometime in the future, you never know.' He looked at me hopefully and I averted my eyes.

I stood up. 'I'd better get back to Camilla. She's a bit jittery at the moment.'

'She'll get over it. These things take time.'

I looked at him. 'I hope you're right.' Sean was walking towards me now and I was tempted to say that I so hoped I was doing the right thing but no way was I going to give Sean the chance to stop me. 'The thing is I would never have believed that someone as seemingly strong as Camilla could become so vulnerable.'

'Hmm, the power of the mind.' Sean rested both hands on my shoulders and very gently kissed my mouth. It seemed only right to let him do so. He added, 'I didn't like that witchdoctor at all.'

'Nor me. I wish you good luck with her.'

He grinned. 'Have no fears.'

I grinned too. 'Don't let her cast her spell over you.'

He laughed and then became serious. 'The only person who's done that is you.'

I hugged him then and whispered, 'I do still love you.'

He hugged me back. 'I know you do. Trouble is it's nowhere near as much as I love you.'

No, I thought, that sort of love belonged only to Charlie.

Brighter Orange

The stewardess checked our seatbelts and removed our glasses of champagne. 'I'll pour you more when we're airborne.' She assured us.

I smiled and said, 'Yes, please.'

Camilla leaned over and even though our seats were spaciously apart she reached out to nudge me. 'Something else, this first class, isn't it?'

Playfully I winked. 'The only way to travel.'

She smiled and I was so pleased to see that the smile reached her eyes. 'Thank God you're rich, Diana. I can't wait to be away from this place.'

'But we'll be back for holidays and things.' I said cheerfully and then hastened to add, 'When you're feeling better, that is.'

She sighed. 'I don't think I ever want to come back.' She put a hand on her chest as the plane started to draw away. 'I can't tell you how this place gives me the creeps.'

I'd now heard this so many times and honestly wondered if Camilla would ever return to her old confident self. In fact, there were grave doubts in my mind.

She asked me for the hundredth time. 'Sean won't give Rachel our new address?'

'No, Camilla. Definitely not.'

'You did tell him that?'

'Yes. Besides, Sean knows exactly the situation and will act on your behalf. Not Rachel's.'

'It's just - well, I could see her turning up in California.'

'Camilla, listen, Rachel will not know we're in California. In fact, she won't have a clue where we are *ever.*'

She bit her lip. Nothing more was said and with my hands on my tummy I settled myself down for the journey.

1984

Los Angeles Olympics
Ice dancing partners Jayne Torvill and Christopher Dean win gold medal
The first untethered space walk from Space shuttle Challenger
Boy George – Britain's latest pop idol
Sir John Betjeman; best loved poet died
Eric Morcambe died
Richard Burton died
JB Priestley died
James Mason died
IRA bomb blasts Tory conference HQ
Prince Harry is born
Mrs Gandhi shot dead
Chelsea FC rise once more to First Division

Warm Orange Glow

It is July and my son Charlie is four now and the most lovable child a mother could ever wish for. To say I adore him would be the biggest understatement in the universe! What's more, he's an all-American boy who speaks with an accent that never fails to tickle me pink. I now know what *warm orange glow* means; I only have to look at my son to feel it. What's more he so resembles his father. When Ivor and Winnie come out to Oceanside which is about twice a year they comment on the likeness and bring photographs of their Charlie when he was a boy. In fact we have photographs of Charlie Senior absolutely everywhere alongside photographs of Charlie Junior with Camilla; with me; with Ivor and Winnie; with Sean; with my mother and Aunt Fi and, yes, even with Natasha. Angelica is the only person who has continued to reject me and as far as she is concerned I don't give a damn.

Sean visits often (Mel now lives in Paris close to her mother; all paid for by her father!) and after Charlie's first birthday we've flown home to Cambridge about twice a year. Camilla stays in Oceanside; even now she hasn't the will to fly home. From the very beginning I wrote to Natasha every week sending her photographs of Oceanside and I rang her every week; always at different times to stop Angelica blocking me. She would never let me talk to my daughter if she answered the phone but Natasha would sometimes pick up and eventually she relented; curiosity maybe. I like to think it was because she liked Oceanside and my new lifestyle intrigued her.

But what really sealed her approval was our first visit to Cambridge when Charlie was one. I arranged with Natasha's school that I would be there just before home time. I had to see Natasha, who was eleven at the time, without Angelica around and thankfully the school was very accommodating and when I walked in with my son so many of Natasha's friends fell over themselves to coo over him. With his blonde curls and blue eyes he is pretty irresistible and Natasha saw this and immediately took control. After all, he was her American brother. I think she too fell in love with Charlie because ever since she's wanted him in her life. In fact when she visits with my mother Natasha reminds me of how Angelica was with her when she was born, obsessive, and I have to admit to an uneasy feeling. But I've been such a rotten mother to my daughter that I push these feelings aside. Besides, most of the time she is thousands of miles away.

Next: my darling Camilla. But first let me explain about our position here in the sunny county of San Diego. Oceanside, together with Vista and Carlsbad is part of the tri-City area just south of US Marine Corps base camp Pendleton which just happens to be the busiest military base in US; not that you'd know that living in peaceful Oceanside. And we arrived here at exactly the right time, albeit unintentionally, because there has been a boom in property ever since starting with single-family homes. Even in my pregnant days I couldn't resist dabbling in property – with Sean's help that is.

We live down Oceanside Strand in a fabulous two-storey six bedroom/six bathroom house overlooking the ocean. We have Rita, a Mexican lady and her husband

Fabio to look after us. Rita's position changes day to day because she is our housekeeper cum cook cum baby-sitter cum friend and Fabio looks after the garden, the pool and maintenance of our property. They don't exactly live in but they're not far away and I couldn't imagine our lives without them. All four of their children, three girls and a boy, are now grown up but we know them so well. Camilla, in particular, takes great comfort in the presence of Rita and Fabio.

I think that Oceanside, with its fabulous beach; great for surfing; and 596 metre pier built in 1888, is one of the friendliest places you could wish to be. I have to thank Ben for his business links in California because this has meant that with the passage of time I am now rich beyond my wildest dreams both in England and here in California. Sean and I do good business in real estate; we are established; I'm now well accepted. The Americans do not want immigrants who are a drain on their resources and we are certainly not that. Both Camilla and I have our green cards and are now waiting for citizenship. In particular it means a lot to Camilla.

It took a while for her to settle down, about a year, but eventually she stopped looking over her shoulder and quizzing Sean about his dealings with Rachel. Sean sold Camilla's flat amidst much acrimony. Rachel insisted she had the right to live there even though she paid no rent. She said she'd looked after Camilla for years in return for the right to live there. What lies! What sort of person was she? Very clever with words, that's for sure, but Sean got her out in the end; it took over a year, but the wait proved beneficial because he sold the flat for a very good price. Afterwards somehow or other Rachel found out our address in Oceanside and sent Camilla another long epistle. When Camilla saw the letter her face turned to stone and I shuddered to think what sort of set-back it was going to create but as luck would have it Rachel's letter was filled with vitriol and hatred and had a contrary effect on Camilla. It shored her up; she finally realised that Rachel, as she had said in her letter, had never loved her; just pitied her. According to Rachel Camilla was a cipher.

'What's a cipher?' Camilla asked.

'She's one for sure.' I said disdainfully and then added. 'A nobody.'

Camilla nodded wisely. 'You're right; she certainly is a nobody now.'

Boy, was I glad.

With the proceeds from the sale of her flat Camilla opened a hairdressing salon bang in the middle of Oceanside. It's a smart building; very modern and she now has four stylists working for her, some of them part-time. She fits well into the friendly world of a place where women (and men!) catch up with each other. Camilla never lost her touch with styling hair; she just needed the confidence to try again. Her salon is often booked weeks in advance and she sends her stylists and herself on refresher courses continually.

Through this Camilla met Suzy. Suzy is a surfing instructor by day and works in a bar at night. She's about as different from Rachel as you can get. Skinny, blonde, the opposite of erudite and very self-deprecating; I liked her straight away and this pleased Camilla enormously. Camilla trusts me and I think I deserve that trust. Anyway, she still lives with us down the Strand but stays over with

Suzy who lives downtown when it suits. Suzy also stays here with us sometimes. It's an easy life; no rules and regulations; even Sean visibly relaxes when he visits.

Then there's Hettie. My beloved four-legged friend; and yes she had to suffer the six-month quarantine in order to be with us. I had the choice; did I leave her with Winnie and Ivor or bring her out to my new home. But really there was no choice. She's mine. We didn't visit her in quarantine because we were advised not to. It's too upsetting for the dog who thinks you've come to take her home and then you leave. I was nearly nine-months pregnant when I finally brought Hettie home and she was so very pleased to see me. After that she never looked back and adores her life in Oceanside.

Camilla once asked me why I never told Charlie that I was rich. I had to think about my answer carefully but maybe it was because I didn't want money to feature in my life with Charlie, as least not initially. As Ben often said I had no real respect for wealth; actually, I now have enormous respect for it but one thing's for sure; it doesn't buy happiness.

Then there's Sean whom I've said visits often. And last time we visited England he took Charlie and me to Stamford Bridge to watch Chelsea! It was a complete surprise! Hooliganism is getting a bit out of hand there but Sean made sure we had great seats; how he did it I'll never know; I didn't ask because I want Charlie to like Chelsea Football Club in the same way his father did. Via Sean I follow their progress all the time and I'm pretty hooked myself these days.

In the five years since Charlie's death I've come to terms with a lot; I'll never love anyone as I loved him and Sean knows that. But the love I have for Sean is different and very, very deep; I understand that now. It's based on trust and kindness, laughter and caring. He loves Charlie junior and Charlie junior loves him. What I'm trying to say is that Sean is always going to be in my life and I'd love another child. We still hope that we might achieve that one day. Maybe.

Chrissa lives in Suffolk with her husband. They have three sons and three grand-daughters. Honey, their eldest granddaughter, is in the photograph above taken by artist Sophy Bristol. Warm Orange Glow is Chrissa's fourth published book.

Printed in the United Kingdom by
Lightning Source UK Ltd., Milton Keynes
139977UK00001B/3/P